Operation

Blind Spot

A Jock Miles WW2 Adventure
By
William Peter Grasso

Novels by William Peter Grasso:

Operation Blind Spot
Book 4 in the Jock Miles WW2 adventure series

Operation Easy Street
Book 3 in the Jock Miles WW2 adventure series

Operation Long Jump:
Book 2 in the Jock Miles WW2 adventure series

Long Walk To The Sun:
Book 1 in the Jock Miles WW2 adventure series

Unpunished

East Wind Returns

Book design by Alyson Aversa
Cover photo courtesy of United States National Archives
Map data: Google

Operation Blind Spot is a work of alternative historical fiction. Apart from the well-known actual people, events, and locales in the narrative, all names, characters, places, and incidents are products of the author's imagination and are used fictitiously. Any resemblance to current events or locales or to living persons is purely coincidental. Time lines of actual events depicted may be modified. Events that are common historical knowledge may not occur at their actual point in time or may not occur at all.

Author's Note

This is a work of alternative historical fiction. In actual events, the seizing of Manus Island (and the neighboring island of Los Negros) from the Japanese by the US Army's 1st Cavalry Division played a significant role in safeguarding MacArthur's quest for the Philippines and beyond. The storyline of this novel explores a very different method for eliminating the threat those islands presented to the Allies in early 1944.

Two fictional Nisei GIs play pivotal roles in the story you are about to read. It is a common misconception that Nisei soldiers—Japanese-American volunteers—in the US Army did not serve in the Pacific Theater during WW2. In fact, over 6,000 did. Their exploits are little known, since they were not organized into a homogenous unit as were the Nisei serving in the European Theater. Google *Nisei in the Pacific Theater* to find a number of books and online narratives discussing the topic.

The designation of military units may be actual or fictitious.

In no way are the fictional accounts intended to denigrate the hardships, suffering, and courage of those who served.

Contact the Author Online:
Email: *wpgrasso@cox.net*

Connect with the Author on Facebook:
https://www.facebook.com/AuthorWilliamPeterGrasso

Dedication

To the reluctant warriors...
Who fight not because they want to
But because they have to

SW PACIFIC AREA OF OPERATION
FEBRUARY 1944

Manus Island

Bismarck Sea

Latangai Island

Bougainville Island

New Britain

Solomon Sea

Papua New Guinea

Lae

Port Moresby

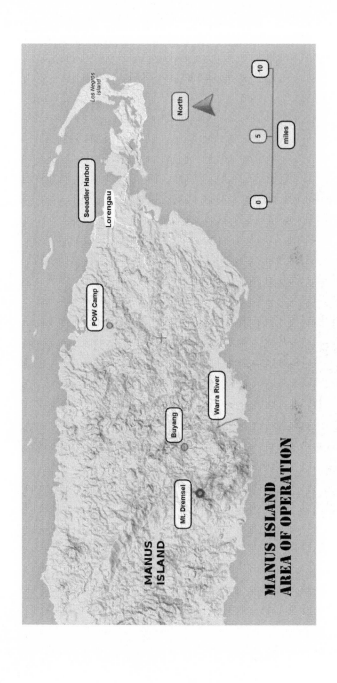

MANUS ISLAND
AREA OF OPERATION

Chapter One

He was starting to remember things…like the airplane's call sign: *Nightingale 12. That's the plane that was flying us GIs to the big hospital at Port Moresby.*

I guess we didn't make it.

Remembering his name was easy. All he had to do was read it off the dog tags around his neck: *MILES MAYNARD J…but everyone calls me Jock, I think.*

Native women fluttered around his low-slung hammock, their bare, dark breasts swaying like pendulums with every movement. They seemed surprised he was awake—or maybe surprised he was still alive. They were jabbering a mile a minute. It sounded like pidgin, but it was spoken so rapidly he couldn't follow it. The women wore shiny olive drab skirts that must have been made of parachute cloth. Somewhere on each skirt was a block-letter "US" printed in black.

The hammock looked like it was made from parachute cloth, too, strung between poles in this open-sided hut. Outside, he could see a few other huts clustered together, all with thatched roofs and built on stilts to keep them level on the steeply sloped terrain.

We're in a mountain village. In a rainforest. Somewhere.

He could've seen more of his surroundings if he'd been able to sit up. But he was too weak…

And every part of me hurts. Did we crash? I don't remember.

The native women stood aside as a man's voice

boomed from the hut's entryway, speaking a language Jock Miles could understand. "Well, laddie," the voice said, "I hardly recognized you with all that hair on your face. Did you Yanks forget how to shave?"

Jock could see the man now. He recognized him: the old Australian coast watcher who'd been his guide, his advisor, and his friend since he first set foot in Papua. But try as he might, he couldn't remember the man's name. A thin, embarrassed smile was all he could offer.

A spry, middle-aged white woman joined the old Aussie inside the hut. "Don't you worry about a thing, Jock my boy," he said. "Ginny and I will have you back where you belong in no time. Your Army might not give a bloody damn what happened to you—but we certainly do."

Ginny...that key unlocked a flood of names in Jock's memory. The man standing over him was Commander Trevor Shaw. *Ginny* was Ginny Beech, Shaw's right-hand woman. But there was one name floating above the rest, riding the last crests of his consciousness. His voice frail, Jock asked, "Jillian...is she...?"

He could tell by the looks on their faces. They might have found him, but Jillian was still gone. One last, painful memory came alive, the note that said the woman he loved was *missing...presumed drowned.*

Presumed...

And then he slipped back into unconsciousness.

Jock awoke to the drumming of rain against the tarp

suspended over his stretcher by wet and glistening native porters. His rescue party had stopped its descent on the mountain trail to wait out the torrential downpour. The tarp was barely large enough to shelter the stretcher. A thoroughly soaked Trevor Shaw stuck his head beneath it and said, "Ahh, good, laddie…you're awake. It's time for your medicine."

"What…what medicine, sir?"

Reaching into his rucksack, Shaw uncapped a brown bottle, its label in Japanese. "The quinine, Jock, for your malaria," he replied, offering a rather large pill like a priest giving Holy Communion. "Courtesy of the Nips. It seems your native friends came into a rather large stash those yellow bastards left behind."

He slid the bitter pill into Jock's mouth, and then held a canteen to his lips to help get it down. "Without it, you'd have been dead a while ago, buried up on that mountain with the rest of the poor souls on that plane."

"We…crashed?"

"Yes, Jock, you crashed."

"How long?"

"About three months ago, in January. It's April 1943 now. And the war's not near over yet."

"Where…where are we?"

"About a two-day walk from the south coast road. From there, we'll hitch a ride with your military back to Port Moresby."

"How…did you…find me?"

"It's simple, laddie," Shaw replied. "Unlike your Army, we pay attention to what the locals have to say." He paused, and then added, "Still, once your Air Force stopped looking for the crash site, it took us a month to figure out where you were."

The rain's ferocity began to ease. Shaw patted Jock on the shoulder and said, "Now don't you worry about a thing, Major Miles. We'll be moving again in short order."

As Trevor Shaw hurried his party back to the trail, he said to Ginny Beech, "The lad's in worse shape than we reckoned, girl. Pray he doesn't die on us."

Chapter Two

September 1943—Camp Cable, Queensland, Australia

The young Army doctor was having a rough time understanding his patient's attitude. Usually, when you told a soldier he was being sent home, the man showed delight to the full limits of his physical capabilities. But this major sitting on the bed before him was anything but pleased by the news.

"That's ridiculous," Jock Miles said, "I'm perfectly fine now."

The doctor shook his head. "The decision of the review board is unanimous, Major. True, the gunshot wound in your shoulder has healed nicely and your malaria seems to be well under control, but you suffered severe head trauma in that plane crash—"

"Come on, Doc. I haven't had so much as a headache in weeks."

"Regardless, Major, you've been classified as no longer fit for combat duty. The only reason you've been in this hospital as long as you have is you weren't deemed fit to travel. But now you are. The ship leaves in two days. You'll be transported to Brisbane Harbor tomorrow."

Jock smirked and slumped back against the pillows. "Sure, Doc," he said, "whatever you say." The words weren't an expression of defeat, just his way of indicating the conversation was over.

Once the doctor had finished his rounds in the ward

tent, Jock hopped out of bed and approached the duty nurse, a harried young second lieutenant fresh from the States. She looked up from the paperwork on her desk and, sounding not terribly sure of herself, said, "Major Miles, you know you're not supposed to be out of bed."

"Sorry to bother you, Lieutenant, but I need to borrow your phone for a minute."

"But sir, this phone is for hospital business only. I could get in a lot of trouble if—"

"I'm sure General MacArthur will consider it *hospital business*, Lieutenant," he said, trying to sound as officious as possible standing there in baby blue pajamas.

She looked like she was about to cry. "You can't call back home on this line, you know," she said. "Guys ask me that all the time."

"I don't need to call home, Lieutenant…just the other side of camp."

"Well….maybe just this once, sir." She slid the phone across the desk and added, "Try not to let anyone else see you, okay?" before scurrying off.

From his ward tent, Jock watched as Captain Theo Papadakis parked the jeep on the far side of the ramshackle hut housing the officers' latrine. Carrying a large paper sack, the *Mad Greek* went inside. Jock, still in hospital pajamas, made the short walk and joined him.

"Here we go, sir," Papadakis said, pulling clothes and shoes from the bag. "A fresh set of khakis and low quarters for you. Got all your decorations up to date, too."

Shucking the baby blue pajamas, Jock replied, "Good work, Theo. Just in time, too."

The *Mad Greek* looked concerned, though. "You really think we'll be able to pull this off, sir? I mean, you've got orders back to the States and all."

"Just get me out of this damn hospital, Theo, and let me worry about the rest."

"You know, sir, a whole bunch of us back in Papua tried to go looking for you with Commander Shaw and Miss Ginny…but Division put the screws to it. Said if we missed the movement to Australia, we'd be considered deserters."

"That sounds just like something Division would say. But I appreciate the thought, Theo. I really do."

As he watched Jock stuff the pajamas and hospital slippers into the paper sack, Papadakis asked, "Whaddya gonna do with the baby blues, sir?"

"Burn them."

"Roger, sir," Papadakis said, and then peeked outside the latrine tent. "Coast is clear. Let's make tracks."

They drove up to a little wooden sign that said *HQ, 81ˢᵗ Infantry*. Theo Papadakis brought the jeep to a halt and told Jock, "Welcome home, sir. Colonel Molloy is expecting you."

In the regimental HQ tent, Dick Molloy began with a simple question: "Are you sure you're up to returning to duty, Jock?"

"I'm sure, sir, despite all those doctors trying to convince me otherwise."

"Well, fortunately for you—and me, Jock—it's really not up to the doctors. They can't *ground* an infantryman who wants to fight. But I'm curious…why *do* you want to stay? Nobody would think the less of you taking the free ride home. Not after what you've been through."

"That just wouldn't work for me, sir. I owe too much to too many people."

"If you're talking about Commander Shaw and Missus Beech…hell, after the effort they put into bringing you back from the dead, they'd be grateful if you tried staying alive for a change."

Jock shook his head. "It's not just them, sir…"

Molloy nodded. He knew who Jock was referring to: Jillian Forbes. But there was no need to say it out loud. The look on Jock Miles' face—that look of pain, like a dagger had been plunged into his soul—said it all. There was no point making that pain worse by uttering her name.

"If it wasn't for her," Jock said, "my men and I would've died at Buna…"

Molloy finished the sentence in his head: *But she died instead. Tough break, fella…real tough break.*

It was Jock who broke the uncomfortable silence that ensued, asking, "So I can have my battalion back, sir?"

"It's yours if you want it."

"I do, sir."

"Then it's done, Jock. Major Meriweather is a good staff officer…but as a C.O., he's just not cutting the mustard. I'll be glad to get him out of that job before your Sergeant Major Patchett arranges some *accident* to happen to him."

Molloy led him to a large scale map of New Guinea and asked, "How much do you know about the eight months since we seized Buna?"

"I know the Aussies have pushed the Japs back through the jungle beyond Lae and the Huon Peninsula," Jock said, tracing that advance on the map. "I heard they had some help from our Forty-First Division...and we even dropped in paratroopers to take an airfield"—he searched the map for the location—"ahh, here it is...at this place called Nadzab. I'm assuming MacArthur wants to keep pushing westward along the northern coast."

"You assume right, Jock."

"Is our division ready to get back in the fight, sir?"

"Not quite yet. The Thirty-Second was decimated at Buna...but I certainly don't need to tell you that. We've trained our replacement troops as much as we can here in Queensland. In a few weeks we'll be returning to Papua for three months of jungle training." Molloy swept his hand along the map, tracing the entire expanse of New Guinea's northern coast. "And where we go after that is anyone's guess."

Chapter Three

February 1944—Goodenough Island, Papua New Guinea

The little island off Papua's eastern tip was an excellent training ground. Jock Miles and his veterans of Port Moresby and Buna were using it to great advantage. The rookies they trained were receiving an excellent education in how to fight and survive in the jungle. This morning's exercise was a perfect example: the companies of Jock's 1st Battalion slipped through the dense jungle without bunching up or straggling, adjusting the artillery fire clearing the path before them by the sound of its unseen impacts alone. When they reached the base of the hill crowned with their objective, the infantry's advance up its slope was perfectly coordinated with the lifting of the artillery fire. The hypothetical defenders of that hilltop—if they survived the barrage—would've had but seconds to lift their heads before the attacking GIs were upon them, dispatching them with bullets and bayonets.

"Excellent attack," Jock Miles said. Melvin Patchett, his battalion sergeant major, couldn't have agreed more.

Patchett said, "It seems like yesterday...hell, it damn near was yesterday...they wanted us to do this without any artillery support at all."

"And like idiots, we tried to do it, too, Top," Jock replied.

"Goddamn Buna...that didn't go none too well, as I

recollect, sir. Now, the brass are so all fired-up about artillery we even got it shooting out of the landing craft as we hit the beach. I reckon even generals learn…just a lot slower than the rest of us."

A GI from the commo section approached and handed Jock a message form. "It's marked *urgent*, sir," the messenger said.

"Hmm," Jock said as he read it. "It says I'm to be at Regiment at 1300 hours."

"Maybe we're finally getting our marching orders," Patchett said, and then—with a hefty dose of sarcasm— added, "You suppose *The Great One* finally made up his mind where he's gonna try and get us all killed next?"

The Great One—General Douglas MacArthur—had indeed made up his mind. Jock was about to hear his part in it from Colonel Molloy.

"We're leap-frogging all the way to here, Jock," Molloy said, pointing to a spot on the big map. "A port called Hollandia, in Dutch New Guinea. It's a big jump—a couple more amphibious operations just like it and we'll be in the Philippines. Our division is scheduled for the follow-up landings, to head off and trap the Japs trying to counterattack from Wewak…"

Molloy paused, moving his finger slowly north from Hollandia to an island across the Bismarck Sea. "But before that happens, this regiment's been handed a special assignment, crucial to the success of the main effort, right here at this island called Manus. The Japs have an observation post on a mountain peak there. Do you see where I'm going with this, Jock?"

"Yes, sir, I believe I do. This looks like Port Moresby and Astrolabe Mountain all over again."

"Yeah, it's somewhat similar," the colonel said.

It's all too similar, Jock told himself, *and it explains why it's me sitting in this chair right now and not someone else.*

"Obviously," Molloy continued, "when this plan got hatched, your name came up right away. But I don't want you to get the wrong idea here, Jock. I'm not ordering you to go. I'm asking if you'd like to volunteer."

*Volunteer...*Jock tried not to laugh out loud. He'd been in the Army far too long to know how *volunteering* worked. Your commander said something like, *I need a volunteer*, and then pointed to a man and announced, *You.*

"It's just that you've led a mission like this before, Jock...with great success, I might add."

"And if I decline this honor, sir?"

"No problem. Just suggest somebody else as qualified as you."

Colonel Molloy waited patiently for Jock's reply. Nothing in his demeanor suggested he was being anything but honest about the *volunteering* part.

And Dick Molloy's always been straight with me—right down the line.

Jock found himself instinctively fumbling for the West Point class ring on his finger. But there was nothing there—the ring was gone now, lost somewhere in the same fog of war that had claimed the woman he loved.

Knowing what that ring represented, though—*Duty, Honor, Country*—that was not gone. It was altered, no doubt, its high purpose eroded, taking on a jaded character through the filter of war's unspeakable horrors. But not gone. And with that enduring knowledge, Jock Miles was certain—just like Dick Molloy was certain— that it would be impossible for him to say *no, thank you.*

Just like it had been all those times before.

Feeling the weight of the West Point ring on his own finger, Colonel Molloy asked, "What happened to your class ring, Jock?"

"No idea, sir. Probably some native kid up in the mountains thinks it's a magic charm now. Hope it gives him better luck than it did me. One question, though, sir."

"What's that, Jock?"

"I get to pick my own team, right?"

"Damn right you do," Molloy replied. "We'll fly over to Milne Bay first thing tomorrow and get this ball rolling. I'll set up a briefing at Division HQ. There's an Aussie there who was stationed on Manus before the Japs drove them out. He should be a big help. Plan for an 0800 takeoff."

Chapter Four

Seeing the bureaucratic gaggle that was 32nd Division HQ at Milne Bay made Jock glad his battalion was doing their jungle training across the strait at Goodenough Island, away from all this meddlesome hierarchy. Colonel Molloy found himself appreciating the distance, too, as he told Jock, "Sure beats having these pencil-pushers up our asses all the time, doesn't it?"

The briefing was scheduled to begin at 1000 hours but, of course, being on *Army time*, it didn't. A stream of overwrought staff functionaries, each with a last-minute change to some miniscule facet of the agenda, kept racing into the old plantation villa housing the HQ, pushing the start time back. Finally—at 1025—the briefing was ready to begin.

A US Army major, looking barely out of his teens, was the briefing officer. He announced to the dozen or so attendees, "I'm Major Kit Billingsley from the G3 shop, Supreme Allied Command."

Supreme Allied Command—that meant MacArthur.

As Billingsley began speaking, Jock made a not-so-startling revelation: *I remember this guy. He was three years—three whole years!—behind me at The Point, in the class of '38. A plebe when I was a firstie. A real screw-up, too…but his daddy was some hotshot in the War Department. And he's a fucking major already, on the big guy's staff. He's not wearing a CIB on those khakis, so I'm guessing he's seen maybe two days of combat time, if that much—but he's probably got light colonel in the bag already.*

Same old story: it's all about who you know and who you blow.

Well, I sure know a lot of people in this man's army...but I guess I'm a little weak on that second part.

Standing at the big map of New Guinea, pointer in hand, Kit Billingsley thrust himself into his presentation. "If you've been allowed in this room, gentlemen, you're part of a very select group. You already know of General MacArthur's plans for seizing Hollandia. Before we can discuss that operation, however, we must discuss a different objective, one that poses a unique problem for the Supreme Commander."

Billingsley's pointer hit a spot on the map—a tiny patch of brown and green on the northern edge of the deep blue Bismarck Sea. The officers being briefed had to lean closer in their seats to get a decent look at it. "This, gentlemen, is Manus Island, the largest island in the Admiralty chain," Billingsley continued. "It's been of great interest to our General MacArthur as well as Admiral Nimitz, as it sits on the border of their respective areas of responsibility and appears to be very lightly held by the Japanese. But each command has a very different interest in this island."

Dick Molloy leaned toward Jock and whispered, "Oh, brother...we're about to get sucked into a four-star pissing contest."

Pointing to a large anchorage at the island's northeast corner, Billingsley said, "Admiral Nimitz seeks the excellent natural facility that Seeadler Harbor can provide. It can be a terrific asset to our Navy in bottling up the Japanese stronghold of Rabaul, which is less than four hundred miles to the southeast. However, gentlemen, the admiral has already made the case to

Washington that *MacArthur* should take the island *for* him, since the general's forces in New Guinea are so much closer to Manus. Of course, the Supreme Commander considers this an insult and has made his position clear to Washington: his troops will not shed one drop of blood securing territory for Admiral Nimitz. If Washington were to be foolish enough to order him to do so, he would resign his command immediately."

Kit Billingsley paused as a smirk spread across his face. "Naturally, the Supreme Commander has called Washington's bluff."

"*Naturally*," Dick Molloy muttered. "Funny, though…MacArthur's never been worried about spilling our blood before. Only when his pride gets hurt."

Billingsley was far from finished. Working his pointer across the map, he continued, "But at the moment, Manus Island presents an irritant to our Hollandia amphibious landings. In an effort to avoid easy detection by Japanese aircraft operating from bases on the northern coast of New Guinea—such as Wewak—the invasion fleet will sail far offshore as it makes its way west through the Bismarck Sea to Hollandia, close enough to Manus—within fifty miles or so—to be seen from the Japanese observation post we suspect is on Mount Dremsel, the island's highest point."

Jock raised his hand to ask a question.

"Yes, Major Miles?" Billingsley said, managing to make *major* sound like a slur.

"How high is this Mount Dremsel?" Jock asked.

Dismissing the question with a scowl, Billingsley replied, "That's been published."

His face reddening, Jock stood up, ready to lock

horns. "I didn't ask if it's been published or not. Just tell us how high the damn OP on this mountain is. Or do I have to read it off the map myself?"

He didn't mean to sound brusque, but it's hard not to sound that way when you're totally focused on a problem. Kit Billingsley's veneer of imperiousness—a trait every member of MacArthur's staff exhibited, as if emulating their general—began to crack just a little. Perhaps it was foolish of him to talk down to a man of equal rank. Especially one with a bucketful of serious combat time and the contempt for desk jockey bullshit that came with it.

Sounding much less sure of himself now, Billingsley replied, "I believe it's two thousand, three hundred and sixty feet."

Jock did a quick calculation in his pocket notebook. When it was done, he said, "So, with clear skies, you can see to a horizon about eighty-five miles away. Do you agree, Major Billingsley?"

Billingsley gave a sheepish shrug. He had no idea if that number was correct or not.

"Then you're going to have to trust me on it," Jock said, "since I've done this stuff before. So, eighty-five miles…that's nearly halfway to the New Guinea coast. If the fleet sails where you say it will, then yeah…on a clear day they'll be visible from Mount Dremsel to anyone with a halfway decent pair of binoculars. At night, they'd even be able to see the big blinker lights the Navy uses for ship-to-ship commo. So what does the *Supreme Commander* want us to do about it?"

"The Japanese garrison there sends regular radio reports to their headquarters at Rabaul," Billingsley said. "We need to make sure that the Japs at Rabaul or on

New Guinea don't get any warning of the Hollandia fleet's approach…until it's too late."

"That's a pretty tall order," Jock replied, "considering any plane high enough can see a fleet of ships a hundred miles away. Or any idiot with a radio in a patrol boat just might stumble across them."

"Agreed, Major Miles," Billingsley said, "but the Air Force and the Navy are doing their best to minimize those chances."

Jock asked, "Does this mission have one of those inspiring names yet?"

"Yes, Major Miles. The Supreme Commander has named it *Operation Blind Spot*. Very fitting, don't you think?"

Nobody seemed to care one way or the other how fitting it was.

Dick Molloy had a question. "You've been monitoring the Jap radio on Manus," he said, "so you've probably got the transmitter's location pretty well pinpointed. Why doesn't the Air Force just take it out?"

"They've tried, sir," Billingsley replied, "but that transmitter keeps coming back on the air day after day."

"So you're telling me we've got a choice," Jock said. "Silence the transmitter or blind the OP. Either one gets the job done, right?"

"That's correct, Major Miles. In fact, I was instructed to tell you the choice of this mission's objective is yours, be it the OP, the transmitter, or whatever. All we need is to ensure there is no advance warning of the fleet's approach to Hollandia. *How* you do it is totally up to you."

Molloy asked Billingsley, "When do you need this to happen, Major?"

"Three weeks from now, sir. Twenty-nine February, to be precise, thanks to 1944 being a leap year."

The briefing *took ten* for a coffee break. Jock and Colonel Molloy were still a bit shocked by the freedom they were being allowed. Usually, you were ordered to *Depart Point A at such-and-such hour and take a very specific Point B.* Neither man could recall ever being granted such wide-open latitude selecting a mission objective.

Quickly warming to the concept, Molloy said, "Maybe the brass are finally learning, Jock. Just think of the freedom and flexibility it'll give you."

Jock wasn't so convinced. "I don't mind planning on the fly, sir...but if the intelligence we get is the usual half-baked shit, we're liable to run out of options real fast. My back went up as soon as he said *very lightly held by the Japanese.* I've heard that song and dance before."

Dick Molloy wasn't ready to surrender to skepticism just yet. "Before you give yourself a case of the red ass, Jock, let's see what the aerial recon photos show. And I really want to hear what this Aussie who's actually been there has to say about the place."

When the briefing reconvened, the Aussie—an Australian Army sergeant named Burke—limped into the room, supporting himself with a cane. "I guess he won't be coming with me," Jock whispered to Colonel Molloy.

Sergeant Burke told the assembled Americans he'd been a member of the last Aussie unit to occupy Manus

Island: a platoon that manned the observation post on Mount Dremsel. "When the Japanese came in '42," Burke said, "a few of us lucky ones fled into the rainforest and managed to evade the Nips." He tapped his game leg and added, "That's how this happened— fell into a bloody ravine running for my life in the dark. Finally, with the help of some friendly natives, we escaped by sea to one of the nearby islands."

Jock asked, "And how'd you get off that island, Sergeant?"

"A submarine finally picked us up, sir."

Kit Billingsley chimed in, "That's how you're going to Manus, too, Major Miles. By submarine."

Jock wasn't surprised. Still, it wasn't great news: *Submarines aren't even big enough for their own crews. That's really going to hold down on the size of my team and the equipment we can carry.*

"Geographically," Sergeant Burke continued, "Manus is just a very small replica of New Guinea. It's the largest of the Admiralty Islands at sixty miles long and nineteen miles wide, and it's covered by dense rainforests for the most part, a fair bit of jungle, and the occasional swamp and coconut plantation scattered here and there along the coast—"

Major Billingsley broke in, adding, "And very few Japs."

Dick Molloy tried not to laugh in Billingsley's face. Jock resisted the urge, too, asking, "How *few* is few, Major?"

"Two to three thousand."

"That's more than a few, I'd say," Molloy replied.

"But we estimate they're scattered across the width and breadth of the island," Billingsley offered in rebuttal. "The odds of running into large units are—"

"Begging your pardon, sir," Burke interrupted as he turned to the map, "but that's not likely. The Japs will be clustered here, on the eastern half of the island—around Seeadler Harbor, the town of Lorengau, and Los Negros, which is actually a separate island across a narrow passage of water from Manus proper. The western half is fairly rugged, inhospitable, and sparsely populated. And, of course, we expect they're using our old observation post on Mount Dremsel, near the island's center." His finger fell on the concentric contour lines indicating the island's highest point on the map.

"Yeah, we've heard a little about the OP already," Jock said. "Give us all the details you can, Sergeant."

"Of course, sir," Sergeant Burke replied. "It's nothing fancy, as you can imagine. It's about half a day's hike up the trail from Lorengau. We built a fifty-foot tower at the peak to get our line of sight well above the treetops."

"Where was your transmitter?"

"In a plantation outside Lorengau, sir."

"How'd you get the information from the OP to the transmitter?"

"We ran a telegraph line, sir."

"Did you leave that line intact when you escaped?"

"No, sir. We cut it up as best we could. And after being rained on for a couple of years, anything left will be quite useless now."

"I'm sure you're right," Jock said, fixated on the map. "This Mount Dremsel looks like a pretty steep climb."

"It is, sir. The only way to the top is a trail that runs on ridges all the way up and around the mountain, like a spiral staircase."

Colonel Molloy was sorting through aerial photographs. He set one in front of Major Billingsley and asked, "The Jap transmitter location...it's marked here as a goose egg several square miles in size. We couldn't nail it down better than this? No wonder the Air Force hasn't knocked it out."

Billingsley fumbled for an answer, finally admitting, "I can't explain that exactly, Colonel."

"The transmitter might be moving, sir," Jock said. "We've run into that before—a high-powered radio mounted on a truck."

"Maybe so," Molloy replied, and then laid another photo before Billingsley. "This airfield on Los Negros— *Momote*, it's called—it looks deserted. There's scrub growing on the runway. What does the Supreme Command make of that?"

"We believe Los Negros is deserted, sir," Billingsley replied.

Sergeant Burke shook his head. "With all due respect, Major, the Nips wouldn't be foolish enough to do that. I speak from experience, unfortunately. The beaches of Los Negros are about the only decent amphibious landing zones on Manus, too inviting to leave undefended."

Touching his fingertip to a point on the map, Jock asked, "What about here, Sergeant? Could we land here undetected?"

The spot he picked was on the island's southeast coast, the mouth of a river on a small, sheltered bay. Nearby was a trail, part of a network that would lead west to the base of Mount Dremsel—just eight miles away—or in the opposite direction to the town of

Lorengau, some twenty miles distant.

Burke replied, "You should be fine there, sir, as long as you land in the dark so they can't see you from Dremsel."

"This trail," Jock said, tracing the dashed red line. "Is it really there? Can't tell from aerial photos. All I see are treetops."

"It was there two years ago, sir, just like it's shown."

"Can I get to Lorengau inside of a day on it?"

"If you can stay on the trail, yes. But remember, villagers and the Japanese will be using it, too."

Jock asked, "Will the natives support us?"

"Hard to say for certain, sir, but they've put up with Nips for two years now. I'll bet they're getting mighty tired of the yellow bastards."

Colonel Molloy looked up from the aerial photos. He'd heard every word Jock and Burke said—and had a pretty good idea what Jock was thinking.

"You're going for the OP, then," the colonel said.

"Yeah," Jock replied. "It's the only place we can be relatively sure of. And if the Japs aren't up there, they won't see the fleet, anyway. But I've still got two questions—first, how long does the boat ride to Manus take?"

A naval liaison officer provided the answer: "Figure two days on the sub. When do you want to depart Milne Bay, Major?"

"Not so fast, Lieutenant. How long will it take this invasion fleet to *pass in review* off Manus?"

"About twenty-two hours, sir."

"All right, then," Jock said, "I figure I'll need three days on the island to scout and get organized, two more days to hold the OP while the fleet passes, and one day to get the hell out. That gives us a jump-off date of Twenty-Four February. Less than two weeks from now."

Chapter Five

Once the briefing ended, it was time to get down to the serious planning, working out the details which could spell the difference between the mission's success or failure—or the difference between life and death. The Navy had been fairly easy to deal with. In the words of the submarine flotilla liaison, "No problem, Major Miles. A ten-man team, with their equipment, will fit on the sub. It'll be a tight squeeze, but we'll make it work."

The slow-turning wheels of Army bureaucracy proved more difficult. "Absolutely not, Major Miles," the Division Communications officer, a lieutenant colonel, said. "You may not take Sergeant Botkin. He's essential to my operation here at HQ. I doubt he'd want to go on whatever little adventure you're cooking up, anyway."

"I've already spoken to the man, sir," Jock replied, "and he's more than willing to go. He's done some fine work for me before."

"I couldn't give a rat's ass less, Major. Botkin's not going anywhere with you...or anyplace else, for that matter."

Obviously, Jock told himself, *this desk jockey hasn't gotten the word yet.*

Like some timely magic, the colonel's phone rang. The conversation lasted only a few seconds, knocked the wind from his sails, and ended with, "Yes, sir, he's here now. I'll see to it right away, sir." With those words, Jock knew he was getting Stuart Botkin—the young man who had worked electronic miracles back on Cape York—as his commo specialist.

There was one more personnel hurdle to clear: getting two Nisei interpreters. "I know they work in the G2 shop somewhere," Jock told Colonel Molloy. "I spoke with some of them when I was in the hospital."

"What makes you think they'd want to go on this mission, Jock? It's an automatic death sentence for them if they're captured."

"I'm pretty sure it'll be a death sentence for any of us—Caucasian or Japanese-American—if we get captured, sir."

"I don't know, Jock. How do you think your other guys will take to having Japs with them?"

"I think they'll realize we just might need Japanese speakers to pull this off, sir," Jock replied, "just like we did on the mountain at Port Moresby. We got lucky then, with a native kid knowing a little of the language. This time, I'm not trusting it to luck. I'm taking Japanese linguists with me from the get-go."

"Well, good luck with that," Molloy said, as Jock set off to find the interpreters' section.

The G2—a full bird—shared all of Dick Molloy's reservations. Unlike the communications officer, though, he was already aware of the Supreme Commander's wishes: Dick Molloy's people were to get whatever they wanted for this mission.

As they waited for Jock to return, the G2 said, "You say you want them to be *volunteers*, Dick. You are talking *Army-style* volunteers, aren't you? I mean, what *Nip-American* is going to want to lay his neck on that chopping block? And as I recall, one of the terms of their enlistment was they would be kept out of combat with Japanese forces."

"Unless they *volunteer* for that combat duty, Fred,"

Molloy replied. "Unless they volunteer…and we're talking *real* volunteers here, not this *you, you, and you* bullshit. Let's just wait and see what Miles can come up with."

They didn't have to wait long. Jock strolled into the G2's office with two Nisei corporals. They certainly didn't look like they had been forced to accompany the major. In fact, they looked positively eager.

"Every man in the section wanted to come," Jock said. "We had to draw lots, and Corporals Nishimoto and Hashimoto were the lucky winners."

The G2 said nothing, but the look on his face seemed to say, *I am one surprised son of a bitch.*

Dick Molloy was pretty surprised, too. He smiled as he said, "We'd better hurry up and get over to the G1 shop, Jock, and get your new guys' paperwork in order…or we'll be spending the night here."

The slow-as-molasses personnel sergeant was getting on Jock's nerves. Using only two fingers, one lethargic key stroke at a time, the sergeant was typing the orders that would assign Sergeant Botkin and the two Nisei corporals temporarily to Jock's battalion. Every few letters, he would stop, mumble something under his breath, and readjust the paper on the carriage.

"Having a problem with that typewriter, Sergeant?" Jock asked.

"No problem with the machine, Major, but I didn't get my coffee because of this *expedite* on these here orders of yours."

"Oh, I'm so sorry to hear that," Jock replied, with

all the insincerity he could muster. "It must be one hell of a sacrifice having to work in this clean, comfortable office without a fresh cup of coffee. Maybe you ought to come out to the field with us. Coffee will be the least of your little worries."

"We do things a certain way around here, Major," the sergeant said, "and—"

Jock cut him off. "Yeah, I can tell, Sergeant. Creature comforts got you all by the ass. I'll be back in five minutes to pick up my *completed* paperwork. You'd best get on with it."

Jock found Colonel Molloy in the G1's office, riffling through the regimental dispatch pouch. "Having problems?" Molloy asked.

"No, sir…just some poor, deskbound sergeant needed a little guidance."

"And his ass kicked, too, I suppose," the colonel said as he handed some documents to Jock. "Here…this'll be of interest to you."

It was the paperwork on First Sergeant Tom Hadley's Congressional Medal of Honor for his actions at Buna. It had taken a year to wind its way through the chain of command, but the final determination had been made: *Sergeant Hadley's actions, though valorous, do not meet the established criteria for awarding the CMOH.*

The Silver Star was being awarded instead.

"Shit," Jock said, "they didn't even consider a DSC…just kicked it down to a Silver Star. If what Hadley did doesn't qualify, what the hell does a guy have to do?"

"It looks like he only did one thing wrong, Jock," Molloy replied. "He didn't die."

Chapter Six

The sergeant piloting the courier plane—a well-worn, single-engine Stinson L1—turned to his passengers and shouted, "This is gonna be a real close-run thing, gentlemen."

Jock and Colonel Molloy didn't need to be told that. Even though the coastline of Goodenough Island was filling the windshield, the sun was *awfully* low, casting deepening shadows across the land and sea below them. The lower the plane dropped as she made her approach, the more the darkness would envelop her.

Swell way to end up wrapped around a tree, Jock thought, reflecting on those close calls he'd had in another light aircraft over the Port Moresby battlefields. But he'd walked away from all those without a scratch. It was the crash of a big plane—the C-47 high up in the mountains of Papua, the one that cost the life of everyone on board but him—that he couldn't remember at all.

When the little plane finally skimmed over those last treetops—nothing but jagged, colorless blurs against the burnt orange sky—and bounced down on the darkened grass airstrip, the sighs of relief that escaped the plane's occupants in near-perfect unison didn't seem enough of a celebration. A hearty round of applause seemed more in order.

Sergeant Major Patchett was waiting with the jeep. "I thought for sure y'all weren't gonna make it. You get Botkin?"

"Yep," Jock replied, "I sure did. He'll fly over tomorrow. You got my other six guys lined up, Top?"

"Yessir, all ready and willing....the damn fools."

"Look who's talking," Jock said. "You're one of those *damn fools*, aren't you?"

Patchett replied, "Affirmative, sir. Who else is gonna keep you straight?"

"I've got some news about Hadley's CMOH, Top."

"Yeah, word beat you back here, sir. He already knows he's getting a Silver Star instead."

"How'd he take it?"

"Like a man. Said right out he doesn't give a damn about medals. Just wants to get him and his boys home alive. Made me damn proud to hear it."

They dropped off Colonel Molloy at the regimental CP and then began the short but slow drive to their battalion bivouac, inching along the few feet of road barely lit by the jeep's blackout headlight. Patchett asked, "How long you figure we gotta keep driving with these Mickey Mouse lights?"

Jock replied, "Until the Jap airbase at Rabaul runs out of fuel."

"Maybe that happened already. We ain't had a *night visitor* overhead here in weeks."

"Let's hope, Top."

"This mission we're going on, sir...it got a name?"

"Yeah. They're calling it *Operation Blind Spot*."

"That ain't real inspiring, sir," Patchett said.

"It's just a name, Top."

"And you're gonna do this with eight men, counting yourself?"

"Make that ten, Top."

"Ten? Who's the other two, all of a sudden?"

As Jock spoke the names of the two Nisei, Patchett slammed on the brakes, nearly throwing his commander onto the hood in the process. In the darkness, Jock couldn't make out the expression on his sergeant major's face. But he didn't need to see it to know the man wasn't happy.

"Them names," Patchett said. "They sound awful *Japanese* to me, sir."

"They're Nisei, Top. Japanese-American troopers. Volunteered for *this man's army* just like you and me. Now it's been a real long day, so let's get this jeep moving. We can talk about this back at the CP, if you like."

"Don't see much to talk about, sir," Patchett said, sounding as if he was slamming a door on an unwelcome visitor.

As the jeep began its slow rumble again, Jock could sense a wall between the two of them, men who—until a moment ago—had trusted each other with their lives for three combat campaigns in this war. Suddenly, that trust seemed to have vanished—and Jock blamed himself.

He looked over at Melvin Patchett in the driver's seat, now just a faint outline in the night.

How the hell could I have been so wrong about Top's reaction to the Nisei? Have I just ruined one of the finest working relationships I've ever had in this Army?

Or can it still be saved?

They pulled up to the CP tent and went inside without saying a word to each other.

"Clear this tent, on the double," Jock said. The battalion staff members working there weren't surprised by that order in the least. The tension between the commander and the sergeant major was sucking the dank jungle air from the CP. They all felt it.

Once they were alone, Patchett asked, "Permission

to speak freely, sir?" He sounded like he was addressing a stranger.

"Absolutely, Top. There's no other way we're going to get to the bottom of this."

"It's real simple, sir," Patchett began. "The only thing I ever agreed with that sumbitch Roosevelt on was when he locked up every last one of them yellow bastards in prison camps."

"Internment camps, Top, They're internment camps."

"Same fucking thing, sir. Now, as far as them *Nisei* go"—he made *Nisei* sound like a cuss word—"I don't care if they swear allegiance to Uncle Sugar on a stack of bibles a hundred feet high—they're still fucking Japs. And I don't—no, I *can't*—trust 'em. What I don't understand is how the hell can you, a guy who's been through hell and back because of them lowlife, cannibal bastards—you do remember 'em eating our dead at Buna, right? And you was there at Pearl Harbor, too. How the hell can you want to play ball with 'em now?"

"Because we need them, Top, just like we need our German-American and Italian-American troopers. You don't suppose those GIs who fought in North Africa—or the ones fighting in Italy right now—give a rat's ass where the parents of the guy fighting next to them came from? In fact, *we* don't seem to care much, either—"

"Until now, sir. This is a whole different ball of wax."

"Because they don't look like us, Top?"

"I don't care what they look like, sir. I care what they done. Let me ask you something...you planning on giving them weapons?"

Jock found that funny. "Don't be ridiculous. Of

course I'm going to give them weapons."

"Then that's another mistake you just made."

There was a silence—brief as the blink of an eye, but thunderous as any explosion— before Jock said, "That's just about enough out of you, Sergeant Major. I'm going to assume from our conversation you're *un-volunteering* for this mission."

"Whoa! Hang on a minute, sir. I didn't say nothing about that."

"Well, *I* just did. Return to your regular battalion duties, effective immediately."

Chapter Seven

This long day that had begun with the flight to Milne Bay was refusing to end. It was just past midnight when Jock, sprawled on his cot at long last, saw the outline of a short, muscular man hovering outside the tent's mosquito netting. He told himself, *With a fireplug shape like that, it can only be one man—Captain Theo Papadakis.*

"Come on in, Theo," Jock said. "Something on your mind?"

"Didn't mean to disturb you, sir, but the rumor's all over camp. They're saying the sergeant major's not going. Is it true?"

Jock sat up and rubbed his tired eyes. "The rumor mill's quicker than usual," he said, "but yeah, it's true— Patchett's not going."

Jock figured the next thing out of *Pop's* mouth would be *Why?* He wasn't expecting him to say, "Then I volunteer to go in his place, sir."

"Theo," Jock replied, "I've already told you *no* once. I'm not taking any company commanders. You guys are critical. I need you getting your troops ready for the follow-up landings at Hollandia."

"But you're taking Tom Hadley, sir. Aren't first sergeants just as critical?"

Jock shook his head. "As long as Lee Grossman's in command of Charlie Company, we can cover Hadley for a couple of weeks."

Papadakis said, "Speaking of Grossman, I think he's coming to see you, too."

"If it's about *volunteering* to take Patchett's place,

tell him to save his breath."

In the shadows, Jock couldn't make out *Pop's* expression, but his body language was unmistakable: Captain Theo Papadakis was desperate to go on this mission.

Theo's a natural fighter, Jock told himself. *Guys like him always want to be picked for the special missions.*

Papadakis' desperation then took a surprising turn: he began to unfasten the captain's insignia on his collar. "I tell you what, sir," he said, "I'll take off these *railroad tracks* right now if it'll get me in on this fight."

"Knock it off, Theo," Jock replied. "Privates are a dime a dozen but company commanders as good as you don't grow on trees. Do me a big favor—stay a captain, please."

Papadakis knew when he was licked. His head hung low; his shoulders slumped. "One question, sir," he said. "Who *is* gonna replace Patchett?"

"Nobody, Theo. Nobody *can* replace him."

Chapter Eight

Their official name on the operations order was *Scout Team Blind Spot*, but every one of the nine men on that team—Jock Miles included—hated it. *Blind Spot* had the stench of delusional blundering by the high command about it, something they knew from hard experience got soldiers killed in vast numbers very quickly. They took to calling themselves *The Squad* instead. It fit: numerically, they were too small to be an infantry platoon and too big to be considered a section. Squad said it best.

The men of *The Squad* were becoming a close fit, too. They'd been training together for three days now and Jock could sense the camaraderie growing. Integrating Sergeant Stuart Botkin, the commo specialist, back into the unit had been no problem at all. It was like he'd never left, even though it had been two years since he fought as one of Jock's men at Cape York.

Integrating the Nisei had been rockier. Corporals Roy Nishimoto and Bruce Hashimoto barely had time to drop their duffle bags before Bogater Boudreau was in their faces. "You better be worth it, *mes frères*," the Cajun sergeant said. "A man I'd really like covering my backside ain't coming on this little trip because of you two."

"Let me guess, Sergeant," Nishimoto said. "Is it because he doesn't think we're American enough?"

"Something like that."

The two Nisei just shrugged. "He wouldn't be the first to think that," Nishimoto replied, "and he'd be just as wrong as all the other..." He stopped himself: he'd almost finished the sentence with the term *rednecks*.

Boudreau took a menacing step forward. "All the other *what?*" he asked.

"*Misinformed*, Sergeant," Nishimoto replied. "All the other misinformed."

Boudreau took a step back and smiled. He took Nishimoto's diplomatic choice of words as a victory. "What part of Japan you from, anyway?" he asked.

"I'm not from Japan, Sergeant. I'm from San Francisco."

"And I'm from Oakland," Bruce Hashimoto offered.

"Hmm...California boys," Boudreau said. "What team y'all root for?"

"The New York Yankees, of course," Nishimoto replied.

"How come the Yanks?"

"Because that's where Joltin' Joe plays."

Boudreau had to think for a minute. "You mean DiMaggio?"

"Of course, Sergeant. Who else?"

"Still doesn't answer my question...How come?"

"Because Joe DiMaggio's from San Francisco, too."

"You're shitting me. He's really from San Francisco?"

"That's a fact, Jack...I mean *Sergeant.*"

Bruce Hashimoto gave Boudreau a quizzical look and asked, "You sure you're an American, Sergeant? I mean, Joe DiMaggio...Come on! And that accent of yours...Where are you from?"

Boudreau's face turned red. "I'm a Cajun from *Loosiana*, you...you..."

Tom Hadley burst into the tent and said, "All right,

all right, ladies. That's enough happy talk for today."
He'd been watching the exchange—greatly amused—
from just outside. "Now which one of you guys is
which?"

The Nisei introduced themselves all over again.

"Those names," Hadley said. "They sound too damn
much alike. Could cause a lot of confusion when the shit
starts flying. Tell you what we're going to do"—he
pointed to Roy Nishimoto—"I'm going to call you *Moto
One*."

Then he pointed to Bruce Hashimoto. "And you're
Moto Two."

Bogater piped up, "Why don't we just make it real
simple and call them *One* and *Two*, Top?"

"Because these men have names, Bogater, not
numbers. Confusing names, I grant you—but names
nonetheless. Now, have either of you ever fired a
Thompson?"

"You mean the submachine gun, First Sergeant?
The Chicago Typewriter?"

"The very same."

"No," *Moto One* replied.

"Me, either," *Moto Two* added.

"Then you've got two minutes to get your gear
squared away, after which you will double time your
sweet asses to the CP, which is two tents thataway.
Sergeant McMillen will get you checked out."

Walking out of the tent, Hadley turned to Boudreau
and said, "You sure you're an American, Bogater? Joe
DiMaggio....for cryin' out loud. Who doesn't know
everything about Joe DiMaggio?"

By the third night, the bonding of *The Squad*
seemed complete. From his tent, Jock watched and
listened as a raucous, eight-handed poker game raged
next door, beneath the faint, red glow of blackout
flashlights. He laughed as he realized the men from his
battalion were learning a lesson the hard way: the two
Nisei were crack poker players.

It's a good thing they're only playing for cigarettes,
Jock thought. *The "Moto Brothers" are cleaning them
out. Listen to Bogater complain! He must be losing his
shirt.*

By that point in the game, Bogater Boudreau had
already lost his shirt and more—but had, apparently,
gained newfound respect for the Japanese-American
GIs. Jock could hear him quite clearly as he shouted
over the din of boisterous voices: "The hell with this
Moto One and *Moto Two* noise! Since these *Nips*
are...wait, can I say that? Can I say *Nips*?"

Bruce Hashimoto shuffled the cigarettes before him
into a formidable pile and said, "As long as we're
beating your ass this bad, Sergeant, you can call us
whatever you like."

"Okay, then," Boudreau continued, "as I was
saying, since these *Nips* are such good card sharps, I say
their *Squad* names should represent their special
skills...something more fitting than *Moto One* and *Moto
Two*. I propose we christen these two *Ace* and *Deuce*."

Suddenly realizing he might be stepping on First
Sergeant Hadley's toes—the man who had given the
Nisei their *Moto* nicknames—he added, "I mean, if
that's okay with you, Top."

Tom Hadley just smiled. He didn't seem to mind at all.

Neither Jock nor the poker players realized that someone else was watching, too. Alone in the darkness, concealing the glow from his cigarette in a cupped hand, Melvin Patchett was taking it all in.

He wasn't smiling.

"Listen to them zipperheads," he mumbled to the night, "treating them fucking Japs like they was just one of the boys."

PFC Joe Youngblood was surprised he didn't have the rifle range all to himself. He'd made a point to skip breakfast so he could be there at sunrise. Sergeant Major Patchett had beaten him to it.

Patchett squeezed off three quick rounds from his .45 pistol, the *powhh powhh powhh* of the shots shattering the morning quiet on Goodenough Island. The short target—only twenty yards away—was unscathed.

"Sumbitchin' piece of Colt shit," Patchett muttered as he eyeballed the sight alignment. Then he turned to look at the approaching Joe Youngblood.

"I heard you coming a mile off, *chief*," Patchett said. "I thought you *injuns* was supposed to be light on your feet. Real sneaky-like."

Joe Youngblood was big-boned, over six feet tall, and weighed just shy of one hundred eighty pounds. He'd weighed two hundred when he enlisted, before the GI diet in the Southwest Pacific Theater had worked its usual, slimming magic. Still, he could never imagine himself as *light on his feet*, regardless of the silly myths white people chose to believe about Indians.

"I'm about as sneaky as a bulldozer, Sergeant Major," Youngblood replied, "and I'm not a chief. Very few of us are, you know."

Patchett went back to inspecting the pistol in his hands. "What're you doing out here at the crack of dawn, anyway, Youngblood?"

"I've got to zero this M1. Major Miles picked me and Allred to carry Garands on the Blind Spot mission."

"I thought all you boys would be carrying Tommy guns."

"No, Sergeant Major. Major Miles wants two M1s along in case we need to actually hit something at long range. You aren't going to do that with a Thompson." He glanced at Patchett's unblemished target and added, "Or that pistol, either."

"All right, wise guy," Patchett said, "let's see what you can do with that musket there."

Youngblood promptly got down to business. His first shot—at the hundred-yard target—struck the ground right in front of the man-shaped silhouette, spraying dirt all over it. He gave a twist to the sight adjustment knob and fired again. Gazing through binoculars, Patchett said, "You're on the target, a little low."

"Okay, just a *skosh* more, then," Youngblood said, giving the knob another twist.

"*Skosh*...that some *injun* word?"

"Nope. Picked it up from Ace and Deuce playing cards last night."

"So, y'all are picking up some lingo from them Jap boys now. What's next? They gonna have y'all eating fish heads and rice, too?"

Joe Youngblood gritted his teeth as he said, "You know, Sergeant Major, all this nasty talk about Japanese-Americans doesn't mean anything in my book. Every swinging dick around here's got a hyphen in his nationality—everyone but me. I'm the only real American in this outfit. My people were already there long before yours were getting off the damn boat."

Youngblood took aim at the far target. He fired once—twice—three times. The bullet holes formed a tight triangle right where a man's heart would be.

"Hmm…nice shot group," Patchett said, with a nod of respect. "Real nice."

"Damn right it is, Sergeant Major."

Chapter Nine

Melvin Patchett parked the jeep off the trail and, with a folder full of unimportant papers, set off on foot into the thick woods. *The Squad* was training in that part of the rainforest—somewhere—so he'd taken it upon himself to deliver the humdrum daily dispatches to Major Miles, a job usually detailed to a PFC clerk.

For Patchett, this was a personal quest: he needed to see just how well this little team—with this very big mission ahead of it—was managing without him. As he crunched through the underbrush, he told himself, *I just can't believe a li'l ol' cobbled together bunch of dogfaces is shaping up as fast as they want me to believe. Even if I did train every last one of them NCOs myself.*

And if they had *shaped up* that fast, he knew it only meant one thing: *They don't need me one little bit no more…and that'd make me just another stripe-heavy geezer with a load of bullshit war stories and a desk to put his spit-shined combat boots up on.*

Even though it was 1000 hours, with the blazing sun climbing above wispy clouds in a brilliant blue sky, it was like dusk on the rainforest's floor. The thick canopy of treetops conspired to keep out much of the light. Bruce Hashimoto—*Deuce*—was amazed how difficult it was to see GIs only twenty feet away. But he could still hear just fine, though—and there was definitely someone making his way toward *The Squad's* concealed perimeter.

He scurried on hands and knees to tell Sergeant Mike McMillen, his team leader.

"What the fuck are you doing here?" McMillen said. "Get back to your position."

"But there's somebody coming, Sarge," Deuce replied.

"Good. Let him keep right on coming. Just remember, this is a *recon* exercise. We don't engage unless—"

McMillen was cut off by the dull *pop* of a blank round being fired from somewhere on the perimeter. Quickly came the *clack-clack* of a rifle's bolt being cycled, another *pop*...and then Melvin Patchett's angry voice saying, "Just who the fuck do you think you're shooting at, numbnuts?" He grabbed PFC Cotton Allred by a shoulder strap of his web gear and jerked him to his feet. Pointing to the waxy yellow spots on his breast pocket—right over his heart—Patchett said, "You dumb cracker. You ever see a blank take a man's eye out at close range?"

Allred drawled his reply. "Couldn't tell it was you, Sergeant Major. I though you was part of the exercise. Besides, I wasn't aiming at your eyes."

Jock Miles scurried out of the shadows, yelling, "ANYBODY HIT?" Then he saw Melvin Patchett— waxy stains and all—and asked, "Sergeant Major, what the hell are you doing here?"

They walked out of the men's earshot to talk in private. Patchett launched into a song and dance about the regular clerk being at sick call, the XO wanting Jock's guidance before dealing with a few of the directives in the folder, Regiment needing some answers right away…and any other baloney that came to mind.

Jock listened to it all in silence, all the while fixing his sergeant major in a glare that said, *Don't bullshit a bullshitter, Top. I know why you're here.*

When Patchett's string of excuses finally ran out of steam, Jock kept that glare blazing, still not saying a word. He didn't let up until the sergeant major was squirming in desperation, picking vainly at the waxy blobs on his fatigue shirt, deposited there by PFC Allred's blanks.

"You want this mission real bad, don't you, Top?"

"Yes, sir. This has all been a terrible misunderstanding between you and me."

"Cut the shit, Top. What about the Nisei, then? Have you changed your mind?"

"Well, sir, let's put it this way. I still ain't crazy about them—"

Jock interrupted, "I'm not asking you to *like* them, Top. I'm asking you to *lead* them…as you would any other GI."

"Affirmative, sir. I can do that for you. I'd be proud to do that for you."

Jock offered his hand. "Then welcome to *The Squad*, Sergeant Major."

As they shook on it, Jock took in the residue from the blanks on Patchett's chest. "Looks like I picked the right man to be a sharpshooter," he said.

"Shee-it, sir," Patchett replied, "I couldn't have been more than twenty feet from him. Even my grandma was a dead shot that close."

In six days, they'd be on the submarine to Manus Island. Jock was glad—no, make that relieved and delighted—to have Melvin Patchett back on the team. This day's training focused on taking a mountain top, something Jock felt fairly sure they'd have to do on Manus.

As the pre-attack briefing wound to a close, Patchett told *The Squad*, "This ain't no step for a stepper, even for an itty-bitty unit like ours." As he spoke, he prowled around the sand table, where a replica of Mount Dremsel—the suspected OP on Manus—had been used to illustrate the path of attack. "To repeat, the only way for us to do this thing right is attack it from two sides—one team opposite the other—and not end up shooting each other when we get to the top."

"That's where radio coordination is going to come in," Jock added. "Sergeant Botkin, are all the walkie-talkies up and running?"

"Affirmative, sir," Botkin replied.

"Very good. Here's the deal…we're going to run this attack twice today—now, in daylight, on Hill 157; and after supper, we're going to run it again—in the dark."

Tom Hadley raised his hand. "The attack in the dark, sir…that'll be on Hill 157, too, right?"

Jock and Patchett exchanged tight-lipped smiles, delighted Hadley had unwittingly played the straight man so perfectly. Jock delivered the punchline: "Of course not, First Sergeant."

There was a collective groan from *The Squad*. Night attacks in the mountainous rainforest were difficult enough, but they were a little easier if you'd covered the ground once before—when you could actually see a couple of feet in front of you.

But life—and the enemy—rarely deal you an easy hand.

"Shut up, ladies," Patchett said when the groaning persisted. "You'll find out your objective for the night attack once it starts to get dark."

"When we stand a good chance of not even finding it," Hadley mumbled.

"That's exactly the point," Patchett replied. "Sergeant McMillen, Sergeant Boudreau, have your teams ready to move out in one-zero minutes." Then, that coy smile still on his lips, he added, "Best of luck to y'all, now."

The only issue plaguing the daylight mock assault of Hill 157 was noise discipline. Sergeant Mike McMillen's team made such a racket coming up the hillside that Tom Hadley, serving as umpire, stopped them halfway and changed roles, becoming mentor instead. "Listen up," Hadley said, "you guys sound like a train pulling into the station. If someone told me four GIs could make so much noise when they were supposed to be tactical, I would've said they were nuts. But you guys just proved me wrong."

A frustrated McMillen asked, "So what the hell do you want me to do, Tom? Send them to bed without their supper?"

"Don't smart-mouth me, Mike. For openers, they can stop talking out loud. Did you forget how to use fucking hand signals?"

"No..."

"Okay, so use them. Another thing...their gear is clanking like cowbells because there's metal-to-metal contact like crazy. Muffle those fittings better—half the cloth tape you put on has fallen off already. Be more generous with that tape...we've got shitloads of it for this exact reason."

"All right, Tom, all right," McMillen replied, "I get the message."

Hadley's critique wasn't finished, though. "And for cryin' out loud, knock off the fucking coughing and throat clearing. Make up your mind right now what you'd rather deal with—a frog in your throat or a bullet in your gut. Learn these lessons now—it's going to be too late once we get to Manus. Are there any questions?"

McMillen's team uttered a collective mumble: "No, First Sergeant."

There was the soft crackle of a voice from McMillen's walkie-talkie: Bogater Boudreau was reporting his team in position to seize the peak.

"Okay, then...let's get moving," Hadley said. "We're holding up the damn show here."

The night attack problem was every bit as difficult as the men of *The Squad* feared. Just finding the right place to start their ascent of Hill 123—whose peak was this attack's objective—was kicking the ass of even an experienced scout like Sergeant Bogater Boudreau. As his team plunged farther into the pitch black of the rainforest, it was becoming more obvious by the second something was wrong.

"We don't seem to be climbing no hill, Bogater," Melvin Patchett, the umpire for Boudreau's team, said. "What's that tell you, son?"

Boudreau knew he was lost. The extra minutes it had taken for his cocky self-confidence to falter and admit that simple fact had only gotten his team farther off course. "We're gonna have to backtrack to the trail," he told Patchett, "get our bearings…and start over again."

Patchett shook his head. "Hang on a minute there, boy, and think this through. Take a look at this map here." He spread the map on the ground and lit it with the dim blackout flashlight. "You know damn well where the trail you set out from is—y'all got to recon that before the sun went down. Now, once you're moving east off that trail, where's the only place you're gonna hit flat terrain like this?"

Bogater studied the map for a moment and then circled an area with his finger. "Right here, Sergeant Major," he said.

"Correct. And what does that tell you?"

"We left the trail too soon. We should be farther north."

"That's exactly right, Bogater. So there's no need to drag our asses all the way back to the trail and start over again, is there? That'd just be a fuckload of wasted time, right?"

"Right, Sergeant Major."

Patchett leaned in close and whispered so none of the others could hear. "Look, Bogater, I seen this a whole lotta times before. You was real hot shit when you was just a regular little dogface, not responsible for nothing but your own ass. But now you've got that third stripe on your sleeve and it's got your head all turned around. All of a sudden, you're in charge of a bunch of people and every swinging dick above and below you got some opinion or another about how you're running your little show…and it's making you fuck up. The Bogater I used to know would've never made a navigation error like you just did…I don't care how damn dark it was."

Melvin Patchett waited in silence for Bogater's response, knowing it would go one of two ways. He might be belligerent, denying with all the misguided certainty in the world the error was his fault. Patchett hoped this wouldn't be the case, because it would mean Boudreau still had a long way to go to becoming an effective combat NCO.

Or he could just accept his mistake, learn from it, and move on.

Patchett waited a little longer, until Bogater finally said, "Yeah…my head's so far up my ass I can't see shit. Thanks, Sergeant Major…*merci.*"

"*De rien,*" Patchett replied, the French drawled but unmistakable.

Boudreau's jaw dropped. "*Vous parlez francaise,* Sergeant Major?"

"I was in France in '18, remember? The hookers can't take advantage of you so easy if you know a little French. But no matter now…get these men of yours moving on the double, Sergeant, before McMillen and his boys pull off this attack without y'all."

As Boudreau quickly reorganized his team, Melvin Patchett breathed a sigh of relief and told himself, *That young man just might make it as an NCO after all.*

The radio traffic on Jock's walkie-talkie made it clear: his two teams were nearing the peak of Hill 123. In his sand-bagged OP on the hilltop, he threw back the safety guard on the detonator box, exposing several rows of switches. It was time to give this exercise a dose of realism.

He toggled an entire row of switches with one bump of his forearm. Before he could count to *one*, a ring of artillery simulators circling the peak—huge firecrackers, really—began to *bang*, shattering the silence of the night. Both teams came to an abrupt stop.

Like the blink of a photographer's flash, the momentary light from the explosions allowed Melvin Patchett to catch the three experienced infantrymen in Bogater Boudreau's team fling themselves to the ground and then crawl on their bellies to cover behind the nearest tree. One man still stood in place, though: Corporal Hashimoto—*Deuce*. His head and shoulders seemed to lurch in one direction and then the other but his feet remained planted.

That boy's got no earthly idea what he's supposed to do, Patchett told himself. *Probably shitting his pants, too.*

Deuce nearly leaped out of his skin when Patchett snuck up behind him and said, "You better make up your mind which way you're going, son. Darkness don't stop no bullets." A new round of explosions—strings of firecrackers simulating automatic weapons fire— punctuated the end of his sentence perfectly.

His voice quivering, the Nisei corporal said, "I don't

know what I'm supposed to do."

"Well, for openers, try going *down*."

Before Deuce could process that guidance, a quartet of flares popped over the peak, each bathing a quadrant of the hillside with shimmering light and flickering shadows. One of those flares seemed dedicated to spotlighting Deuce, who had just figured out what the sergeant major had been trying to tell him. *Down* he went.

"No! Not Now! Too late," Patchett said. "You don't never ever move when you're caught in a flare, son. The enemy probably can't see your silhouette, but I guaran-damn-tee they can see your movement."

Deuce began to stand back up but Patchett pushed him back down.

"NO, NUMBNUTS! I SAID DON'T YOU MOVE WHEN THERE'S A FLARE BURNING. WHAT'S WRONG WITH YOU, BOY?"

"You're confusing me, Sergeant Major," Deuce said.

"You can't be confused no more, son, 'cause you're dead a couple times over. And that's a real shame, because we don't need you dying on us just yet..." He finished the sentence in his head: *At least not until you do what the major wants you to. After that, I don't give a rat's ass.*

"I'm calling this attack successful, Sergeant Major," Jock said as they conferred on the peak of Hill 123. "But, obviously, we've still got a few problems."

"One I can think of right off, sir," Patchett replied.

"The one called Deuce ain't no infantryman, that's for damn sure." He looked to Tom Hadley and asked, "How'd the other one do?"

"Ace did okay," Hadley replied, "but..."

He paused, as if trying to hedge his next words or wishing he hadn't said the last one.

"But *what,* Tom?" Jock asked.

"Nothing, sir. He did a good job. He'll be all right."

"You're sure?"

"Positive, sir."

They could hear the mutter of a deuce-and-a-half's engine on the trail near the hill's base—their ride back to bivouac. Gathering his gear for the downhill trek, Patchett said, "Looks like it's a good thing you got two of them Jap fellers, sir. We just might need that li'l ol' cushion."

Sprawled on the bed of the deuce-and-a-half, the men of *The Squad*—all except Jock Miles and Melvin Patchett, who were in the cab with the driver—tried to relax as they bumped and lurched back to camp and their bed rolls.

"Listen up, all of you," Tom Hadley said. "Mess Section will have a midnight snack ready for us, but Major Miles has ordered there will be no coffee. He wants all of us to get a good night's sleep. That means no card playing, either. Tomorrow's going to be another busy day. Any questions?"

One voice rose above the grumbles of men resigned to compliance. It was Roy Nishimoto—*Ace*—who said, "I have one, First Sergeant."

Hadley bristled. He hadn't expected anyone would have the balls to actually ask a question. Especially not one of the new guys.

"This better be good, Ace," Hadley said. "Go ahead."

Every man sat up, shut up, and leaned in closer. They wanted to hear this impertinent rookie get taught a lesson at the hands of First Sergeant Hadley.

"I'm puzzled by one thing in the chain of command here," Ace said. "We've got *two* top sergeants—you and Patchett. You both wear six stripes with a diamond. Who outranks who?"

Hadley growled his reply. "What the hell do you care, Corporal?"

"Well, I just need to know if one of you gives me an order and then the other gives me a conflicting order, which one do I obey?"

"Kinda big with the hypotheticals, ain't you?" Hadley said. "What on earth makes you think that's ever going to happen?"

"It seems quite possible to me, First Sergeant. I saw how confused everything got on that mountain and—"

"That wasn't any *mountain*," Hadley interrupted. "We've been up on mountains. That was just a tiny little hill."

Polite but insistent, Ace continued, "Regardless, First Sergeant, there were more than a few times one hand didn't know what the other was doing."

That made Tom Hadley laugh. "Better get used to that. That's what combat's like."

But he could see the Nisei's point. New to the unit, Ace had no appreciation of how the men of this battalion—some of them veterans of three campaigns—

gelled as a unit. To him, *rank was rank* and this special unit—*The Squad*—had two senior NCOs with an equal number of stripes.

Hadley decided a courteous explanation would do far more good than an ass-chewing. "Let me put it this way," he said. "There's only one *top* in *The Squad*, and that's Sergeant Major Patchett. He and I might wear the same number of stripes but he was soldiering, in combat, when I was still sucking my mama's tit. So let me make this perfectly clear to you new guys—Sergeant Major Patchett is second in command to Major Miles. I come in third. Maybe someday the Army will get smart enough to make *sergeant major* more than just a title and kick in another stripe and more pay. But for now, that's the way it is." He paused before asking, "Are there any more damn questions?" Once again, he expected none—and this time, that's just what he got.

Chapter Ten

"At least none of my men got seasick yet," Patchett said as the submarine's mess steward poured him another cup of coffee. "Y'all been treating us real fine. We appreciate it, son. We surely do."

"No problem, Sergeant," the steward replied. "Captain's orders—treat you like honored guests. Breakfast is at two bells."

"What do you reckon that is in Army time?"

"That's 0500, Sergeant. Two hours from now. Make sure your guys wake up on time because they get to go to the front of the chow line."

The steward started to make his way down the narrow passageway and then turned back to Patchett. "Can I ask you something, Sergeant?"

"Sure can, son."

"The Nips you got with you…you guys don't mind that? The crew's pretty pissed off over them being onboard."

"Don't much matter if we minded it or not. The major says we need them for this mission, so they're here."

The steward looked confused. "It just…just don't seem right," he said.

"Right for who, son?"

"I don't know…for everyone, I guess. For you guys, first off, having to trust them. And them, having to fight their own kind…"

"They volunteered for this duty, son, just like you and me. Lord knows why, but they did. Nobody forced 'em."

Alone with his coffee, Melvin Patchett had little doubt why the Navy was being so courteous to the GIs: *I heard some of them swabbies talking. They think we're on some damn suicide mission. Stupid bastards...*

Like Patchett, Jock couldn't sleep. Between the mission plans swirling in his head and the unfamiliar *thrum* of the submarine, he was condemned to be wide awake. He climbed topside, joining the sub's captain on the conning tower's bridge as the vessel plowed through the emptiness of the sea at night. The moon offered what little light it could as it floated in a black dome of twinkling stars.

"We cleared the Vitiaz Strait about an hour ago, Jock," the sub's captain said. "That puts us in the Bismarck Sea now. We're about halfway to Manus, right on schedule. How are your guys holding up?"

"They'll manage this little boat trip just fine, Hank."

"I'm guessing you and your guys have all seen a lot of action, right?"

"Yeah," Jock said. "All but the Nisei."

"You taken many casualties?"

Jock gazed into the darkness as Jillian's memory stabbed him in the gut for the hundredth time that day. The words of that final message kept haunting him:

Missing...presumed drowned.

The most haunting word of all—*presumed.* So tentative—so indefinite.

But no matter how much you mince the words, Jock, she's still gone.

He needed this topic of conversation to end. Hoping

a terse reply would do the trick, he said, "Yeah, Hank. We took a lot of casualties. A whole lot."

It worked. In the awkward silence that followed, Jock took in the panorama of the conning tower at work: the cramped, exposed platform where he stood with the boat's captain—a lieutenant commander—and his assistant officer of the deck (AOOD)—a lieutenant. Three seamen acted as lookouts, two standing in narrow, waist-high cages on either side of the periscope masts, their feet at the level of Jock's head as they scanned ahead and laterally, and the third on the *cigarette deck* at the rear of the bridge, scanning aft. He wondered if these Navy men could see something in the night he couldn't.

The AOOD clamped the headset against his ears and announced, "RADAR REPORTS CONTACT BEARING THREE-TWO-ZERO, FOUR MILES, MOVING LEFT TO RIGHT."

In a few moments, the port-side lookout reported, "CONFIRM—TWO DESTROYERS..."

Jock's eyes strained as they searched the black emptiness but saw nothing. He cursed himself for leaving his binoculars below with the rest of his gear. *Maybe if I had those binos,* he told himself, *I might at least see their bow waves glowing.*

The AOOD was already calling the info to the man on the torpedo data computer when the captain stopped him. Sounding dejected, the captain said, "Forget it, Mister Shafter. Come left to two-eight-zero."

The lieutenant looked stricken. "But sir," he said, "we've...we've got them dead to rights."

"Yeah, dammit, I know. I gave you a command, Mister Shafter. Execute it."

"Aye aye, sir."

As soon as the sub cut its shallow arc to the new heading, the captain ordered, "All stop."

Jock could sense the bitterness in the AOOD's voice as he relayed the command to the helm. The bitterness wasn't lost on the captain, either.

"We have no choice," the captain said as he kept a wary eye on the two Japanese destroyers now slipping away to the northeast. "You remember what our orders said, Mister Shafter—*clandestine operation, take no action to compromise the Army's mission.*"

"But sir," Shafter said, "we're still a couple of hundred miles from Manus. They'll never know—"

"You understand what *clandestine* means, don't you, Mister Shafter? Even if we got lucky and sent them both to the bottom—and that's a big *if*—there'll probably be planes looking for us come sunrise. We're too close to Rabaul, too close to New Guinea...and we've got to stay on the surface as much as possible to get these guys there on time. Can't be playing hide and seek right now. End of discussion."

As the easy quarry slipped away, the captain gave it a long, lingering look through his binoculars. When that look was finished, he muttered, "Shit."

Sergeant Botkin had a theory. Once onboard the submarine, he quickly made friends with the ship's radio chief and set out to prove his theory correct. It had taken hours of twisting the radio direction finder's dials and plotting on a map taped to the bulkhead of the sub's closet-sized radio compartment, but he believed he now had his answer.

"It's simple, sir, really," he told Jock. "They could never pinpoint the Manus transmitter's location because they've been chasing two different signals, thinking they were the same." He swept his hand across the plots he'd made on the chart. "We've actually got two distinct transmitters—I've been listening to the operators' Morse and their fists are completely different. I can't believe our SIGINT guys missed that." He pointed to two locations on the map. "And now that we're closer, the locations don't plot out to some big, vague goose egg, either. The weaker one is right around Mount Dremsel, sir. Probably right on it. The stronger one—their main transmitter, I'm sure—sits over here, outside Lorengau."

"Could you copy any text from their transmissions?"

"We sure could, sir. They don't even bother to code them. All Ace and Deuce had to do was translate. The Mount Dremsel set would transmit a message and then the Lorengau set would include that exact same message along with a bunch of other ones..."

"Like a relay?"

"Exactly, sir," Botkin replied. "The station on Dremsel probably isn't strong enough to work Rabaul reliably—especially in daylight—so the station at Lorengau rebroadcasts it with a more powerful set, which I'll bet is using a directional antenna, too. That's why both signals sound equally weak at the monitoring stations in Papua. The main Jap antenna's beaming the stuff the other way."

"It all makes sense, Sergeant," Jock said. "This is outstanding work you've done."

"No problem, sir...but the best thing about it, I think, is it proves what you've been saying all along."

"What's that?"

"That there's an OP on Mount Dremsel, sir, for sure. Just hold it for a couple of days and we've got this mission knocked."

Sergeant Major Patchett appeared in the passageway. "We got a problem, sir. Something's wrong with Private Youngblood."

They found Joe Youngblood lying on the catwalk of the forward torpedo room, his feet elevated by his GI pack, covered with a blanket. Deuce seemed to be completely in charge as he crouched beside him, checking his pulse. An annoyed Navy corpsman was propped against the compartment's aft bulkhead, looking like he wanted to wash his hands of the whole affair.

"Fucking Nip thinks the guy's going into shock," the corpsman mumbled loud enough for most everyone in the compartment to hear. "Don't see how. That redskin ain't injured."

"The man's traumatized over something," Deuce said. "It's just a precaution."

"Traumatized, my ass," the corpsman replied. "Leave it to the Army to stuff a claustrophobic ground-pounder into a submarine."

"All right, that's enough," Jock said. "Somebody want to tell me what happened here?"

Deuce provided the explanation. "We were all sound asleep, sir, when Private Youngblood suddenly sits up and starts wailing like some crazy banshee, saying things like *she's coming for me* and *I'm not ready*. I think he was just having a dream, sir...a real bad one, but just a dream."

Patchett leaned over the catatonic Joe Youngblood, took a good look at his face, and said, "I ain't never seen no dream do this to a man before. He's off somewhere in Section Eight-land. How'd you know what to do to calm him down, son?"

"I worked as an orderly in a hospital," Deuce replied, "and I was premed at Stanford before—whoa!"

Youngblood snapped to a sitting position despite Deuce's attempts to keep him prone. "It's okay, *Corporal Deuce*," he said, embarrassed by the attention he had garnered. "I didn't mean to cause any trouble."

The Navy corpsman was no longer annoyed. Now he was disgusted. Turning to leave, he said, "You gotta be shitting me. No fucking trouble at all. Not a damn bit."

As the corpsman tried to nudge past on the narrow catwalk, Patchett grabbed him lightly by the arm and whispered some advice in his ear: "I'd work on that attitude, swabbie, or you and me's gonna lock asses. Didn't the Navy tell you we're all on the same side here?"

The corpsman—clearly disinterested at the prospect of *locking asses* with this hard-boiled top sergeant— stuttered something like an apology before fleeing aft down the passageway.

Jock helped Private Youngblood to his feet. "Let's go see if we can find a quiet place to talk about this," he said.

Youngblood replied, "I don't think there is such a place on this submarine, sir."

"Maybe I can work something out. Give me a minute."

As Jock stepped through the bulkhead door, Patchett asked, "Did you know that Deuce feller had medical training, sir?"

"Not until after I picked him, Top. Bit of luck, eh? Considering we don't have room for a medic on this trip."

"Luck? You're just dipped in it, ain't you, sir?"

The sub captain had no objection to Jock bringing one of his men out to the cigarette deck for *a little chat*, as he put it. "Just make sure you both remember how to get your asses below deck on the double if we've got to dive. The last Navy man through is dogging that hatch. If you're still on the other side...well, that's too damn bad."

As soon as he emerged topside, Joe Youngblood took a moment to enjoy the starry night and fresh sea air. "Too bad the other guys can't come up here," he said.

"Yeah," Jock replied, "but we're in the crew's way enough as it is. It won't be too long before we'll be getting all the fresh air we can stand. You're from Oklahoma, right?"

"Yes, sir. Near Ada."

"What were you doing before the war?"

"I was working as a farmhand. Taking night courses at the college there, too."

"What were you studying?"

"Education. I wanted to be a teacher."

"I think you'd be a good one, Joe. You'll get your chance when all this is over. But for now, *teach* me about this dream of yours that got you all riled up."

"It was more than a dream, sir. It was an apparition. From my people's stories."

"So let me hear it."

"It's not easy to tell, sir…not something white people want to understand."

"Give me a try."

Youngblood unfurled the story of *The Woman in White*. The tale boiled down to this: in the course of the life of each and every person in his tribe, a woman in white—a spirit—would appear three times. Each appearance would herald a fortuitous event. The first two could happen at any time. The third happened when you were about to die.

"Dying? That's a *fortuitous* event to your people?"

"That's what I've been told ever since I was a child, sir. *It's the natural order of all things*, they say."

"You don't sound convinced of that, Joe."

Private Youngblood didn't need to reply. He stood at the ship's rail, staring silently into the night's emptiness. The picture left no doubt in Jock's mind the man wasn't sold on the concept of death ever being a welcome thing in someone's life.

"And I'm guessing you've seen her three times, Joe?"

"Sort of. Twice for real—the first time was in the big drought. Some of us saw her walking calm as could be through the fields, through the parched, dying crops, barefoot in that simple white dress, long black hair flying in wind like the blast of a furnace. We all hoped it meant the drought would end…and the next day, the rains came. The second time, I'd been arrested on some trumped-up charge. A grocery store got robbed…the storekeeper said some tall redskin kid did it. The police chief hated all Indians, so I was as good a suspect as any to him, even though I was nowhere near the place at the time. And I could prove it."

"I'm sure you could, Joe. So what happened?"

"Late that night, I looked outside through the barred window of my jail cell and saw that same spirit woman walking down the street, singing one of the old songs of hope and courage, her dress glowing white hot in the moonlight. The next morning, just as they were about to take me to the courthouse for arraignment, there's this big commotion at the police station. A bunch of federal marshals were arresting the police chief. Seems he'd been running cover for the local moonshiners...might have even killed a couple of people who got in his way. My charges got dropped the next day. They just went away, like the whole thing never happened."

"And the third time," Jock said, "that was in the dream you just had?"

"That's right, sir. In my dream."

"So you didn't actually see her three times."

"No, sir...but I think it was telling me the third time's coming. In the dream, she was on an island." He pointed in the direction they were sailing. "Maybe *that* island."

"You mean Manus, Joe?"

He nodded. "If she's there, I guess there's not much I can do about it."

"Yeah, there is, Joe. You can try to calm down and—"

"Begging your pardon, sir, but I'm quite calm."

There was no arguing that point. Joe Youngblood was calm...and seemed resigned to a fate Jock refused to accept.

"I've seen this so many times before, Joe. Fear can make us all believe strange things."

Again there was no reply. Jock struggled in the darkness to read the look on Youngblood's face. As near as he could tell, it was a scowl—a look of dismissal. The words the young Indian had said just a few minutes ago echoed in Jock's head: *not something white people want to understand.*

A thin strip of pale gray began to paint the eastern horizon. Soon, the golden light of dawn would shine on their lone submarine as she sailed through the hostile waters of the Bismarck Sea.

"I need you to get below now," the sub's captain called to Jock. "If any planes pop up, we'll need to dive in a hurry. I'd hate like hell to leave you behind."

Chapter Eleven

Jock wiped the river of sweat from his eyes and checked his wristwatch. It was still two hours to sundown—and that meant two more hours just like the last twelve, submerged and loitering off Manus Island, waiting for the darkness which would allow them to surface undetected by the very OP they intended to seize. They'd have to stay drenched in sweat and breathing the sweltering air of the buttoned-up submarine a little longer.

Pressed face-first against the periscope, with his arms draped over its handles like an ardent dance partner, the captain asked Jock, "You want to take a look? You can't see a whole lot...but you'll get a pretty good idea where we are."

Jock took his turn to dance with the periscope. The captain was right: you couldn't make out any coastal details, but it was obvious they were getting close to where they needed to be. The looming conical mass of Mount Dremsel jutting out of the sea to the northwest made that quite clear.

"How far offshore are we?" Jock asked.

"About four miles," the captain replied.

Jock pivoted the periscope a few degrees right. "So I'm guessing the mouth of the Warra River must be right about there. I want to take the rubber boats up that river if I can. You can still get us to within a mile of it when we launch?"

"Yeah, but no closer. It starts to get shallow real fast. You should be able to row to shore in about twenty minutes, though. The current will be pushing you in the right direction, too."

Jock backed away from the periscope. "Okay, then," he said, "I'll be with my men until we're ready to surface."

"MAN OVERBOARD," a seaman on the sub's deck cried as he threw a life ring into the water. The GI it was aimed for, PFC Cotton Allred, never got to grab it. Sergeant Major Patchett already had a firm grip on his shoulder straps and was pulling him out of the water and into the rubber assault boat.

"If you let go of that damn weapon, zipperhead," the sergeant major said, "I'm letting go of you, too." Once Allred sloshed onboard, Patchett added, "Just how clumsy are you, boy? Even the...even the Yankees managed to get themselves into these blow-up toys without going for a swim." He'd almost said, *Even the damn Nips managed...*

From the other rubber boat, Jock called out, "Everything okay, Sergeant Major?"

"Everything's just peachy keen, sir," Patchett replied. "A little wetter than necessary, courtesy of our *cracker* sharpshooter here with his soaking wet weapon"—he put his face inches from Allred's—"which he will not even think about disassembling to clean until we're on dry land. Is that clear, boy?" Turning back to Jock, Patchett concluded, "But otherwise, sir...peachy keen."

That didn't comfort Jock very much. "Please tell me the radio didn't get wet," he said.

Sergeant McMillen, in Patchett's boat, had already

made sure of that. "The walkie-talkie is dry and serviceable, sir," he reported.

"Excellent," Jock replied. "Let's get moving."

Oars began to dig into the water.

"Good luck," the sub captain called after the boats. "Be back for you guys in six days."

"We're counting on it," Jock replied.

They'd been rowing through the darkness for ten minutes. In the bow of the lead boat, Jock studied the compass in his hand. The two GIs on the oars—Deuce Hashimoto and Bogater Boudreau—seemed to be keeping right on course. Sergeants Hadley and Botkin huddled at the stern with the walkie-talkie rigged as a radio direction finder. Botkin fiddled with the loop antenna and shook his head. "Something's not right," he told Hadley, who moved to the bow to relay the news to Jock.

"Sir," Hadley said, "the transmission we expected from Dremsel at 2200...we didn't get it. Just dead air."

"Maybe they changed frequency," Jock replied. "Did you check?"

"We'd just be guessing, sir. And the set would be down for a few minutes every time Botkin has to change crystals. We'd probably miss everything."

"How about the Lorengau station? Did they transmit as usual?"

"Yes, sir. Botkin's getting the bearing to it now. But with only one signal..."

Hadley stopped himself. He didn't need to tell Major Miles that with only one radio signal from the

Japs, they couldn't get a good fix on their boat's position. It took two.

"What are we going to do, sir?" Hadley asked.

"We're going to stay on this compass heading…and keep our fingers crossed good and tight."

A minute later, the lead boat's bow bumped against something quite solid, and it came to an abrupt stop. Low waves lapped against its stern, spinning the craft so it bobbed broadside against whatever was holding it fast. "This can't be right, sir," Hadley whispered, shining a blackout flashlight into the wall of stilt roots scraping the rubber hull. "This is a mangrove…and it looks so thick you probably can't even walk through it."

Bogater Boudreau said, "Maybe we can just ride the crocs through it."

"Knock if off, Bogater," Hadley replied. "That ain't funny."

"Wasn't meant to be, First Sergeant. I tell you what, though…right this minute, I fear the croc more than the Jap. No man's crazy enough to be out here…'cept us, of course."

"I thought you Cajuns weren't afraid of crocodiles," Hadley said.

"Not when we can see 'em…or when we're not in some glorified inner tube they can rip apart with one bite."

"Knock it off, both of you," Jock snapped. "Stay alert, dammit."

Patchett's boat materialized out of the darkness, bumping into the lead boat with the low moan of rubber sliding against rubber. "A little premature for a landfall, ain't it, sir?" the sergeant major said. "Either that, or you guys just set a new world's record for the one-mile row."

"No shit," Jock replied as he studied the map in the red glow of Hadley's flashlight. "Come here, Top. Take a look at this."

Patchett hopped into the lead boat. "Botkin couldn't get a fix from Dremsel like we hoped," Jock said. "But we know where we set out from and we sailed a pretty constant heading—"

"*Pretty* can be an awful inexact word, sir."

"Tell me about it," Jock said as he circled a spot on the map. "The question is, are we east or west of the Warra River? Assuming the current was exactly what the Navy said it was...I'd say we hit land here, somewhere near this old mission. If that's true, we're east. What do you think, Top?"

Patchett took a minute to study the map. When he finally looked up, he said, "I'm not so sure, sir. Lots of variables, like the Navy's info, for openers..."

"Yeah, sure, Top...but look at it this way. When the sun comes up, we'll get our bearings real quick one way or the other. We won't be able to miss Mount Dremsel standing up there like a giant statue. But if we take our best shot now and actually find the river, we can ride it almost all the way to the bluffs below Dremsel and save ourselves a whole lot of jungle walking...and a whole lot of time."

"So what are we gonna do, sir?"

"We're going to start rowing west along this mangrove. If I'm right, the coastline will turn north and we'll hit something that feels like a river pretty soon."

Patchett had doubts he didn't dare voice in front of the men: *If we actually find the river, and if there are any Japs around, we'll be sitting ducks in these boats. Then again, floating along under cover of darkness sure*

*beats the hell out of humping it through a pitch-black
jungle. And we can't turn back. Hell, there's no "back"
to turn to...so it's time for some "unity of command," I
reckon.*

"You heard the major," he hissed at the oarsmen,
his arm a signpost pointing west. "Get these damn boats
moving thataway right fucking now."

They could hear little as their boats slid along the
mangrove, just the soft slapping of the oars against water
and the gentle burble of wakes, sounds so light not even
the birds nesting in the mangrove's trees stirred. They
could see even less. To their right, the shadowy outlines
of the gnarled, tangled stilt roots could—to ten pairs of
apprehensive eyes—look like the talons of giant birds of
prey or perhaps prison bars as depicted by artists on the
edge of insanity. To their left, there was nothing but the
invisible sea.

Like Patchett, Sergeant McMillen was having his
doubts, too. Taking a turn on the oars with Joe
Youngblood, he mumbled, "Are we even sure this is
Manus we're rowing around?"

"Hard for it not to be, Sarge," Youngblood said,
"considering we were only a mile away from it when we
left the submarine, and it's sixty miles long."

PFC Allred—the sharpshooter who had fallen into
the water trying to get off the submarine—kept a wary
eye on the land slipping past. He had doubts, too: *Will
this weapon even fire after I dunked it? Sergeant Major
won't let me take it apart in the boat...too easy to lose a
part into the water, he says. Just shake it out and dry-*

*fire it a couple of times, he says, until we get on dry
land. It won't rust up that fast, he says. As I live and
breathe, he'd better be right. If some Jap pops up along
here, I want to be holding something in my hands that
shoots better'n my pecker.*

In the lead boat, Bogater Boudreau had no doubts,
just questions. "How come we took two of these boats,
sir, when we could've all fit in one with a little room to
spare?"

Jock replied, "So we've got a hundred percent better
chance of getting out of here if we lose one. I'd have
taken three if they could've fit in that damn submarine."

It seemed like much longer, but only five minutes
had passed before the mangrove to their right suddenly
dissolved into the darkness. "Turn right," Jock said,
pointing to a new course. "Yeah, that's it…come around
a little more. There—now we're heading north."

In a few moments, the unmistakable outlines of stilt
roots jutting from the water reappeared. "Okay," Jock
said, "this is looking better. If I'm right about where we
are, in about ten minutes the land is going to bend back
to the west…and we'll be at the mouth of the Warra."

Hadley asked, "How are we going to know for sure
we're at the river, sir?" The question wasn't a challenge,
just an honest expression of concern.

"The Warra's not that wide, a little less than a
hundred yards at the mouth. We'll row diagonally across
it until we hit the far bank. That's the bank we need to
be on, anyway—the west bank. It should only take a few
minutes."

"And if we don't hit it, sir?"

"Well, Tom, we're going to have to get out and
walk on this island at some point. It's just a question of

where we do it."

It had all come together. They were definitely rowing up a river now—the men on the oars could feel the current fighting them, slowing them down. All the assumptions of time, distance, and geography had become hard facts. This had to be the Warra.

One more calculated assumption remained: how long it would take to reach the river's unnavigable headwaters. Just where these headwaters lie was in itself a guess. Jock figured they'd be able to row for about four miles until they reached a point where the elevation began to rise and the river turned to shallow rapids. Even at this slower pace, they'd make it to those headwaters just before dawn. Then they'd become infantrymen again and have to cover the six uphill miles to Mount Dremsel on foot.

They heard the *hiss* of the rapids sooner than they expected—Jock estimated about two miles sooner. "Fucking Aussie maps," Patchett said as they pulled the boats ashore. "Can't even get contour lines in the right place."

"I'm not complaining, Top," Jock replied. "The maps were good enough to find this damn place in the dark just by feeling our way along." He checked his watch. "We've got an hour to sun-up. Give the men a rest stop until then, half on perimeter, half off. Once we've got some light and we can see what the hell we're doing, we'll stash these boats."

Chapter Twelve

"Well, no surprises here," Patchett said as he slithered down the tree he'd climbed to get a visual fix on their location. "Dremsel's right where it oughta be. And it's sunny as all hell, too, not like this tomb we're in down here."

True, the thick canopy allowed only a fraction of the tropical sunlight to reach the rainforest's floor, but at least now—unlike last night's blind journey on the boats—they could see their surroundings. "Looks, feels, and smells just like that damn Papua to me," Bogater Boudreau said as he checked how well the men of his section had cleaned their weapons. "Get more oil into this trigger group," he told Cotton Allred as he tossed the M1 back to him. "That sea water you gave it a bath in makes a pretty poor lubricant, *mon frère.*"

Tom Hadley emerged from a nearby thicket. "I found a good place to hide the boats, sir," he told Jock. "There's a depression just beyond those trees with all kinds of low vegetation growing over it. It'll be natural camouflage. The Japs would have to stumble right over them to actually see them."

"Good work, Tom," Jock said. "Just make sure *we* can find them a few days from now."

"No problem, sir. We'll be marking the trees on our way out of here *Hansel and Gretel style.*" He pulled his machete from his web belt and slashed two small cuts into a tree trunk to illustrate his point. A random observer wouldn't think twice about them, but to the men of *The Squad* they formed an arrow as good as any signpost.

"How long do you want me to keep cutting these marks, sir?"

"Until we hit a landmark," Jock replied. "That trail about two miles north of here should do."

Patchett joined the conversation. "Just make sure them boats get hidden real invisible-like from any direction."

Hadley took in the wilderness around them and said, "Sure, Sergeant Major...but this ain't exactly Grand Central Station we've got here. I mean, there's nobody around...nobody at all."

Patchett replied, "That could all change, son...in a li'l ol' heartbeat."

The Squad walked north through the dense rainforest, a column of ten men in olive drab barely distinguishable from the wilderness around them. Their first objective was to find the trail winding its way around the eastern half of the island. Even fighting the uphill terrain, cluttered with underbrush and the fallen detritus of the forest, they should get there in less than an hour.

Forty-two minutes had elapsed when Boudreau, the point man, stopped, crouched down, and raised his clenched fist—the signal to *halt*. Without any need for further instruction, the GIs formed an oblong perimeter, each man in the prone firing position, as Jock made his way forward.

"This must be the place, sir," Boudreau whispered when Jock arrived.

They were among stout trees just yards from a well-used trail.

"Look at all them tracks, sir...ox carts, all kinds of animals...looking pretty fresh, too. We gonna walk on it?"

"Nope. You know that's not the plan, Bogater. Can't risk getting spotted."

"I know all that, sir. It's just that...well, you gotta admit it would be so much faster on that trail than crawling through this jungle. And it's happened before where plans changed all of a sudden when opportunity knocked."

"It isn't going to happen right now, Bogater. Keep your eyes peeled while I huddle with the sergeant major."

As Jock scuttled back, he saw the perimeter had shrunk, with Patchett, Botkin, and the two Nisei crouched in the middle, all listening intently to the walkie-talkie.

"Lorengau station's come up on the usual frequency, sir," Botkin said. "Ace and Deuce figured out what they're saying. They want Mount Dremsel station to report. They've sent that same message three times now."

Patchett added, "That could mean that something's wrong with the radio up on that OP, sir."

"Maybe," Jock replied, "but one thing's for sure. Lorengau doesn't know what's going on up there." He paused before adding, "And neither do we, dammit."

"It could mean something else, too," Patchett said. "We just might climb up there and find nobody's home."

Jock shook his head. "Or we find a platoon, maybe a company, poking around, trying to figure out why the radio went silent."

Botkin's face blanched as Jock's words took hold. The Nisei's did, too. Patchett's optimism crumbled like a sandcastle battered by a gathering storm. "I get your point, sir. We was better off when they had a routine we could monitor."

"Yeah," Jock replied. "Routines lead to complacency. We learned that a long time ago."

"So what do you propose, sir? Are we going up there anyway?"

"Damn right we are, Sergeant Major. We have to."

They had turned west toward Mount Dremsel, walking parallel to the trail but far enough from it to be concealed in the forest. So far, the map—augmented by the intelligence the Aussie sergeant had given them back at Milne Bay—was proving fairly accurate. *Close enough for government work,* as Patchett would've said out loud, if they weren't keeping strict noise discipline. If the map really was *close enough,* Dremsel was still five miles away.

The going got tougher. Steep ridges bounded the island's central plateau, from which sprouted Dremsel and several lower peaks. The trees had thinned slightly as the elevation rose, providing less shelter from the baking sun of late morning. The men of *The Squad* had slept little in the last three days. Laden with weapons, ammunition, K rations, canteens, ropes for scaling cliffs and crossing streams, and seven days' worth of bulky radio and flashlight batteries, they were already tired. The physical effort to climb the ridge was pushing them to exhaustion. At the steepest face, it was necessary for two men to strip off their gear, ascend the ridge like mountain climbers armed only with rope, tackle, and bayonets, and rig a crude "pulley" system to haul the others up.

Once on the plateau, the sparser tree cover allowed the men to keep Dremsel in view. Even though they had been walking toward it for two hours, the mountain seemed no closer. It loomed in the distance like an inverted cone, bedecked with low trees sprouting from what seemed near-vertical walls. They were all convinced it was mocking them.

Jock signaled the column to *halt*. The men needed to rest and eat. This shady patch, on a rise giving them fair visibility in all directions, was as good a place as any for a break. As they tore into K ration packages, Jock asked Patchett, "Is everyone tanked up on water, Top?"

"Yes, sir. Every man filled up at that last stream we crossed. I watched the Halazone tablets go into each and every canteen, too."

"Good, because it doesn't look like we cross any water for a while. When it rains, we'll stop and catch what we can. Next question—should we leave Boudreau on point?"

"Nah, give him a rest. Let Hadley walk point for a while."

"Sure," Jock said. "Get him over here. I want to show him something on the map."

With Hadley seated on the ground beside him, Jock pointed to a spot on the map and said, "There should be a village straight ahead, Tom. In the aerial photos, it looked like about fifteen or sixteen huts right on the main trail to Lorengau. I want to stay downwind of it so neither man nor beast will smell us. We're getting a little *ripe*."

"Roger, sir. When do you want to kick off?"

As he checked his watch, Jock noticed Patchett doing the same, his fingers rising in sequence as if counting off minutes. Or hours.

"What's your suggestion, Sergeant Major?"

"Well, sir, I know you're all fired up to get to that mountain there, but if we hold off a bit…take a li'l ol' *siesta* right in this fine place, we'll be able to work into nightfall a whole lot better."

It only took a moment for Jock to realize Patchett was right: he *had* wanted to push off immediately for the mountain—and if they did, by nightfall the men would be completely exhausted. Too exhausted, in fact, to make good use of the one ally they'd have when climbing that mountain: the cover of darkness. *We should wait here*, he told himself, *get to the mountain a little bit later…but a lot better rested.*

Hadley wasn't convinced. "It's half a day's walk from Lorengau to the mountain, right? Isn't there a good chance a detail checking on the OP is already there?"

"Not likely," Sergeant Botkin said as he joined the circle. "Lorengau station just sent another message requesting Dremsel's status, sir."

"Sounds typical," Patchett replied. "From what I've seen, Jap HQs don't work no different from ours. They gotta jaw about something for a day or two before they do anything about it. I don't expect they sent nobody out of Lorengau yet. Not if they're still trying to raise them on the radio. And it's for damn sure they ain't got no working telephone up there, neither."

"I've got to agree with the sergeant major," Jock

replied, "and I'm liking his suggestion more and more. How about we push off in about three hours, then...say around 1600?"

Patchett nodded. "I think that would work out just fine, sir."

Jock didn't know what startled him more: being shaken awake by Tom Hadley or the fact he had fallen asleep in the middle of the day. No one could fault him—it was his turn to take the *siesta* Patchett had prescribed. But he had never been able to sleep when a mission was on the line, especially one like this, which put them out on a limb farther than they'd ever been before...and totally on their own.

"We need you to take a look at this, sir," Hadley said. "We're not sure what to do. Take a gander over there."

Just outside the perimeter stood three native tribesmen—two young, lean, and strong, the other old and pot-bellied—wearing only loincloths and symbols painted on their skin. Each held a spear taller than he was, the tips pointed skyward, posing no immediate threat. A short distance away, two GIs—Sergeant McMillen and PFC Allred—crouched behind trees, their weapons pointed at the tribesmen. Their gazes locked, each side seemed to be waiting for the other to make the next move.

"How long has this little standoff been going on?" Jock asked.

"A couple of minutes," McMillen replied.

"Did you try talking to them?"

"Yes, sir…but I don't understand a word they said. Sounds like some sort of pidgin, but I don't know what the hell it means."

"Let me try," Jock said. Taking a few steps toward the trio, he aimed his words at the elder tribesman, saying, "*Poroman…pren…wantok.*"

McMillen asked, "What the hell does that mean, sir?"

"They're the only pidgin words I know for *friend*. Maybe one of them will ring a bell for these gentlemen."

There was no response from the natives at first. The staring contest went on for a few moments more before the elder said, "*Austrelia.*"

It sounded like it might be a question.

"No," Jock replied. "Americans." He pointed to himself and repeated, "American."

The elder insisted, "*Austrelia.*"

Oh, what the hell…

"Ya, ya," Jock said. "Australia."

That seemed to satisfy the elder. He swept his arm in a panoramic arc and said, "*No gut birua ami.*"

Hadley said, "I think I know what that means, sir."

"Yeah, me too. I think he's telling us the Japs are everywhere."

The elder became even more talkative. In the barrage of words he spoke, the Americans picked up only a few: *bilong em…nogat…tekewe.* Coupled with the gestures he made toward the younger men by his side, they figured it could only mean one thing: "Those two are his sons," Jock said, "and the Japs haven't managed to take them away yet."

"Yeah," Hadley replied, "that's what I make out of it, too, sir. I guess the Japs are using the natives here for forced labor just like on Papua."

Patchett approached, waking sleeping soldiers for the next watch. He came to Deuce Hashimoto, who was asleep in the underbrush just a few yards from the encounter in progress with the tribesmen. His eyes popped open and, still lying down, said, "What's all the noise? Aren't we still tactical?"

"Got a few visitors, son," Patchett replied.

Deuce rose to his feet and got a good look at the tribesmen. They got a good look at him, too. In a split second, they were fleeing. Even the elder was fast on his feet.

Allred drew a bead on one of the tribesmen. Before he could pull the trigger, Jock grabbed the M1's muzzle and jerked it skyward.

"They aren't the enemy, Private," Jock said.

"But they're getting away, sir! They'll rat us out!"

"To who? They already think we're with the Japs. Let's not make things even worse by actually killing some of them."

Deuce seemed startled—and a little disheartened— by the whole affair. "I guess it's just not white people who think we all look alike," he said as he shuffled to his place on the perimeter.

Nobody else seemed thrilled with the turn of events, either. Patchett said it best: "All that help we was getting from the natives back on Papua...I guess we can kiss that goodbye on this damn island."

"Put a lid on that talk, Top," Jock said, quiet enough for only Patchett to hear yet harsh enough to convey his annoyance. "One little minus doesn't wipe out that real big plus of having the Nisei with us."

Chapter Thirteen

The *siesta* came to an end all too soon. The GIs shouldered their gear and headed west in the descending sun of late afternoon toward Mound Dremsel. The rest period had made some of the men surprisingly energetic; the head of the column was moving quickly—*too* quickly—with the distance between the lead and trail elements growing minute by minute. Jock gave the hand signals to *slow down* and *close it up.* They'd be losing light steadily from now on. It would be easy for a man to become separated from the column in the thick rainforest. Like Melvin Patchett had always preached, *A man you can't see is a man you can't control...or help out if he gets in deep shit.*

They'd been walking for an hour. Dremsel, its near face in shadow now as the sun settled behind it, finally seemed to be getting closer. They heard no sound but the gentle *thump* of their footsteps and the *squawks* of birds.

One might dare call it *peaceful.*

That's why it was so startling when point man Tom Hadley threw himself to the ground. Only the two men close behind him in the column—Jock and Botkin—could see Hadley disappear into the underbrush...

It took a microsecond for their minds to process *something's wrong*—and then they were on the ground, too.

A few more seconds passed before the entire column—like a row of toppling dominoes—was prone in the dirt.

Low-crawling to Hadley, Jock was halfway there when he saw what was happening: two Japanese

soldiers—*did they even have weapons?*—were
blundering straight toward the column.

"What do we do, sir?" Hadley whispered. "I don't
even think they're armed."

"Capture them."

Boudreau and Youngblood lay behind trees ten feet
back, adrenaline masking their fear, their senses razor
sharp. They still had no idea why they were on their
bellies. Jock signaled them: *Don't shoot. Follow me.*

The Japanese soldiers never saw Jock, Hadley, or
Botkin. They walked right past them...

Right into the middle of the five-man trap.

"NOW," Jock said.

In a blur of rushing bodies, the Americans charged
the startled enemy soldiers and tackled them to the
ground.

A cloud of rice silently exploded from rucksacks
torn from the captives...

But no grenades.

No pistols.

No bayonets.

No weapons at all...

And no resistance, either.

"Ain't no fight in these sumbitches," Boudreau said.
"Shit...they seem downright happy we caught 'em." He
rolled his captive face down and tied his hands behind
his back, just like Hadley was doing to the other.
"What's the deal with these guys? Out here in the jungle
without even a machete? Ain't never seen me an
unarmed Jap before."

"And you're not seeing one now," Ace Nishimoto
replied, arriving too late to do anything but watch.
"They're not Japanese. They're Korean."

The two captives became terrified when they saw the faces of the Nisei.

"How the hell can you tell that?" Boudreau asked.

Jock added, "Koreans? Are you sure?"

"Trust me, sir, they're Korean. Asians don't all look alike to me. I'll bet they speak very poor Japanese, too. And look—the silly bastards are scared shitless of me and Deuce."

Bogater Boudreau was totally confused now. "What the hell are *Ko-reans* doing all dressed up like the Emperor's finest?"

"Korea's been occupied by Japan for over thirty years," Ace replied.

"Yeah," Jock said, "but I didn't know they were using impressed Korean troops off the Asian mainland."

"You're not alone, sir," Ace said. "We never heard that mentioned at G2, either. Do you want me and Deuce to see what we can get out of them?"

"Hell, yeah, Corporal. That's why you're here."

It took a while for Ace and Deuce to break through the Koreans' terror and win their trust. Once they did, though, an unbelievable story—in fractured Japanese—began to spill out with startling enthusiasm.

Deuce told Jock, "We think they're saying they were *servants*, sir, to the Japanese officers up on the OP."

"How many are up there?"

Ace posed the question in Japanese, then struggled to understand the torrent of words forming the answer.

"He's saying *none*, sir."

Jock shook his head and said, "How the hell could that be?"

Another exchange in Japanese. Ace and Deuce were dumbstruck by the Koreans' response. Deuce asked, "Did you get that? Did they really say *kirā*?"

"Yeah," Ace replied, "I think they did."

Kirā. Killer.

As the Koreans smiled proudly, Ace relayed their reply to Jock. "There were six men on the OP, sir—these two plus four officers. They're saying they shot the officers to death."

It was Jock and Patchett's turn to be dumbstruck for a moment, until Patchett asked, "And I'm guessing they did this last night sometime?"

"That's right, Sergeant Major. That must be why their radio went dead."

Patchett checked his watch: *1720 hours. About an hour until sunset...*

"We better get our asses up that damn mountain on the double, sir."

"I couldn't agree more, Sergeant Major."

Patchett pointed his Thompson toward the Koreans. "What about these two?"

Jock replied, "They're coming with us."

Under his breath, Patchett muttered, "Well, ain't that just fucking dandy..."

As *The Squad* raced toward Mount Dremsel with their two Korean *guests*, the interrogation continued on the fly. "Try and find out *why* they killed their officers," Jock told the Nisei.

When they reached the foot of Dremsel, the path leading to its peak looked just as the Aussie Sergeant Burke had described it back at Milne Bay—a *spiral staircase* that wound its way around and around the steeply-sloped mountainsides. As they started the long, uphill climb, Ace and Deuce thought they had pieced together the answer to Jock's question.

"If I'm hearing them right," Ace reported, "the Japanese are preparing to pull out of Manus, so they're getting rid of their excess baggage. These two thought they'd be killed rather than be taken off the island, so…"

"What made them think that?" Jock asked.

"Apparently, there's a POW camp here…and the Japs have been killing off the prisoners. When they're done with that, the rumor is they'll kill off the Korean guards—"

"And these two as well, I suppose," Jock said. "Where's this POW camp?"

"Just this side of Lorengau, sir."

Patchett could see the wheels in Jock's head turning—and he didn't like it one bit. He pulled close to his major and whispered, "I know what you're thinking, sir. You best put a notion to freelance out of your mind right now. Rescuing POWs ain't our mission here." He stopped himself from adding, *Don't get your hopes up, sir. She ain't gonna be here in no POW camp. You said yourself Miss Forbes is dead.*

Jock shrugged him off. "First things first, Sergeant Major. After that, we'll play it by ear."

"We lose focus here, sir, and we just might all get dead. Plus them GIs landing at Hollandia get dealt a real bad hand."

"Tell me something I don't already know, Sergeant

Major. Like I said, we're going to play it by ear. End of story."

"With all due respect, sir—"

Jock's icy glare cut him off. "Give it a rest, Top. I haven't forgotten what *with all due respect* really means."

The last rays of sunset still lit the peak when Jock and his men got there. The OP's layout looked quite like they expected. The watchtower the Aussies built was still standing, well-weathered and rickety but serviceable, its apex looming high over the treetops. The radio—a low-power unit, just like Botkin suspected—sat unmolested inside an open-sided wooden shelter. Several tents housed living accommodations. In one of them were the bodies of the four slain officers: three lieutenants from the Imperial Japanese Navy, one captain from the Army. All had been shot to death. Squadrons of flies and battalions of maggots were laying claim to the corpses.

As Ace Nishimoto spun the cranks of the radio's generator, Sergeant Botkin hunched over the set's dials with headsets pressed to his ears. It only took a moment for him to jump up and announce, "We're in business, sir. The set's working."

"That's great," Jock said. "Tell Lorengau we had radio trouble but we're back on the air."

Ace and Deuce composed the message in Japanese Morse. Botkin sent it. The reply from Lorengau was immediate. After quickly translating it, Deuce read it out loud.

"The captain-in-charge has been warned not to let the radio malfunction again," he said, stifling a laugh. "And they want to know if his section needs relief before Three March."

"That sounds almost too good to be true," Jock replied. "By Two March we'll be long gone. Tell them *the captain* is doing just fine. No relief necessary."

They exchanged messages with the Japanese at Lorengau again. "One more thing, sir," Deuce said as he scrawled the translation. "They say to make sure we transmit the usual status report at 2200."

Patchett had other things on his mind. "We gotta get rid of them rotting bodies, sir...and that lousy death tent they're in, too."

"Have the Koreans dig some graves downslope," Jock replied.

"You sure that's such a good idea, sir? I mean, untying them and all?"

"They're not going anywhere, Top. They think they hit the jackpot running into us."

"I ain't so sure about this, sir..."

"Besides, Top, there's probably a lot of intel we can get out of them."

Patchett blew out a chestful of frustration. "You're thinking about trying to save these damn POWs, ain't you, sir?"

"I don't know if we can save anyone or not. But we sure as hell are going to find out what the story is. We just got handed a gift—we're on top of this mountain, without a fight, two whole days ahead of schedule. We're going to make good use of that extra time."

"It still ain't our mission, sir."

"We're doing our mission, Top. Hell, it's damn near

done already. But maybe—just maybe—we can do a little bit more. Even if we can just pinpoint the POW camp so our flyboys don't bomb it."

And just maybe we get ourselves all killed chasing rainbows, Patchett thought.

But he didn't dare say that out loud.

All he said was, "As you wish, sir. As you wish."

"By the way, Top...after what's happened so far, do you still think the minuses of having the Nisei outweigh the pluses?"

"Still a little early to tell, ain't it, sir?"

Chapter Fourteen

It poured all night, turning the OP at Mount Dremsel's peak into a replica of the soggy rainforest floor far below. Without being told, the Koreans had taken over the water collection duties, catching the rain in outstretched ponchos, diligently ensuring everyone's canteens were filled to the brim. The stash of water jugs the Japanese had used on the OP were topped off, too. Watching the captives bustle about as dawn broke, Patchett told Jock, "Even if it stops raining right this minute, we should be good on water for our planned stay up here, sir. These *Ko-reans* are working their asses off…but I still ain't trusting them one li'l bit. Something really puzzles the shit out of me, though."

"What's that, Top?" Jock asked.

"There was Nambus and Arisakas laying all over the place when we got here," he said, pointing to the pile of Japanese pistols and rifles the GIs had gathered and secured. "How come they didn't take any when they made their getaway?"

"They were trying not to look hostile, Top. Their only chance at survival was getting taken in by some natives."

"That'll never happen, sir. Given half a chance, the natives'll run spears right through 'em, I reckon."

"Maybe so, Top. But they're in your hands now. You sure you've got enough guys to cover this OP and keep an eye on the Koreans while we're gone?"

"Yes, sir. Me and Allred, with Botkin and that Nip Ace on the radio, should do the job just fine…but you sure you want to give me Ace?"

"Why not him?"

"He's the one Hadley says is the better fighter, sir. Wouldn't you rather have a better fighter where you're going?"

"Nah...I just need a translator. You need both."

"Okay, sir...if that's the way you want it."

Hadley walked up with a walkie-talkie. "Botkin's got me all checked out on changing the frequency on this thing, sir."

Patchett had that skeptical look on his face. "What the hell you gonna do with that thing, sir? You'll be out of range with us in no time."

"True," Jock replied, "but we can still receive your nightly 2200 broadcast to Lorengau. If you don't transmit, we know you're in trouble."

"Hmm...pretty clever," Patchett said. "So I'm guessing you're expecting to be gone a while, then?"

"Maybe. The earliest we'll be back is midday tomorrow, Top."

"And if you're not?"

"Hold this OP until sunrise of Two March, then get the hell back to the boats."

As soon as Jock and his men headed off down the mountain, Sergeant Botkin had a question for Sergeant Major Patchett: "Do you think the major's got his hopes up about finding Miss Forbes? I thought everyone said she was dead."

"She's *presumed* dead, son. Big difference."

"What do you think, Sergeant Major?"

"If she was a POW, she probably would've still

been in Buna when we finally took the place. But we didn't find no POWs there…not live ones, anyway."

"But couldn't she still be in a camp someplace else?"

"Who knows, son? You don't get no cards and letters from POWs."

Jock and his five men were halfway down the *spiral staircase* when it finally stopped raining. As they walked, each man used the army green towel looped over his neck to wipe the water droplets from his weapon—all except Deuce Hashimoto. He seemed preoccupied and very uncomfortable as he tugged at his crotch.

"What's the matter, Deuce?" Tom Hadley asked. "A bug crawl up your ass?"

"No, First Sergeant. I'm itching like crazy."

As Deuce pulled the wet fabric of his trousers tight against his buttocks, Hadley saw the distinct outline of another garment below. "Holy shit, Deuce…are you wearing underpants?"

"Yeah…I am."

"For cryin' out loud, how long have you had them on?"

"Since the submarine, First Sergeant."

"Shit. How many times do we have to tell you? *No fucking underwear in the tropics.* That's guaranteed crotch rot. Take those goddamn things off right now."

Deuce shed his gear and his pants. When he slid the underpants down his legs, he was embarrassed to find Hadley squatting before him, ready to check him out.

"Damn!" Hadley said, eyeing Deuce's wares. "Seen worse, but that's a pretty good irritation." He pulled a packet from his first aid kit. "Here...put some sulfa on it. Didn't they teach you anything in that medical school?"

"Crotch rot wasn't much of an issue in San Francisco, First Sergeant."

"You ain't in Frisco anymore, Corporal. Pay attention when we tell you something. And make it snappy, before Major Miles kicks us both in the ass for straggling."

Deuce did as he was told. Once he donned his gear again, though, he tossed the underpants to the side of the trail.

"Pick those lousy drawers up and take them with you," Hadley said. "They've got your fucking name in them. In English! Why don't you just leave the Japs a calling card that we're here?"

Bogater Boudreau was where he felt he belonged: walking point, the lead man in the column. *Ain't nobody got the instinct like me. I'd rather be point man all day long, every damn day, than trust some other touch-hole with the job.*

No sooner did that thought pass than the razor-sharp instinct had him flat on his belly. There was something on the trail ahead, right at the base of Mount Dremsel. The five men behind him followed his lead and dove for cover, too.

An anxious Jock, a few paces back and unable to see what his point man could, whispered, "What the hell's going on, Bogater?"

"I don't rightly know, sir."

Jock crawled forward to take a look.

There was a native man sitting cross-legged smack in the middle of the trail. He was grinning broadly as he waved a hand in greeting.

"You come back, Aussie," the man said. "I be waiting long time."

"We're not Australians," Jock replied. "We're Americans."

"Same thing. You kill Japanese, yes?"

"We sure try."

Jock figured the man to be in his thirties, but like most island men who'd reached that age, he looked older. It was the weathered and leathery skin that did it.

At least this guy still seems to have some of his teeth.

The man popped to his feet like a spry youngster. He was barefoot and wore a tattered Australian Army shirt over baggy shorts. A web belt laden with ammo pouches hung around his waist. When he stood, his slender frame was barely over five feet tall.

I'll bet he weighs about eighty pounds soaking wet.

"My name is Oscar Solo," the man said. "I am here to help you take back Lorengau."

Jock asked, "How the hell did you know we were here?"

"You make much noise."

Tom Hadley voiced what everyone was thinking: "You think we can trust this guy, sir?"

Oscar seemed injured by the question. He asked, "Don't you remember me? I am *Number One Fuzzy-Wuzzy.*" His chest puffed with pride as he said it.

Fuzzy-wuzzies: what the Australians called the island natives.

"I have proof," Oscar said. He reached into his breast pocket and produced what looked like the leaf of some jungle plant. Folded within it was a stained and brittle piece of paper. He opened it carefully and offered it to the Americans.

Jock read the paper slowly, trying not to damage it any worse than time and nature already had. It certainly looked like an official Australian Army letter, granting Oscar Solo a commendation for *Meritorious Service* in support of His Majesty's Australian Forces on Manus Island.

This looks like the real deal.

Jock leaned close to Hadley and whispered, "Keep Deuce out of sight until I tell you. Let's not spook this guy like those other tribesmen. Maybe he can do us some good."

"My rifle is ready, sir," Oscar added.

"Show me, Mister Solo."

"No *mister*, sir…you call me *Oscar*, please." He led Jock off the trail. Stashed behind a tree was an Enfield Rifle, its stock engraved with the royal crown of the British Empire.

"Please, sir…inspect it. But careful…it is loaded."

Jock gave the rifle a quick but thorough going over. When he was done, he said, "This weapon is in fine shape. How many rounds do you have for it?"

Oscar patted his ammo pouches and said, "Many more than these, sir."

"Very good. My name is Miles…Major Jock Miles, US Army. That tall fellow over there is First Sergeant Tom Hadley. Now let's have ourselves a little talk."

Jock told Oscar why they were there and what they planned to do. When asked if he knew a way to the POW camp that would keep them off the main Lorengau trail, avoiding all the villages along the way, he replied, "Yes. There is another way...very quick-quick, too, Major Jock. No one see us."

"Can you guide us there, Oscar?"

"Yes, Major Jock, yes! We go now, okay?"

"Not quite yet," Jock said. He proceeded to explain there was a Japanese-American soldier with the patrol, finishing with, "He's a friend, Oscar. Not your enemy." Then he signaled Hadley to bring Deuce forward.

Solo didn't seem in the least bit concerned. He pointed to the Nisei and said, "If you not kill him, I not kill him."

Deuce took little comfort in that sentiment: *Great...the others just ran away. This one would just as soon finish me off.*

Oscar asked, "Sir, your other men on the mountain. They stay?"

"How the hell did you know about *other men*?"

"I count you when you go up last night. Six here now, six up there."

"Gee, you don't miss a trick, do you?"

The little tribesman's reply was a proud, beaming smile.

Jock signaled the patrol to its feet. "All right, Oscar," he said, "you lead, we'll follow."

Following Oscar Solo was proving quite a challenge. He covered ground rapidly, plunging Jock's patrol deeper and deeper into an impenetrable wall of green as the rainforest thinned and yielded to jungle.

Wasn't expecting terrain like this, Jock told himself. *This place is full of surprises. I hope to hell I didn't fuck up taking this little guy on as a guide.*

Rarely did Oscar bother to swing his machete, instead slipping his small, lithe body through the tangled vines as if they were no more than sinewy curtains. When he did lash out with the blade, it was more often to slice a particular vine from the undergrowth. Without slowing a step, he'd squeeze the clear fluid within the vine into his mouth. The jungle was his canteen.

The taller, broad-shouldered Americans couldn't navigate this murky wilderness quite so easily. Bogater Boudreau and Joe Youngblood, the next men behind Oscar, often had to hack their way through the stubborn patches inch by inch. Then all the GIs would jog through the newly cut openings to catch up to their guide. The machete wielding was exhausting, too. Boudreau and Youngblood were ready to let someone else swing the blades for a while.

Hadley brought up the rear of the column so he could better police up stragglers. During passage through some relatively open ground, he sprinted to the column's head to ask Jock, "You have any idea where the hell we are, sir?"

Compass in hand, Jock replied, "All I know is we're headed east-northeast. That's where we want to be."

"How much ground you figure we've covered so far, sir?"

"I have no idea, Tom. But I'm guessing this little hike is going to last about six hours."

"Shit," Hadley said as he checked his watch. They'd

only been walking for one hour...

And we're just going deeper and deeper into this jungle. The fucking insects are the size of small airplanes. And those big snakes ain't too shy of people, either. I guess they own this neighborhood. And if they don't, I hate to think what the hell does own it.

On his way back to the rear of the column, he checked each man he passed in turn. They were all doing okay—except for Deuce Hashimoto.

"How's the crotch holding up, Deuce?"

"Itches like crazy, First Sergeant."

"I'm real sorry to hear that...but we need you out here. Don't even think about dropping out and going back to the mountain."

Going back...the thought of making his way back to Mount Dremsel—alone—sent a shiver down Deuce's spine. He had decided many tortured steps ago to endure being filthy and wet all the time, broiling in the heat, and battling the enormous bugs and snakes. He'd endure the crotch rot, too.

"Who the hell wants to go back, First Sergeant? I'm staying right here...with all you guys."

Chapter Fifteen

Jock's estimate of a *six-hour hike* proved to be right on the money. It was just past 1600 hours when Oscar Solo pointed ahead and said, "Over there, Major Jock. Prison camp just across river."

They could hear the river but not see it. The source of that watery burble might have only been thirty or forty yards away, but the jungle hid its secrets well.

"Good," Jock replied, glad for the brief chance to rest and regroup. Watching his exhausted men flop into a defensive perimeter, he added, "My men and I are running on fumes. You're a tough man to keep up with, Oscar."

Solo didn't approve of the rest stop. "You want to see prison camp before dark, no?"

"Of course," Jock replied.

"Then we must walk fast more. We sleep later."

*Sleep later...*the GIs would have been happy to take a nap right now, but they knew better. "Fat load of good this perimeter does us," Sergeant Mike McMillen grumbled. "We can't see five feet in this fucking jungle. Keep your eyes peeled, you guys. Any numbnuts I catch dozing off gets my size ten right up his ass."

Their canteens were running low. It had only rained once—*poured*, rather, and briefly at that—as they struggled to make their way. They had only managed to catch a little in their helmets as they walked—barely enough for a refreshing swallow. At least now a plentiful source of cool, fresh water—the river—was nearby. They celebrated its presence by taking last gulps of lukewarm water from the canteens and then dumping whatever was left on their sweltering heads. Oscar laughed as he watched them.

Jock took the map from his helmet liner, unfolded it, and asked the question all his men were thinking: "Okay…now where the hell are we?" Along their direction of travel, the map showed a crooked blue line, indicating a wide creek or river. "Looks like we're *here*," he said as his finger fell on a point along that blue line. That point was just a little more than halfway between Mount Dremsel and Lorengau. "The trail to Lorengau—and two villages—should be less than a mile south of here."

Oscar didn't bother to look at the map. "Yes, Major Jock, villages that way," he said, pointing south. "Trail, too."

"Then we're almost ten miles from Lorengau," Jock said. "Why the hell did they put the camp way out here, in the middle of nowhere?"

Oscar just shrugged. Then he said, "But we must hurry. Sun go away soon."

Bogater Boudreau returned from his scouting detail at the river. He was shaking his head. "We gotta go farther upstream, sir," he reported. "Too many damn crocs in these parts. Water looks to be about chest high—just how they like it."

Shit, Jock thought, *more daylight wasted.*

"You have rope," Oscar protested. "We make rope bridge. Cross here."

"Negative," Jock replied. "Somebody's still got to wade across to rig the far side. Sergeant Boudreau's my resident croc expert…and there's nothing he'd like better than to shoot one of those ugly bastards in the head. But a gunshot right now is as good as waving a big flag at the Japs. We're going farther upstream."

They were bunched together now, each hanging on to the pack of the man in front of him, afraid of being separated and lost in the thick undergrowth. It took almost an hour of hacking through one tangled vine after another until they found a safe place to cross. There, the water was shallow—only ankle deep—and ran swiftly. "Ain't gonna find no crocs here," Boudreau reported.

They crossed the river, filling their canteens as they did. Hadley kept an eagle eye on the process. "That's right, boys," he said, "two Halazone tablets in every one of those canteens. Let 'em dissolve real good. First man I see trying to cheat, I'm gonna let die in a pool of his own runny shit."

The journey south along the river had brought them close to one of the villages drawn on the map. They could see several shafts of wispy, grayish smoke rising above the trees. Oscar plucked from the air an aroma only he could distinguish. Rubbing his empty belly, he slipped into excited pidgin and announced, "*Kaikai! Kukim pik!*"

Hungry, exhausted, and miserable, Deuce asked, "What did he say? It was about food, wasn't it?"

"Yeah," Hadley replied. "Some lucky bastards are roasting a pig over there."

"That doesn't seem fair, First Sergeant. These natives—these *primitives*—eat better than we do."

Hadley replied, "What's not fair? They killed the pig, they get to eat it. If you kill a pig, you'll get to eat it, too. And who said they're natives? They could be Japs.

Stop feeling sorry for yourself and stay alert, dammit."
He pointed toward Oscar Solo and added, "Don't be
knocking these *primitives*, either. In Australia and
Papua, they saved our asses more times than I care to
remember."

Once across the river, they moved more slowly—
more cautiously—as they made their way back up the
opposite bank toward the camp. They couldn't see any
of it yet, but the sounds of human activity filtered
through the trees like whispered warnings. As they drew
still closer, those whispers grew and became
recognizable: the rumble of vehicles, the neighing of
horses, voices shouting in Japanese.

Jock pulled Deuce to his side and whispered, "What
are they saying, Corporal?"

"Just marching commands, sir…and telling
someone to hurry up."

Jock asked Oscar, "How much farther to the barbed
wire?"

"Very close, Major Jock."

He was right. After ten minutes of silent struggle
through the thick vegetation, the Americans could catch
fleeting orange glints of the setting sun reflecting off the
tin roofs of the camp.

They crawled forward, silently enduring the pain of
prickly thorns tearing skin right through their clothes.
Mike McMillen bit his tongue as his arm was sliced by
another of nature's barbs: *Gotta get some sulfa in these
cuts real soon or we're all going to die of jungle
infections. But I'll take getting scarred up…just so I
don't see another fucking snake.*

Then, just short of the wire, like a curtain being
drawn back, they earned their reward: a broad view of

the prison camp from well-concealed front-row seats.

"Just like what I figured," Jock whispered to Hadley. "Twenty, maybe thirty acres of cleared land, watchtowers in the four corners. We've got to get around the east side for a good look at those buildings."

"Something's funny, though, sir," Hadley said. "That handful of prisoners over there near the wire, digging those holes—they aren't white like we expected. They're Melanesian. Sure, they've got shorts and shirts on instead of loin cloths, but still...what the hell are they doing in there?"

"Let's ask Oscar."

The native guide's answer was simple: they were islanders who had worked for the Australian administrators before the Japanese came and had failed to show the proper *switching of allegiances*. Mostly clerks, merchants, kitchen help, and menservants—about a hundred of them.

"So they're in the *nick*," Oscar said.

"They didn't just kill them?"

"No, Major Jock. They only kill ones like me, who fight. The rest...hostages."

"Are there any white men in there?" Jock asked.

"Some."

Then Oscar pointed to the natives on the digging detail. "And those not *holes*, Sergeant Tom," he said to Hadley. "They are graves."

"Those guards," Hadley said, "are they Japanese or Korean?"

"Go ask Deuce," Jock replied.

Hadley returned quickly with the answer. "He can't tell, sir. They're too far away. Can't see their faces good."

The Squad moved slowly east along the camp's southern wire. Progress through the thick jungle growth became tougher: the fraction of daylight that managed to filter through the canopy was fading as late afternoon slid into evening. Jock and Oscar were in total agreement on one point: they'd stop for the night before they lost the light completely. It would be too dangerous to try and keep going in the dark.

We'll make noise...we won't be able to help it stumbling around in the blackness.

And Japs could be less than fifty yards away.

There was still some daylight when they reached the southeast corner of the camp, enough to see the soldier manning the watchtower. His gaze was focused on the camp's interior. He never once turned to look into the jungle beyond the wire.

"I guess they're not much worried about people trying to get *in*," Hadley whispered.

As the GIs turned north to skirt the camp's eastern edge, Oscar pointed to their right and warned, "Be very careful. Big *pundaun* that way."

Pundaun...that word was beyond the GIs' knowledge of pidgin. Oscar could tell right away by the confused looks on their faces.

"Come. I show."

"No, wait," Jock said as he studied the map. "It's almost dark. We don't have time."

Oscar made a motion with his hand—a downward tuck with flattened palm—like a diver plummeting.

"You mean we're going to fall?"

"Ya, Major Jock. You fall far."

"I guess we would," Jock said, his finger tracing a line on the map. "Looks like we're on the edge of a real big drop here, men…the eastern edge of this island's central plateau."

It was starting to make sense to Jock why the Japanese put this prison camp so far outside Lorengau: *Pretty unique location, even for this part of the world. So many natural obstacles. If someone manages to slip through the wire, they get their choice of thick, nasty jungle, a river full of crocodiles, or a chance to fall off a cliff. I wonder if anyone's even tried?*

And if they did, how long did they survive?

"Come on," he urged his men, "let's try to get near those buildings while we can still see a little."

They made it just as the sun dropped behind distant trees. Though nestled close together in the undergrowth, they were almost as invisible to each other as they were to the Japanese. Exhausted and bleeding, they had made it to their objective, at least. Now, it was time for a new revelation: this was where they'd be spending the night, in easy range of the enemy, surrounded by nature's tropical horrors. There would be no going back once darkness fell.

Bogater Boudreau held up his bayonet. Stuck to its point was the largest crawling insect he'd ever seen—a centipede of some sort, almost a foot long, with a body like an armadillo. "Think we can eat this?" he asked Joe Youngblood, waving the impaled, writhing creature in his face.

Youngblood pushed the bayonet away. "Be my guest, Sergeant."

"Well, maybe not." Boudreau replied. With a flick of the bayonet, he launched the creature far into the tangled green web surrounding them.

Insects and food were the farthest things from

Jock's mind at the moment. Peering through a veil of broad leaves, he and Hadley couldn't take their eyes off the scene unfolding before them.

Just beyond the gate in the camp's wire stood several barracks-like buildings and a house surrounded by a veranda. The house's tarnished tin roof reflected what little it could of the sun's last light. A Japanese officer stood on the veranda, looking down at a small circle of his soldiers—*ten, maybe twelve* at a quick count—and a barefoot man at the center.

Definitely not Japanese or Melanesian. Those rags he's wearing look like what's left of an Aussie flyer's uniform. I think I can still see the wings sewn on.

His arms were bound to his sides.

He was blindfolded.

One of the soldiers stepped to the blindfolded man and forced him to his knees.

He drew a sword...

Like a batter awaiting the pitcher's delivery, he cocked the sword behind his ear...

Just a glint as the shiny blade vanished in a horizontal blur...

And buried itself in the Aussie flyer's neck.

"Holy fuck!" Hadley said. Immediately, he covered his mouth, afraid he'd said it too loud.

The executioner put a foot on the Aussie's back and pulled the sword free. The decapitation was, at best, partial.

He took another swing—this time, a vertical hack straight down.

The head bounced and came free.

It pivoted on its face and rolled one full turn in the dirt.

Two soldiers dragged the headless body to a cart. A third lifted the head, using an ear for a handle. It, too, was flung into the cart.

"Holy fuck," Hadley repeated, much quieter this time.

"Miserable, low-life savages," Jock whispered.

Oscar said, "See? I tell you…holes are graves."

A few minutes later, the GIs found themselves wrapped in the cloak of night's darkness.

Chapter Sixteen

The only light the men of *The Squad* could see were the few oil lanterns burning in the camp, like stars hung low in the sky. The moon seemed to cast no glow this night. Even if it did, none would have penetrated to the jungle floor where they lay.

Tom Hadley turned off the walkie-talkie. "The 2200 report from the OP just went over the air, sir."

"That's good. At least all's well with Patch and his boys."

Hadley asked, "How many Japs you figure there are in that camp, sir?"

"From what we saw, Tom, I'm thinking no more than a platoon or two."

"You think we could take them?"

"Not unless we could knock out all four watchtowers first...and that's not likely. Looks like they've got Nambus up there."

"Yeah, I noticed that, too." There was an awkward pause before Hadley added, "So what are we going to do, sir?"

Without hesitation, Jock replied, "Right now, I have no earthly idea, Tom. Maybe when the sun comes up we can see a little more...and maybe—"

"Seems kind of risky, sir. We don't know if there's any more of our guys left in there to save. That guy they just killed...suppose he was the last one?"

"Wake up, Deuce," Sergeant McMillen whispered.

"Your turn on watch."

"I'm awake, Sergeant. Who the hell can sleep out here, anyway?"

McMillen cupped a hand over his red flashlight, letting it cast a dim, ghostly light on Deuce's face. The man looked scared out of his mind. It wasn't just the deep shadows making him appear that way.

"You've got to loosen up a little, Deuce. Nobody's shooting at you yet."

"I just...I just can't stand being out here, Sergeant. All these insects...these snakes..."

"Are you shitting me? We just watched a guy get his head cut off and you're worried about *bugs*? I think you need something to keep yourself busy, so get on the stick and go relieve the Indian over there."

Tom Hadley had just come off watch. He crawled through the blackness like a blind man looking for Jock—*He should only be a couple of feet away!*—but he couldn't find him. Not until he stumbled right over someone hunkered under a ground sheet.

"Oh, shit," Hadley whispered, "is that you, sir?"

"Yeah, Tom, it's me. Come in here for a minute. I think I've figured something out."

Beneath the ground sheet, Jock was using a flashlight to study the map and make notes without lighting up their position to the Japanese.

"Thick as this jungle is, sir, I'm not sure the Japs would see one li'l ol' red flashlight, anyway."

"Let's not take that chance, Tom. Now look at this...we've seen every part of that camp except the north side. We haven't gotten a good look at those buildings...or who's in them. At first light, I want you and Youngblood to scout up that way."

"Why Youngblood, sir?"

"He's our sharpshooter. I want him to see the two towers on that end up close, so he can figure out which of the four are the easier to take out." He tore a page from his notebook and handed it to Hadley. "Here...I made you a diagram of the camp as we know it so far. I've got one just like it. Go have a look and fill in the blanks, Tom."

Hadley stuck the diagram inside his helmet. "Good plan, sir. I'll take care of it."

"Just be extra careful about one thing, Tom. That trail that runs into the camp...you're going to have to cross it somewhere. Pick a good spot so you won't get..."

A strange sound suddenly filled the air, stopping Jock's words cold. It was music—and it sounded so out of place in this brutal jungle. Someone in the camp was playing a piano, and a well-tuned one, at that.

"What the hell?" Jock said. "That's Liszt...one of the *Hungarian Rhapsodies*."

"How the hell do you know that, sir?"

The answer was almost too painful to think about, let alone say out loud: "Because Jillian—*Miss Forbes*—used to play it all the time. She loved Liszt."

Hadley wished he had never asked the question. Every man in the unit tiptoed around any mention of Jillian when Jock was near. She had helped them in so many ways on Cape York and again on Papua—and now she was gone. That knowledge was just as painful to the men as it was to Jock.

She might have been the major's woman...but they all loved her.

"Who do you think is playing that, sir?"

Jock shook his head. "I wish I knew, Tom."

Hadley and Youngblood cursed their luck. A Japanese truck—led by a colonel on horseback—was moving up the trail toward the prison camp. It snarled in low gear as it slowly climbed the steep trail up the ridge, trying to keep a respectable distance from the horse walking before it. They were about to cross the trail when they heard the racket of the truck coming and threw themselves back into the undergrowth. There they lay, well concealed, waiting for this noisy little parade to pass just yards in front of them.

"How many trucks you count, Joe?"

"Just one. Troops in the back. Not too many, though. Maybe five. But there are two more on horseback bringing up the rear."

That made a total of three horses—a grand white stallion for the colonel, a mottled brown one for a captain, and a black one for a sergeant.

"They'd make much better time if they got rid of the horses," Youngblood said.

"Yeah, and we'd make much better time if they weren't here at all."

Within minutes, the Japanese colonel and his entourage had entered the prison camp's gate. The officer who had presided over last night's execution stood at attention, ready to greet them. In the daylight, his insignia of rank could be read with binoculars.

"He's a captain," Jock said. "I wonder who's really in charge there...him, or this cowboy colonel?"

Bogater Boudreau said, "It probably ain't considered much of a camp if it's just a captain in charge, sir."

As the colonel brought his mount to a halt, the captain stepped forward, speaking quite loudly.

Jock asked, "What's he saying, Deuce?"

"He's saying *greetings,* and *welcome to the such and such camp*...I couldn't make out the name, sir. Now he's telling him that accommodations have been prepared at Headquarters House."

"Yeah," Jock said, "he's pointing at the house with the veranda. Figured that was the headquarters. I guess you're right, Bogater...can't be much of a camp with just a captain in charge."

There was more talking between the Japanese officers but the volume was much lower now. Deuce couldn't make any of it out.

"You know," Jock said, "there isn't a whole lot to inspect at the camp, either. What's that colonel doing here, anyway?"

It was a quiet, sleepy morning on the Mount Dremsel OP. Sergeant Stu Botkin was tying to keep himself awake, listlessly spinning the radio dial. He made sure that every few minutes, though, he'd stop at Lorengau's frequency to make sure they weren't trying to raise the OP.

I can't doze off, he reminded himself. *It's the sergeant major's turn to take a nap. That means I'm in charge.*

Ace Nishimoto was on lookout duty close by, his binoculars scanning east toward Lorengau for any signs of activity. Cotton Allred, the sharpshooter, was posted on the north side of the peak, with a clear view well down the *spiral staircase.* With that clear view came a clear shot at anyone trying to climb the trail to the top. The two Koreans—Park and Sung—sat near Botkin's feet, waiting for something to do.

On the third pass through the Lorengau frequency, Botkin sat bolt upright. The OP was being called. With a frantic wave, he sent Park and Sung to the hand-crank generator. The Koreans scuffled over who would have the honor to turn the handles and power the transmitter.

"For cryin' out loud," Botkin called to Ace. "Tell them to stop jerking around and take turns, dammit. I need transmit power NOW."

Patchett awoke as if summoned by some silent alarm. By the time he reached the radio shack, he was wide awake, watching over Ace's shoulder as he translated the message.

"Get this," Ace reported. "We're having a *command visit.* A *Colonel Yamagura* and his party will arrive tomorrow around midday."

"Ain't that great fucking news," Patchett said. "How many in this *party?*"

"Hang on, Sergeant Major. We're just getting to that."

As he scribbled the message text, Ace added, "You realize if they ever code this stuff, we're fucked?"

Patchett replied, "How do you know it ain't coded right now, son?"

"Hmm...good point, Sergeant Major...but I sure hope that's not true. Anyway, the message says there'll be three in the party..." He paused, struggling to translate a phrase, before adding, "And I think they're saying these three will be on horseback."

"Bullshit," Patchett replied. "Ain't no horse gonna climb that damn trail up this mountain. It's too steep and narrow...they'll spook. That colonel may gallop out here but he'll be climbing this li'l ol' hill on foot, just like everyone else."

Ace asked, "What are we going to do when that colonel shows up?"

"Simple, son," Patchett replied. "We're gonna kill him...and anybody else who shows up with him, too. We've got to. We ain't giving up this OP until we're damn good and ready."

That didn't give Ace much in the way of reassurance. "But what about Park and Sung?" he asked. "What if they turn against us when the shit hits the fan?"

"Then they die, too, son. And how'd you find out them *Ko-reans'* names, dammit?"

"I asked them, Sergeant Major."

"Well, forget them names right now. I don't give a shit who they are...and you better not, neither."

Chapter Seventeen

It started to rain buckets. "Catch all you can," Jock told McMillen, Boudreau, and Deuce. "It'll save us a trip back to the river."

On the north side of the prison camp, Hadley and Youngblood were catching all they could, too. Youngblood found a vine that allowed a fountain-like cascade to descend its length from one broad leaf to another. He inserted the canteens into the steady flow until all four were quickly filled.

"Of course," Hadley said, "we could wring our clothes out at this point and probably fill those canteens, too."

"But our clothes are filthy and mildewed, First Sergeant. Who wants to drink wash water?"

"Just making a little joke, Joe, that's all."

Damn...this Indian kid can be so serious.

The maddening *hiss* of jungle rain subsided as they neared the camp's barbed wire fence. They settled into a natural hide amidst the undergrowth and began to record what they saw.

"What do you think of the watchtowers?" Hadley asked. "Where can you get the best shot?"

"Well, forget the east side, near the camp gate," Youngblood said. "I'd get one tower but then they'd be all over me. And forget the west side, too. I'd have to set up on the riverbank. The crocs would probably get me before I could get a shot off. But from the north or south side, I could take out the two close towers...and they'd never know what hit them."

"The two near ones...that's the best you can do?"

Youngblood looked at him like that was the world's stupidest question. "Yes, First Sergeant. I reckon the far towers would be about five hundred yards away. Low probability of a first-round hit."

In the cooling rain's wake, mist was rising off the camp's buildings and the ground around them. To Joe Youngblood it all looked like a dreamscape...

And then that dream turned into a nightmare.

A white woman had emerged from one of the ramshackle structures near the edge of the camp. She bowed to the two guards outside, and then walked with purpose on bare feet to what appeared to be a vegetable garden. Her loose white dress—a tattered, shapeless shift, made from rice sacks, no doubt—fluttered with every motion she made. Her long black hair—curly, untamed—bounced with each stride.

She stood proudly amidst the garden's plants as if she was Mother Nature herself, the giver of life. But Joe Youngblood knew her real title: *The Woman in White*...

And she wouldn't be giving him life. She'd be taking it.

"I knew she was here," Youngblood said.

"Who? What do you mean?" Hadley replied.

"There. That woman. I told Major Miles back on the submarine."

Hadley swung his binoculars her way and stared for a second...until his jaw fell open and he dropped the binoculars to the ground.

Quickly, he picked them up and looked again.

"Holy shit...that's Miss Forbes! You *knew* she was here?"

"Yes, I saw it on the submarine. She's here for me...to take me away."

"I don't know what the fuck you're talking about, Youngblood. She's here because she got captured over a year ago—and all that time we thought she was dead!"

"No, First Sergeant. The story of my people has been told already. She's here to take me. It's the third time I've seen her. That means—"

"Oh, bullshit. She's not taking you anywhere. We're going to take *her*...take her away from this god-awful place. Come on, we've got to get back and tell Major Miles right fucking now."

Hadley and Youngblood couldn't believe how calm Jock was when they told him. All he said was, "Take me there."

It was near noon when Jock and his men returned to the spot where Jillian had been seen. But the rundown building she had emerged from earlier now appeared empty. Aside from two guards lackadaisically patrolling the barbed wire fence, there was nobody to be seen in this part of the camp. All they heard was the rustle of leaves in the warm breeze until Bogater Boudreau said, "I hear something, sir." He pointed to their right. "It sounds like...I don't know...a bunch of girls singing?"

They struggled through the jungle in the direction of the voices, but those voices had gone quiet now.

"I know it was coming from this direction, sir," Bogater said.

They didn't have to move much farther to prove him right. Just the other side of the wire was a group of women, now in solemn silence, going about their work. They stood in a graveyard of makeshift wooden crosses—several rows, perhaps forty crosses in all. They were tending to the gravesites, pulling out weeds and vines, fighting back against the clutches of a jungle eager to reclaim every square inch of cleared land.

He heard her voice before he saw her face. "Anne Marie," she said, "we need that hatchet over here."

That voice. Unmistakably Aussie. Unmistakably Jillian's.

She rose and turned to take the hatchet. Jock could see her now. His chest tightened as if clamped by a steel band. He couldn't speak, not even a whisper. He wasn't sure he could breathe.

Tom Hadley's hand was on his shoulder now. "It's okay, sir. We're going to figure out how to do this. Let's take it one step at a time."

But it's not okay, Jock thought. *We're here and she's there, on the other side of that wire. But she's okay...and still in charge, as usual, even in a group of prisoners.*

Look at her...still tough as nails.

He felt his breath coming back. He dared to test his voice, too. "Tom," he whispered, "how many guards do you think there are at this end of the camp?"

"I count six, sir...one in each tower, two standing guard over the women, and those two we saw walking the fence."

"Deuce," Jock said, "can you tell if those guards are Japanese or Korean?"

"Sure I can," Deuce replied, Hadley's binoculars still pressed against his eyes. "They're all Koreans...except for that sergeant over there with the sword."

"Even the ones in the towers?"

"Yes, sir."

Jock counted the women at work in the graveyard. *I see eight....Jillian and one other white woman, the one she called Anne Marie. The other six are Melanesian. It looks like there are no prisoners but these women at this end of the camp. All the male prisoners are on the other side.*

"Oscar," Jock said, "are these native women in here for the same reasons as the men?"

"Yes, Major Jock. They worked at Government House."

Hadley asked, "Sir, how the hell are we going to get in there without starting a shootout that gets everyone killed?"

"I don't know yet, Tom. But we'd better not hang around here. I don't think much of this position—there's only one way out. Let's get back to where we were before and think this through."

As they made their way through the jungle back to their old position near the camp's gate, Hadley told Jock, "We may have a problem with Joe Youngblood, sir." Then he related what Youngblood had told him when they first laid eyes on Jillian—the whole *Woman in White* business. "Did he mention all this to you back on the sub, sir?"

"Ahh, shit. He did, dammit. You sure he should be on point right now, Tom? I mean, if he's in some kind of state..."

"Actually, sir, he *asked* to be on point. And he's doing just fine right now."

Joe Youngblood raised a hand—the *Halt* signal—and then dropped to the ground, out of sight in the undergrowth. The rest of the column did the same as Jock low-crawled forward to his point man.

"The trail into the camp is just ahead, sir," Youngblood said. "I hear voices on it."

Jock signaled for Deuce to come forward. "People are going to be walking by here in a minute," Jock told him. "If they're talking Japanese, maybe you can translate for me."

Two soldiers came into view, walking from the camp toward Lorengau. According to their collar insignia, they were both privates. They were in no particular hurry and in very good spirits. Each had a rifle slung over his shoulder. One carried an oil lantern. They both seemed to be talking at once.

Once they passed, Deuce said, "I think they're on their way to have sexual relations, sir. They were making jokes about each other's abilities—or lack of—at intercourse."

"Sure," Jock said, "the *comfort women* must be in Lorengau. Were those two Japanese or Korean?"

"One of each, sir."

"I'm guessing they get a day off now and then to go and get laid," Jock said.

"Why do you think they need a lantern, sir?"

"Maybe they plan on being out in the dark, Corporal."

Jock's guess was correct. Later that night, as *The Squad* lay in their position outside the camp's gate, two soldiers returned on foot, lighting their way up the dark jungle trail with an oil lantern. They strolled through the gate as if they owned the place. Neither of the two guards on duty bothered to challenge them...

And a plan began to form in Jock's mind.

Chapter Eighteen

At sunrise, with Colonel Yamagura watching proudly from the Headquarters House veranda, the Japanese beheaded another male prisoner. "Shit," Tom Hadley said. "Maybe *he* was the last white guy in that camp?"

The moment the body was hauled away, a new flurry of activity began in front of the house. The three fidgeting horses were brought forward to await their riders. The truck that had brought the rest of Colonel Yamagura's entourage sat idling. After a round of salutes, the colonel, his captain, and his sergeant clambered onto their mounts and trotted out the gate. The soldiers who had tended to the animals hurried into the back of the truck, which then took up its lethargic, gear-grinding pace behind the horsemen.

Mike McMillen asked, "Why don't those dumbasses just all ride in the damn truck?"

"I think the colonel likes his horse too much," Jock replied. "Probably thinks he cuts a dashing figure in the saddle."

Bogater Boudreau had a question, too: "Who the hell rides a horse in the jungle, anyway? They ain't fit for that duty."

In a few moments the colonel and his men were out of sight, leaving nothing but clouds of dust floating listlessly in the warm and humid morning air. Hadley asked Jock, "Are you ready to tell him, sir?"

"Yeah. Just him and me, okay?"

Jock sat back against a tree and waited. He was exhausted, running on pure adrenaline. Jillian was so close, yet still out of reach…

And he needed to keep reminding himself of the real reason he and his men were here on Papua: to deny the OP to the Japanese this day and tomorrow, while the US fleet sailed by. It wouldn't matter a bit to the high command he brought Jillian home if the boys invading Hollandia were slaughtered by a forewarned enemy.

Taking the OP on Dremsel so easily and so ahead of plan…please tell me that didn't lull me into a false sense of security…and I've foolishly sacrificed Patchett and his men as a result. And a lot of GIs on those ships, too.

I thought she was dead. I convinced myself of it. It never occurred to me she might be alive…and here…even after hearing that piano in the night. That had to be her playing it.

I can't leave her here.

But how will I explain that to men who'll be dead because of me?

Deuce joined him and asked, "You need to see me, sir?"

"Yeah, Corporal. Sit down."

Jock started talking about his need to rescue Jillian. How it had to be done without starting a bloodbath…and as far as he could tell, there was only one way to do it.

But before he could say another word, Deuce replied, "I know, sir. You need me to masquerade as a Japanese soldier, go into the camp, and bring her out. Sure, I'll do it. First Sergeant Hadley told me all about her. I understand what she means to you."

Jock had been expecting to reason, cajole—even plead if necessary—but here was his Nisei trooper, the one Patchett had branded a washout as a fighting man, suddenly rising up larger than life.

Deuce asked, "Do you want me to go back to Dremsel and get a uniform off the Koreans?"

"No, there's no time for that. In two days we need to be on that sub...and we've got a lot of ground to cover before then. We've got to do this tonight."

"But I'll need a uniform..."

"I know. We're going to get one from the men going to the whorehouse."

Deuce seemed not to understand for a moment. Then he nodded and said, "Yeah. Good idea, sir."

Jock started to thank him but Deuce shrugged it off. "I did *volunteer* for this duty, sir," he said. "Four times, in fact."

"Four times? How do you figure?"

"Once when I enlisted, twice when I asked for Pacific theater duty, three times when I signed on for this mission..."

And now.

The plan to pull off the *uniform snatch* was a simple trick: a deception ending in quiet, deadly violence. Deuce, Boudreau, and McMillen positioned themselves well down the trail, far enough so no one at the camp could hear what was about to happen. There, they would wait, hidden from sight, until Japanese soldiers strolled by.

They didn't have to wait long. Two smiling soldiers—actual Japanese, not Koreans—sauntered into view as if they didn't have a care in the world.

"Poor bastards," Bogater whispered. "They don't know they already done dipped it in the honey pot for the last time. Give 'em about ten more yards, Deuce, then do your stuff."

Ten yards—and Deuce started yelling in Japanese: "HELP ME! HELP ME, COMRADES! OVER HERE! OVER HERE! HURRY!"

Not even bothering to unsling their rifles, the two sprinted into the underbrush, straight toward the voice begging for help...

But they saw no one.

Not even Boudreau and McMillen as they sprang upon them from behind...

Each wrapping an enemy soldier's neck with a garotte made of wire.

Deuce did the only thing he could think of to help: he stripped the slung rifles from the writhing and doomed Japanese. He wasn't sure why he said "Gomennasai"—*I'm sorry*—as he did it.

The struggle went on for minutes on end, but the two Americans had their prey firmly under control.

This silent dance of death could end only one way.

Squeezing tighter and tighter...

Until one last convulsion from each blue-faced victim...

And it was over.

"What a pain in the ass! Too bad we couldn't just slice their fucking throats," McMillen said, "but we don't want to get blood all over these duds now, do we?"

Deuce asked, "Do you think they're going to miss these guys anytime soon?"

"Eventually," McMillen replied, "but they probably ain't the first Jap troopers who overstayed leave. What are they gonna do? Go looking for 'em in the dark? By the time they're ready to kick ass and take names, we'll be done with this shit and long gone." He picked up the oil lantern the pair had dropped and handed it to Deuce. "Don't forget to take this, too."

As they stripped off the dead men's uniforms, Bogater said, "Hey look—one of these jokers is a corporal. You can have some rank on you, Deuce, when you saunter into that camp." Then he got quiet, like he was saying a prayer. When the prayer was done, he said, "Too bad you had to die for your damn clothes, *mon frère*."

"Yeah," McMillen replied. "A cryin' fuckin' shame."

"The real shame," Deuce said, "is having to die in a place as horrible as this."

They looked at him like he was out of his mind.

"Of course it's horrible," McMillen said. "Didn't they tell you this is Hell, pal?"

From the OP on Mount Dremsel, they could see the clouds of dust far below being kicked up by the horsemen and the truck following them. "They're coming, Sergeant Major," Ace Nishimoto said. "The fucking Japs."

The fucking Japs...those words erased any doubt Melvin Patchett still harbored about the allegiance of his Nisei trooper.

"How many, son?"

"Three on horseback, I think...and a light truck, Sergeant Major."

"Okay, boys," Patchett said. "You know the drill. Nobody squeezes a trigger until I say so."

The ambush site at the top of the *spiral staircase* was textbook perfect. Allred was centered on the kill zone with his M1, concealed only ten yards from where his targets would shortly be. *Eight-round clip, eight dead Japs,* he told himself.

Patchett covered the high end of the trail, Ace the low end. Botkin was hugging the steep downslope on the other side of the *staircase*, ready to pick off any Jap trying to flee that way.

The two Koreans were out of sight, tied to trees on the other side of the peak and gagged with GI socks.

Don't matter whether it's one or a dozen Japs come up that trail, Patchett thought. *We got it covered.*

But when the Japanese came, only three walked up the trail.

"I told you there wouldn't be no damn horses," Patchett muttered as he squinted for a better look at the still-distant targets. *Let's see who we got here...*

A colonel led the way—no doubt, the *Colonel Yamagura* mentioned in the radio message. A captain and a sergeant trailed close behind. All three were armed only with pistols and swords, still hanging on their belts.

Fucking turkey shoot, y'all.

Patchett let them get close enough to count the buttons on the colonel's tunic.

"DO IT, ALLRED!"

The last split second of their lives...not even enough time for the Japanese to register surprise when they heard Patchett's shout.

Three shots, three dead Japs—that was all it took. Standing over his victims, Allred asked Patchett, "What if more come, Sergeant Major? They heard that shooting down the mountain for damn sure. Thought them reports would never stop echoing."

"If they come, they come, son. Take up your old post and keep your eyes peeled. Can't be more than a handful of 'em...just one li'l truck's worth."

Allred tapped the dead colonel with his foot. "What should we do with these?"

"Just drag 'em out of sight and leave 'em for now. When I feel good about untying the *Ko-reans*, we'll let them do the burying. They got plenty of practice already with the four they done in."

Allred didn't want to view the results of his handiwork much longer. The sergeant major was right, though—this wasn't the time to worry about burying:

More shit could be hitting the fan anytime now.

Patchett said, "I'm going up in that tower to have me a little look-see. If our Navy's keeping on schedule, they should be in sight right about now. Sergeant Botkin, keep an ear to that radio in case Lorengau wants itself an update on that dead colonel's arrival."

At the base of Mount Dremsel, a bewildered Japanese corporal and his equally bewildered men had been wondering for over an hour what those shots from the mountain were all about. "They only had pistols," a private said. "Those were rifle shots."

The corporal scoffed. "The detachment on the OP had rifles. That's what you heard. Probably just a salute for the colonel's arrival."

Another private said, "That didn't sound like Arisaka rifles to me."

The corporal slapped him across the head. "How

would you know? You're an animal handler—a stupid farm hand—not a weapons expert. Our orders are to remain here and care for these horses…and that's exactly what we're going to do."

"But we were supposed to be back in Lorengau tonight, Corporal."

The Corporal slapped him again. "The plans have been changed, idiot."

"What if the colonel doesn't come down off the mountain, Corporal?"

"That is *not possible*, Private."

Atop the swaying, creaking tower, Patchett smiled as he looked out to sea with binoculars. A fleet of tiny, far-off ships—of all types and sizes—had appeared out of the east, creeping slowly westward toward their destiny at Hollandia.

"Now ain't that a pretty sight?" Patchett said to no one but himself. "Looks like hundreds of 'em. And I'm the only sumbitch on this shithole of an island laying eyes on 'em."

His contentment was shattered by the faint snarl of high-flying aircraft. He scanned the sky until he found them—and was able to breathe a sigh of relief. The blue and white insignia beneath their silver wings marked them as US Army Air Force, providing an umbrella of air cover for the invasion fleet. Unchallenged, they seemed to rule the sky.

And all I gotta do is keep the Japs off this mountaintop for another twenty-two hours—until 1000 hours tomorrow—and then this whole parade will be out of sight...and we can go home.

Chapter Nineteen

As the day dragged into dusk, the pronouncement of the Japanese corporal was looking more and more shaky. What he said was *not possible* seemed indeed possible now—the colonel had still not come down from the mountain. Even if he did come down right now, they'd never make it back to the prison camp, much less Lorengau, before darkness and the jungle enveloped them.

To ease his grumbling men, the corporal made an announcement: "Let the horses graze along the trail until sunset, but don't go too far in case the colonel returns. We have sufficient food and water for the night. We will make plans to camp here."

High above on the OP, Allred told Patchett, "No sign of that Jap truck moving or any of them horses, neither. I reckon they're all still right down there."

"I tell you what," Patchett said, "if they don't want to come up, I think at first light you and me'll go down and pay 'em a little wake-up visit."

"Hey," Allred said, "maybe we get rid of them and use their truck to make our getaway."

"Bad idea, son. I'm betting by this time tomorrow—when that colonel don't show up wherever he's supposed to be—the road out to here's gonna be crawling with them sumbitches. We'll be getting out of here the same way we came, I reckon—through the woods."

The moon cast its velvet glow across the prison camp, making the oil lantern Deuce Hashimoto carried seem redundant. Walking on shaky legs, he cursed that moonlight, a lone imposter in a dead man's uniform, toting a strange weapon he'd never fired and hoped he never would. He wasn't sure what force kept him moving forward.

I carry a weapon but I've never felt so vulnerable. A weapon can only protect you from death by dealing death...

And he had no doubt if it came down to *dealing death* tonight, he, the rest of Major Miles' men, and the woman they hoped to rescue might be the ones dealt the losing hand.

It all boils down to how well I can pull off this charade.

Two gate guards, both privates...the Korean looks like he's asleep on his feet, but the Japanese man smirks at me and asks, "Feeling better, *gochō?*"

Gochō...what the hell does that mean?

Maybe it means corporal. It couldn't be some insult, could it? He wouldn't dare—this uniform says I outrank him.

I'll just nod and keep walking into the camp like I own the place...wobbly knees and all.

The guards quickly lose interest in me.

I'm at the women's barracks all too quickly. I need more time...How do I talk myself in?

The lone Korean guard by the door makes it easy for me. He says, "Are you my relief?"

Shit! Is this shift change time? If I get rid of him

does another guard show up any minute?

I'm in too deep now.

I tell him, "Yes. I'm your relief."

No need to say that twice. Within seconds, he's a shadow vanishing deep into the camp.

The walls and door are nothing but screens. I can see the women inside. Some are undressing.

I knock on the door frame.

An angry voice replies in English, "Go away, wanker!" *The Australian accent is unmistakable. That same voice shifts to Japanese and, still angry, says,* "Acchi ni ike!"

Different language, same message: Get lost!

Softly, in English, I say, "I must come in. Major Miles sent me."

A swirl of activity inside...bodies moving quickly...footsteps racing toward the door.

It flies open...

At the threshold stands a fierce-looking white woman in a white shift, dark hair falling around her face in tight curls. The same one we saw in the cemetery yesterday. The group's leader.

She looks me up and down and says, "What the bloody hell are you?"

"I'm an American soldier, ma'am, here to rescue you. Come, we must hurry."

I don't think she believes me.

"You said *Major Miles*...is he here? Is Jock here?"

"Yes, ma'am." I point toward the barbed wire fence. "Just over there."

"Is he now, laddie? Tell me...what outfit is he from?"

A test...

"He commands First Battalion, Eighty-First Infantry, Thirty-Second Division."

Obviously the right answer. But she still seems wary...

So I show her my dog tags..

"Let me get this right," *she says.* "You're Japanese, but you're in the American Army?"

"Yes, ma'am, that's correct."

"Then we have to get you out of here, bucko, and right now. If they catch you in that uniform, they'll cut your bloody head off on the spot."

"You really don't need to tell me that, ma'am. If you'll come right this—"

She interrupts, ignoring me as if command of the situation has just passed to her.

"Come on, ladies," *she says to the seven other women gathered around.* "The bloody Yanks have come to save us at long last."

"Wait a minute, ma'am! My orders are to bring just *you.*"

"Fuck your orders, laddie. It's all of us or nothing. Anne Marie, grab your medical kit."

Not the time for discussion. Stick to the plan. Hope for the best.

I hold the lantern high and wave it back and forth three times...

An eternity of seconds passes...

And then a brilliant flare from the Very pistol pops and arcs high over the far end of the camp.

"Follow me," *I say.* "Walk straight for the watchtower. Don't run. Don't make a sound."

The Australian woman hesitates. "But the guard in the tower..."

"He'll be looking the wrong way," *I answer, praying my words are true.*

"What if he's not?"

"Then he'll be shot."

"Why don't you just shoot him now?"

"Because then they'll know for sure we're here. Now please, ma'am...hurry!"

The women follow my commands without further questions. Confused voices shout in Japanese throughout the camp. We're at the fence beneath the tower in a dozen quick steps. Oscar Solo is there—he's spread open the barbed wire with a tree branch. He helps the women step through.

First Sergeant Hadley is just beyond the wire. He seems shocked as the number of escapees grows far past the solitary one he expected. When Oscar finally closes the gap in the wire, Hadley says, "This looks like a little more than we figured on...but let's all get the hell out of here. That flare won't keep them spinning in circles much longer. Can't believe we didn't have to fire one stinking shot."

They crashed through the pitch black jungle with McMillen in the lead, feeling his way along the discarded telephone wire Oscar had strung to mark the trail. As the shouts of the confused Japanese in the camp fell farther and farther behind, Hadley said, "Hold up here. Everybody down...give the major and Youngblood a chance to catch up."

Jillian crawled up next to Hadley and said, "I didn't get a chance to do this before, Thomas." She hugged him and planted a kiss on his cheek. "I can't tell you how good it is to see you tossers again...and I can't thank you all enough."

If it hadn't been pitch black, she could've seen he was blushing. "Don't thank me, Miss Forbes. It was Deuce—our Japanese-American guy—who made it all happen."

"Oh, believe me, he was the very first one I thanked. Now where the hell is Jock?"

They didn't have to wait long for him. Two men approached out of the darkness, the *crunch* of their hurried footfalls heard long before their dark shapes came into view. Jock and Joe Youngblood exchanged passwords with McMillen and joined the others.

Jock picked out Jillian's silhouette among those of the crouching women. He would have known her anywhere. Their embrace was silent, brief...but its power unmistakable, drawing them together like the opposing poles of magnets, pulling everyone and everything with it.

Close by, Joe Youngblood felt the power, too. But rather than attracting him, it was pushing him away, propelling him down a dark, endless tunnel from which there would be no return.

He knew who *The Woman in White* was: a spirit, here to take his earthly life.

The wire marking their escape path came to its end. "All right," Jock said, "this is where we stay until sun-up."

He dispersed his GIs and native guide into a tight

perimeter with the women huddled at the center. Once satisfied with their position, he sat down next to Jillian. There was so much he wanted to ask her—and tell her—but this wasn't the time. Their survival hinged on more immediate matters.

"How am I going to protect and feed all these other women, Jill?"

"You won't have to. When the sun comes up, the native women will scatter to their villages. They all come from somewhere here on Manus. That'll leave just me and Anne Marie. She's Dutch but speaks bloody good English. You can handle her, right?"

"Yeah...probably."

"Good," Jillian replied, "because you'll need her. She's a bloody good nurse. And we just stole a bagful of medical supplies. We've even got quinine."

"Quinine? Who's got malaria?"

"We all do, silly. You and all your lads must have it, too, long as you've been in these parts."

He nodded.

"I thought so. Probably still taking that Atabrine...and it's still making you all as yellow as the Japanese, too, I'll bet."

"Yeah, it has. Wait until you see us when the sun comes up."

They settled into a comfortable stillness totally out of place in the mayhem, savoring the fact they were nestled against each other once again. It had been a year since they were together like this, a year of which they knew next to nothing about the other's suffering. All that mattered was they were both here—if even for the briefest of moments—until fortune and war would, no doubt, tear them apart once again.

"Jock," she whispered, "are we beating those bastards?"

"Yeah…we're pushing them back everywhere now."

"But did we win at Buna?"

When he replied, "Yeah, baby, we did, thanks to you," she pressed herself against him even tighter. For one brief moment, she seemed quietly content in their tiny world.

Then Jock added, "You've gotten so thin, honey."

"I'm not exactly skin and bones yet, Yank. And you're quite lean yourself."

Another few moments of silence before he said, "Jill, that graveyard back at the camp…"

"Those were the women who lost hope. Or weren't *useful* anymore."

He was afraid where her explanation might be going. "Useful?" he asked. "How? What do you mean?"

"No, silly boy. I don't mean it *that* way. They had their *comfort women* for doing the naughty, and we convinced them we were *unclean* from the very beginning…kept showing them bloody rags until they lost interest. That was Anne Marie's idea, by the way. She was useful to them because she was a nurse. I was useful because that shithead of a camp commander loved the music…another bloody Jap who studied in Europe before the war and got infected with Western culture."

"So you played for him?"

"Every bloody night. That's why I'm still alive, I suppose. I was just about to go perform when your man Deuce showed up at our door."

In the dim glow of the radio's dial lights, Ace looked like a student stumped by a tough exam question. His pencil scratching feverishly at the pad, he kept reworking the Japanese characters written there, trying to make some sense of them.

It was no use. He slid the headphones down to his neck and said, "We've got problems, Sergeant Major. Their last transmission—the reply to our 2200 report—it's in some kind of code. It reads like a weather report for the Himalayas. I have no idea what Lorengau's really saying."

Patchett replied, "Ain't that code book we found on that dead sergeant helping any?"

"I don't even know what half the characters in that book mean, Sergeant Major. If we don't come up with the right answer, they're going to know something's really wrong up here."

"And you've got no idea what that *right answer* is, son?"

Ace shook his head.

"Then fuck 'em," Patchett replied. "Don't send nothing. Maybe they'll think our transmitter crapped out again." He checked his watch. "It's gonna get real interesting around here, boys…and fast. Our Navy's still gonna be out there in plain view for about four more hours after the sun comes up. That's how long we gotta hold this OP."

Cotton Allred asked, "Those guys at the bottom of the mountain…we still gonna take them out at first light?"

Patchett gave it a moment's thought before replying, "I reckon we oughta. But they may be the least of our troubles now."

Chapter Twenty

Patchett and Allred braced themselves against trees on the steep slope just above the base of Mount Dremsel. The first rays of dawn broke through the treetops, revealing the truck parked on the trail below. The three restless horses were tethered just beyond it.

Japanese soldiers were nowhere in sight.

"You got line of sight on the truck, son?" Patchett whispered.

"Yep," Allred replied.

"What do you reckon the range is?"

"Seventy-five yards, Sergeant Major."

"Sounds just about perfect for you and that M1." Patchett looked at the Thompson in his hands and added, "Way too far for this thing, though."

"You want to get closer?"

"Let's play it by ear, son. Just remember, we need to shoot us some Japs…not waste bullets killing trucks and horses."

The driver's door opened and a groggy Japanese soldier stepped out.

"Want me to take him?" Allred asked, peering down his rifle's sights.

"No. Let's see how many there are first. Look…he's headed to the back of the truck. All right…he's yelling at them in there. I reckon he's the man in charge."

One by one, four men emerged from the canvas-topped truck bed. They seemed just as bleary-eyed as the man who woke them.

"The leader," Patchett said. "Take him before he puts on that fucking helmet he's got in his hands."

Allred squeezed off a shot. The leader's head ruptured and sprayed its red-pink contents on the other soldiers like a watermelon splattered against the wall.

"Keep going, son," Patchett said.

In the second it took the four Japanese still standing to override their disbelief and flee, Allred got off two more shots.

Two more Japanese went down.

The other two ducked behind the truck.

Patchett said, "I think they're gonna try to get away on them horses. Stay here, take your best shot. I gotta get closer." He stood and tried to run down the steep incline.

But it was too steep. Patchett lost his balance and went tumbling down the slope, losing his helmet and the Thompson along the way.

Allred couldn't see the Japanese—*But I sure as hell can see them horses.*

He leveled his sights on the first horse—the fine white stallion—pulling frantically at its tether. Patchett's words echoed in his head: *We need to shoot us some Japs...not waste bullets killing horses.*

I got five rounds left in this clip...two Japs, three horses...

I can do this.

A mottled brown horse shot from behind the truck. A rider clung to his side, using the horse as a shield just like the matinee cowboys in the movies.

Allred aimed at the barrel of the galloping horse and fired.

Shit! Missed!

He aimed and fired again.

The horse's back legs buckled and he went down on

his side—right on top of his rider.

Another horse—a black one, with the last Japanese soldier hugging his back—dodged his fallen comrade at a gallop as he made good his escape toward Lorengau.

Allred squeezed off one more round before the horse vanished around a curve in the trail.

Shit. Missed again.

Patchett had recovered his feet and his weapon. He walked slowly toward the truck, letting the muzzle of the Thompson lead the way into the truck's cab and under the canvas of the bed.

Nobody else home.

He paused to look at the slain leader.

Good head shot...pretty fucking grisly. Pretty fucking dead, too.

The second man Allred shot was obviously dead, too. But the third man was not. He lay on the ground, hands clutched to his throat, blood spurting through his fingers.

Listen to that gurgle, Patchett told himself. *Poor bastard's neck-shot, choking on his own blood.*

"Sorry, *Tojo*," he said, and fired a single bullet into the dying man's head.

He walked away slowly, telling himself, *God, I hate this shit. But these fucking little savages started it.*

Allred came down the slope, managing to keep his feet the whole way. He walked slowly toward the brown horse—still heaving and screaming, trying and failing to stand—and put him out of his misery with a point-blank shot to the head.

He did the same for the struggling man still trapped beneath.

"I fucked up, Sergeant Major. One got away."

"I know, son. Ain't nothing we can do about it now."

They walked back toward the foot of the *spiral staircase*. The white stallion was still tethered to the truck. He was still frantic.

"What do we do with him?" Allred asked.

"Cut him loose, son. We done killed enough helpless animals for one day."

Allred did as he was told. The white horse fled down the trail toward Lorengau at top speed.

Patchett said, "Them dumbasses left their rifles in the truck. Grab 'em, son...they might come in handy."

They hadn't gotten far up the *spiral staircase* when the burst of a Thompson began to echo around the mountainside.

Allred asked, "What the hell could they be shooting at up there?"

"We'd best find out right quick, son. I'll lead, you keep our asses covered."

Jillian was right: at sunrise, the six native women vanished into the jungle. "Good thing," Tom Hadley said. "They ate us out of house and home last night. We've barely got a day's rations left. And only a couple of hours' worth of water."

Oscar Solo returned from a scouting patrol to the POW camp full of news. "Much *hariap* at camp, Major Jock. Much—"

Jock stopped him. "You mean *hurry up*, Oscar? Like they're doing things in a rush?"

"Yes, Major Jock, yes. Many *soldia* go from camp

big rush-rush."

"Well, we expected they'd come looking for us," Jock replied.

"No, Major Jock, no! Not us! Not women, too! They take trail…but not to Lorengau. They go other way."

"Other way? You mean to the mountain?"

"Yes, Major Jock, to the mountain. You leave only six men up there. They could have big trouble quick-quick. We go help them now, no?"

"Yeah, of course we're going to help them."

Jock pulled out the map and did a few quick calculations. It would take them six hours to get back to Dremsel along the route they came—maybe more if the barefoot Jillian and Anne Marie couldn't keep up in the jungle. The Japanese and Korean troops on the trail could probably make it in four. He was so focused on the map he didn't realize Jillian was looking over his shoulder—not until her finger fell on the concentric contour lines representing Mount Dremsel.

"Is this the mountain?" she asked.

"Yeah…and Patchett's at the top."

"So what's the problem, Jock? Let's go help him."

"The Japs will get there way before us, Jill. If we try to use the trail, we'll be too exposed, too vulnerable…and I'm not sure how fast you ladies can go through the jungle on bare feet."

She looked offended as she replied, "Baby, I haven't had shoes on my feet for a year, Anne Marie even longer. Our feet aren't the problem—they're so tough we can walk on broken glass. They'll get us through the jungle faster than any of you wankers." She pointed to the shoeless Oscar. "And bare feet don't seem to slow him down any."

The image of the two women sprinting barefoot through the jungle gave Jock an idea. Pointing on the map to a spot a few miles down the Lorengau trail, he said, "Okay, if we can move that fast, maybe we can get to this point here—ahead of the Japs—and set up an ambush."

Oscar and Hadley leaned in for a look at the map. Hadley said, "There's a village near there, sir. Is that going to be a problem?"

Before Jock could say anything, Oscar replied, "No problem, Sergeant Tom. Maybe big help. We get water there."

Patchett and Allred reached the OP at Dremsel's peak breathing sighs of relief. They hadn't had to fight anyone to get back up the mountain. All seemed peaceful and in order—until they saw the look on Stu Botkin's face. He didn't say anything, just pointed toward the tents, his head hung low like a schoolboy caught red-handed breaking some cardinal rule.

In front of the tents, Ace Nishimoto was hunched over the lifeless bodies of the two Koreans. He held his hand to his face as if trying to shield himself from grief. His Thompson lay on the ground beside him. When he saw Patchett walking toward him, he scrambled to his feet, trying to wipe the tears from his eyes.

The sergeant major asked, "All right, what happened here?"

"They must've untied themselves," Botkin said. "We heard the shooting down the mountain...and the next thing we knew, Park and Sung were in the tent, picking up weapons."

"Which one of you shot them?"

It was Ace who replied, "I did, Sergeant Major. I thought they'd try to shoot us. But...I don't know...maybe they were just..."

He fell quiet, overcome.

Patchett stood silently over the bodies for a few moments. Then he said to Ace, "You did the best thing, son. You did good."

Ace didn't seem so sure. "Did I?"

"I'm afraid you did."

Botkin asked, "Who's going to bury them, Sergeant Major?"

"No one of us, that's for damn sure. We might get real busy here. But we just gotta hang on to this OP for a few more hours...and then we're on our way to that boat going home."

Chapter Twenty-One

Oscar signaled the column to a halt. He was full of pride as he said, "Look, Major Jock, very fine place here to kill Japs."

Jock crawled a few yards forward, popped his head through the dense jungle foliage, and found himself looking at probably the best ambush spot he had ever seen in his life. Here, the trail dropped to a gulley-like run, straight and narrow for almost fifty yards. Being the low point of the surrounding terrain, the natural drainage kept it muddy all the time, a quagmire a man could only *slog* through. A ridge on each side would place his men almost ten feet above the trail's floor, looking down on their hapless quarry from positions of excellent concealment.

It was a perfect killing field. A small enemy unit walking into it could be erased to the last man in a matter of seconds—even by an ambush team as lightly armed as Jock's men.

There was only one problem: no Japanese were in that killing field.

There were none in sight on the trail leading to it, either.

Jock asked Oscar, "They couldn't have gotten past here already, could they?"

"No, Major Jock. They must walk very slow."

Tom Hadley added, "That mud isn't even churned up much. If a bunch of Japs passed recently, it would be."

"No shit," Jock replied. "Oscar, how about that village we talked about? Where is it, exactly?"

"We cannot see, but it's right over there. Right through trees." Oscar pointed down the trail, in the direction of Lorengau...

And that's when the Japanese walked into view.

"Where *soldia* are, Major Jock...that is where village is."

"We might be in business yet," Jock said. "Tom...I'm looking at no more than twenty men. You agree?"

Hadley took a long look with his binoculars. "Yeah. No more than that, sir."

"Okay, then," Jock said, "you, McMillen, and Deuce set up real quick on the other side of the trail. I'll take this side with Bogater, Youngblood, and Oscar. My side will work from the head of their column down, your side from the tail up. Start shooting when I do."

"Got it, sir."

As Hadley gathered his team, Jock crawled back into the underbrush to make sure Jillian and Anne Marie were safely tucked out of the way. Like all soldiers before imminent combat, he was tightly strung and hyper-alert. When he found the women, what they were doing did nothing to ease his tension: Jillian was in obvious discomfort as Anne Marie rubbed some liquid from a bottle on her bared shoulders.

"What the hell's wrong, Jill?" he asked.

Anne Marie did the explaining. "Her shoulders have been dislocated several times. She often has pain there. The liniment helps."

"*Dislocated*? How the hell did that happen?"

"How do you think?" Anne Marie replied. "She was tortured...hung by her arms, sometimes for hours, often with heavy weights dangling from her feet. The only thing that saved her from worse treatment was the camp commander might have missed his precious music."

Jillian offered a pained smile that still managed to radiate a sense of victory. "I never was very good at *obedience*, was I, Jock? Don't worry, Anne Marie will have me fixed up in a minute."

"Good, because a minute's about all we've got. The Japs are coming and we're setting up an ambush. Both of you…get behind those big trees over there…and stay there until someone comes and gets you."

Jillian asked, "Can I have a weapon?"

He pulled his .45 pistol from its holster. "Think you can fire this, Jill? You know the nasty kick it's got, especially if those shoulders hurt."

"Of course I can fire it. A little pain in the shoulders is better than being dead."

"Just stay down," Jock pleaded before hurrying back to the trail.

When he got back to his team, there was another surprise. "They stopped, sir," Bogater Boudreau reported. "They're just sitting there, where that village is supposed to be."

"Maybe they rest," Oscar said. "Fill their canteens. Steal food."

Bogater added, "We sure could use a refill on our canteens, too, sir."

"We've got bigger fish to fry right now, don't you think, Bogater?"

"Yessir. I reckon we do. Didn't mean to—"

"Yeah, fine," Jock snapped. "Let's stay focused here."

Thank God for sergeants. They pick the damnedest times to remind you of stuff you already know full well.

Jock gazed through binoculars down the trail. "Why the hell are they just lounging around like that?"

They all pondered that question for a few moments. Then Oscar said, "Listen...that noise."

Jock didn't hear anything out of the ordinary at first. It sounded like another variation on *wind through the jungle*, a gentle, continuous *swish* that wouldn't have caught his attention. But the *swish* grew louder—and a faint *rumble* began to provide a counterpoint, a contrast that changed this seeming sound of nature into something mechanical.

"Holy shit," Bogater said. "Bicycles."

Not just a few, either. There was a swarm of Japanese soldiers on bicycles rolling up the trail. Like those on foot before them, they stopped at the village.

Bogater asked, "Where the hell did they come from? There weren't no bikes at that prison camp."

"I'm betting they came from Lorengau," Jock replied.

"How the hell many you reckon there are, sir?"

"Too many...*way* too many to try and take on here. Kill zone's too small."

"Yeah," Bogater said, "we hit the front end and the back end will dismount and flank us through the jungle."

"Right," Jock replied. "And if we let most of them pass and hit the back end, then the front end will turn around and flank us."

Bogater shook his head. "Maybe if we hit the back, sir, the front will just keep on running."

"I doubt that, Bogater. And even if they did, that'll put a quick-moving Japanese force between us and the mountain—one we can't even catch up with, let alone stop. Doesn't sound like much of a way to help out

Patchett and his boys, does it?"

Bogater kept trying—and failing—to count the Japanese through his binoculars. "I don't know, sir…it sure looks like a lot of them. Maybe if we could take out half…"

Jock had already made up his mind what they were going to do. He told Bogater, "Sergeant, go round up the ladies. While the Japs are taking their rest stop, we're going to make a break for it up the trail to the mountain. We need to find a better place to try and stop them."

"You mean we're going to stay out of the jungle and use the trail for once, sir?"

"Yep. Now *GO!* And don't sneak up on those women. They're armed, remember?"

As Bogater scurried off, Oscar said, "You want better place, Major Jock? I know where, but it's not close to here."

Jock unfolded the map. "Show me."

The place Oscar pointed to was two miles down the trail.

With Oscar far ahead, acting as lookout, the six Americans—plus Jillian and Anne Marie—*double-timed* down the steamy jungle trail toward the mountain. They had only stopped once—just for a matter of seconds—to fill their canteens from a stream. It was torture not being able to drink the cool water right away. They would have to wait an agonizing ten minutes for the Halazone tablets to dissolve.

Within moments of the last man filling his canteen, though, Mother Nature bestowed a double blessing: a downpour began. All the fresh water they could collect was falling from the sky and it didn't need to be treated. The men caught what little they could in their helmets while on the run, gulping it down as they tried to quench their deep thirst and then passing the helmets to Jillian and Anne Marie. They'd still have the treated water in the canteens for later, and the cooling effect of the rain was very welcome now.

The second part of the blessing was even more welcome: the Japanese would find themselves greatly slowed as the rain softened the trail, forcing them to dismount and push their bikes. Jock's party, unencumbered by narrow-wheeled machines, could still manage a brisk pace, even as the trail quickly turned muddy. For once, being on foot was an advantage.

Two miles, Jock told himself. *We just might beat them there.*

Tom Hadley brought up the rear of the column, making sure there were no stragglers while keeping a watchful eye over his shoulder for the Japs. Jillian and Anne Marie were right in front of him, the bulky medical kit bag suspended by its strap between them as they shared the load. They seemed to be keeping pace with his GIs just fine.

These are some tough ladies, he told himself, *but, hell, Miss Forbes was always tough as nails. We've still got a long way to go, though.*

As he caught up to them, he saw their eyes burning with desperate purpose. "Miss Forbes, Miss Smits…how're you two holding up?"

"Don't worry about us, Tom," Jillian replied, not even breathing hard. "It's amazing what you can do when you're running for your life."

Perched on the tower at the OP, Patchett checked his watch. It said 0930. He picked up the binoculars and scanned the ships still passing far out to sea.

No way those Navy bastards gonna be gone by 1000, like they said. At the rate they're moving, it's gonna be a couple more hours until they're out of sight. That's for damn sure.

Got rain coming, too. That oughta fuck up visibility real good. Can't be sure then if they're out of sight or not.

He climbed down from the tower and walked to the radio shelter. Botkin was diligently sweeping the frequencies, hoping to glean some hint of what might be going on around them.

"What're you hearing?" Patchett asked.

"Not much of anything, Sergeant Major. Our fleet out there's practicing perfect radio silence…not a peep out of them."

"How about Lorengau?"

Ace pulled his headphones off to answer that question. "They're doing their usual chatting with Rabaul…all admin stuff. They're not calling us anymore, though."

"Ain't surprised," Patchett replied. "The jig's up on that little scam of ours. Worked pretty good for a while, though. Tell you what…don't bother monitoring Lorengau anymore. Lock onto the major's frequency and stay there, just in case they're trying to make contact."

"Sure," Botkin replied, spinning the dials on the Japanese radio. "I can do that." Then he asked, "Is our fleet out of sight yet, Sergeant Major?" It was obvious there was another part to that sentence left unsaid: *So we can get the hell out of here.*

"Not by a long shot, son. Y'all sit tight. We ain't leaving just yet."

Chapter Twenty-Two

They'd been jogging down the trail for almost twenty minutes. The brief rain was long over, allowing the jungle's stifling heat and humidity to return and inflict their crushing toll on the human body—even bodies lean, tough, and hardened by constant sacrifice, like those of the men and women in Jock's party. The canteens were nearly empty again—most of the contents had been poured over their heads. Bogater Boudreau defended the improvised cooling method this way: *Sure, it's like we're throwing good water away, sir. But if we don't, our brains are gonna boil over.*

Jock couldn't argue with him. The heat and exertion—coupled with the tension of impending battle—had already given him a pounding headache. He was relieved to see Oscar waiting on the trail ahead, smiling and casually standing around as if waiting for a bus.

"Just ahead is very perfect trap," Oscar announced. "And more water."

It might not have been perfect, but it wasn't a bad start. A narrow wooden bridge—just wide enough for an ox cart, a small truck, or two bicyclists abreast—spanned a fast-flowing stream running deep in its steep banks. It wasn't a very long span—only fifteen yards or so—but it was enough to create a bottleneck for bicycles. The Japanese would have to slow down and form an orderly, double-file queue to ride across, or dismount to ford the stream. The jungle offered the Americans well-concealed firing positions near both ends of the bridge.

"Here's the plan, Tom," Jock told Hadley. "You take Deuce and McMillen and cover the south side short of the bridge. Me, Bogater, and Oscar will cover the north side opposite you. Youngblood is going to cross the bridge and set up beyond it—in that tree line over there—and pick off the lead element while it's crossing. That should create one hell of a roadblock, so your team and mine can have a turkey shoot…at least for a couple of seconds, anyway."

Hadley knew exactly what *at least for a couple of seconds* meant. There would be far too many Japanese cyclists to engage all at once. Since they couldn't trap the entire contingent, their attack wouldn't fit the definition of an ambush. It would be a blocking action— and a brief one, at that. How successful it would be depended on how well the Japanese recovered from the initial shock.

Jock continued, "If what's left of them turn and run back up the trail, well…we've bought ourselves a little more time to get to the mountain without having to fight for every yard."

"Yeah," Hadley said, "but if they don't panic and regroup, we'd better haul ass, and fast. If it comes down to a shootout in the jungle, the law of attrition's on their side. They've got the numbers…in spades."

"I know, Tom. You got a better idea?"

"No, sir…I sure don't."

"Good. Let's do it, then. One more thing…Jillian and Anne Marie, I want you to stay across the bridge with Private Youngblood. Keep our sharpshooter's back covered while he's picking off the Japs."

"My pleasure," Jillian replied as she clicked off the safety on the .45 pistol. "I'm ready."

Joe Youngblood couldn't bring himself to look at her. He asked Jock, "Do they *have* to stay with me, sir?"

"Yes, Private, they do."

Youngblood mumbled, "Yes, sir," and set off across the bridge with the women in tow. Settling into their hide, he took up a prone firing position and put the near end of the bridge in his sights. His eyes still fixed on his target, he said to Anne Marie, "Miss Smits, I need you right next to me." He patted the ground where he wanted her. Several clips for his M1, with eight bullets each, were already stacked there, waiting. "When you hear the *ping*, that means the rifle's empty. Put another clip in my right hand right away." He held up his open right palm to demonstrate where he wanted it. "I won't waste any time reloading that way."

Anne Marie tried to pick up a clip and promptly fumbled it. Her voice trembling, she said, "Jillian's so much better with weapons. Shouldn't she be doing this?"

"No, ma'am." Struggling for a believable explanation, he added, "Your dark dress…it blends in better…all those flowers on it…looks so natural."

He thought that sounded so much better than, *She's the death spirit and you're not.*

"This dress is so faded and wet you can hardly see the flowers, Private Youngblood."

"Maybe…but at least it's not shiny white like hers. Better she stays away, back there, out of sight. Now be quiet, please…here they come."

Youngblood let four pairs of riders fill the bridge before he pulled the trigger. In the few seconds it took for the M1's *ping* to announce he was ready to reload, six of the riders were sprawled on the bridge, their bicycles in a jumble.

Eight rounds fired, six hits...

The two Japanese who weren't down yet were trapped in the maze of toppled bicycles, darting back and forth on the bridge seeking cover that didn't exist.

With Youngblood's first shot, the teams on either side of the trail opened up with a noise like a factory clattering at full, deafening output. The five Thompson submachine guns flung their wild and withering shower of lead, chewing up flesh, metal, rubber, and dirt without discrimination. Oscar's Enfield rifle contributed to the carnage as fast as he could cycle its bolt between shots.

Five seconds...a few hundred precious rounds expended...

And so many Japanese at the rear of their column untouched, prone in firing positions, shooting back...

Abandoning bicycles and dashing into the concealment of the jungle.

Shit. They're well disciplined...and well organized. Maybe we got half...but half a hundred still makes it fifty against seven...

The attrition fight Jock knew he couldn't win.

We've got to get the hell out of here.

As if Jock's hand signal to *Pull Back!* wasn't clear enough, two rounds from Japanese knee mortars came crashing into Hadley's position across the trail, making the point with deadly emphasis.

Hadley's men had already stopped shooting, Jock told himself. *They must have been gone from there and into the jungle before those mortars hit.*

The words were more prayer than certainty.

Both teams would have to ford the stream to get to Joe Youngblood's position. He was still sniping, picking off any Japanese soldier foolish enough to venture back onto the trail. It didn't matter if the range was one hundred yards or more; Youngblood was scoring first-round hits.

Jock made it to the open expanse of the stream before he realized Bogater and Oscar were not with him. He scrambled back into the concealment of the jungle and peered down the trail—both men were running like champion sprinters toward the stream. Their arms were loaded with heavy objects unrecognizable at first.

As they splashed into the knee-deep water, Jock recognized what they were carrying:

Knee mortars! With ammo! They must've swiped it off some bicycles.

When the two reached the stream's far bank, reciprocal justice issued a stern verdict: a mortar shell landed within yards of them.

An eye for an eye...

Jock splashed across the stream, grabbed the two dazed and bleeding men and, pumped with adrenaline, dragged them into the undergrowth on the far side. No sooner did they get there, Bogater popped up as if jolted by electricity. He sprinted back to the stream and recovered one of the mortars and four rounds.

Dropping the swag at Jock's feet, he started back for the rest.

Jock tackled him.

"Knock it off, Boudreau. I need you alive more than I need some pop-gun mortars. Look at you...you're sliced up like crazy. I think the blast scrambled your brains a little, too."

Oscar was in even worse shape. His scalp had been grazed and burned by a shell fragment. Blood was streaming down his face. His outstretched hands felt someone beside him.

"I cannot see," he said.

Jock took the towel from his neck and fashioned a crude bandage around Oscar's head. With the free end, he wiped the blood from his guide's eyes.

"Thank you, Major Jock. Much better now."

Maybe not—there was another fragment sticking out of Oscar's thigh.

"We'll get Miss Smits to have a look at you," Jock said. "But we've got to get the fuck out of here, right now."

Bogater was staring at Jock's trouser leg—a spot on his thigh was slowly turning dark with blood. "What about you, sir? Looks like you caught yourself a piece, too."

"Son of a bitch," Jock said. "I can't feel a damn thing. I guess it mustn't be too bad then, eh? C'mon, you two…let's get moving."

Jock acted as Oscar's crutch. Bogater toted the mortar and rounds for which they'd nearly died.

"Did Hadley's boys make it out, sir?" Bogater asked.

"Don't know."

"We sure kicked them Jap asses right good, though, didn't we, sir?"

"I don't think we kicked them enough, Bogater. Too damn many of them…and this sure as hell isn't their first time under fire, either."

When they reached his position, Joe Youngblood was still picking off the odd Japanese soldier unwise enough to show himself.

"Saddle up, all of you," Jock said. "We're moving south. We've got to link up with Hadley and his men…"

If they're still alive.

Anne Marie took one look at Jock, Oscar, and Bogater. "I need time to tend to all your wounds," she said.

"Time's something we don't have right now," Jock replied. "Get moving."

Youngblood's eyes were still trained on the bridge. "Wait a minute, sir. Look at this."

A cluster of Japanese—eight, maybe ten—were on the bridge, flinging wrecked bicycles over the side, dragging bodies out of the way.

"Should I take them down, sir?" Youngblood asked.

"Save your ammo," Jock replied. "I've got a better idea."

He took the mortar, stuck its T-shaped base into the ground, bracing the weapon with his foot as he knelt on one knee behind it, and angled the tube toward the bridge with one hand.

Youngblood said, "So that's why they call it a *knee mortar*. And here I though it was because you fired it off your knee."

"Nah, that's a good way to break your leg." With his free hand, Jock picked up one of the rounds—a hefty 50-millimeter grenade—and hung it over the open tube. "Here goes nothing. Everyone…turn your face away."

He let the round drop into the tube, and then pulled the firing lanyard.

With a dull *THUMP*, the grenade was on its way.

Six seconds later, after arcing high through the air, it impacted in the midst of the soldiers on the bridge, sending torn bodies, bicycles, and wooden boards flying in all directions.

Jillian patted him on the back. "Brilliant! Great shot, Jock."

"Beginner's luck," he replied.

Bogater asked, "Still think it was a dumb idea to snatch that thing, sir?"

"I never said it was a dumb idea, Bogater. Just that I needed *you* more than *it*...and I still do."

As they started their trek through the jungle, Jillian asked, "Your leg, baby...does it hurt?"

"Not yet, Jill."

Chapter Twenty-Three

I must've only been out for a second or two, Deuce Hashimoto told himself. The stench of explosives was still heavy in the air. Leaves sliced from high branches by flying steel fluttered to the ground like dazed butterflies.

Though knocked flat on his back, his Thompson had stayed in his hand, still hot and smoking from the torrent of bullets it had delivered only moments ago. His other hand flew to his crotch to take inventory: *All there.*

A strange memory floated into his head: how the nurses in the field hospital back on Papua would say, with great certainty, *The first thing a guy checks is the family jewels, without fail.*

All the GIs thought those nurses were pulling their legs...

Maybe they weren't.

He stood up, filled with the dreaded sense he was suddenly alone, caught in the cruel and incomprehensible shift from living and breathing to bleeding and dying...

But I'm not dying. Just this siren screaming in my ears.

Time's all fouled up, though...

Events that had happened just moments ago seemed like ancient history: First Sergeant Hadley had given the order to disengage and pull back. They turned, ran...and everything went dark.

But Deuce was back in the light now, in a tranquil jungle that had been a swirling storm of violence and death just a few, rapid heartbeats ago...

He told me to pull back...
But which way is "back?"
Where the hell is my helmet?
And where is First Sergeant Hadley and Sergeant McMillen?

He started walking and, blundering from the concealment of the jungle, stopped cold when he saw the horror at the bridge. Smashed and useless now, its approach was littered with dozens of dead Japanese and their shot-up bicycles. His stomach heaved with the sickening feeling that some, perhaps *many*, of them had died at his hands...

Bad idea. I'm going the wrong way.

He *about-faced* and headed back into the jungle.

In a few quick steps, he came to a helmet lying on the ground.

But it wasn't his. The name written inside was *Hadley, T.*

They didn't leave me behind, did they?

That question was answered as Tom Hadley suddenly reappeared, struggling to sit up in the undergrowth not ten feet away.

He seemed in a daze. Seeing the Nisei, Hadley leveled his Thompson without a moment's hesitation and squeezed the trigger.

An instinct...

But nothing happened. The weapon's magazine was empty.

Deuce was flat on the ground at Hadley's feet, screaming, "IT'S ME, FIRST SERGEANT! DEUCE! DON'T SHOOT! DON'T SHOOT!"

"*Deuce*? What the hell...*who* the hell..."

Hadley's memory stabbed its way back into his

consciousness. He stopped short of slamming home the fresh magazine. His hands grabbed his noise-damaged ears instead, trying to rub away the maddening shriek within them.

"Deuce…what the hell happened?"

"We got hit with a grenade…or mortar…or something. Hey, your ears are bleeding."

Hadley swiped a finger through the blood and stared at it.

"No shit," he said. "They're ringing like a bastard, too. It must've been real close."

He shifted to get a better look at himself.

"At least the family jewels are still there."

Those nurses definitely weren't kidding, Deuce thought.

McMillen stumbled into view and came closer. Although the smoke of the battle had drifted away, a thick cloud still swirled around him.

The pack on his back was on fire, burning from within. He seemed oblivious as Deuce struggled frantically to pull the pack off him.

His words as rushed as his movements, Deuce blurted, "ANY AMMO IN HERE, SARGE?"

"Hell…yeah," McMillen answered, his speech slow and slurred as if he was drunk.

Once the burning pack was on the ground, Deuce realized the back of McMillen's shirt was burning, too.

He knocked the sergeant flat on his back to smother the flames. McMillen was still too dazed to resist. Or be of any help.

Then Deuce dumped the contents of the pack on the ground, pouring what was left of the water in his canteen on the burning K ration cartons. The boxes of .45-caliber ammo hadn't been taken by the flames yet. He kicked them clear.

The water sizzled and steamed when it hit the hot chunk of mortar fragment that had pierced the pack and started the fire inside.

Hadley was fast overcoming the effects of his concussion. He began sorting out McMillen's various injuries while watching Deuce in quiet amazement.

Look at this guy! He was the one Patchett had written off—said he'd never make a combat soldier. Well, I'd say he's made the grade on this mission, for sure, Sergeant Major. I'm proud to serve with this guy.

Just then, a bullet they never heard fired struck Deuce's head and tore off half his face.

It didn't take long for Jock to find the rest of his men. All he had to do was home in on the intermittent bursts of Thompsons answering the chatter of Japanese weapons somewhere deep in the jungle. When Jock's team intercepted Hadley and McMillen, the two wild-eyed sergeants were on the dead run, fleeing for their lives.

"Deuce is dead," Hadley blurted. "A sniper got him. We tried to bring his body out but they were all over us like stink on shit. We've been playing jungle hide-and-seek ever since."

"Shit," Jock said. But there was no time to mourn. "Any idea how many are chasing you, Tom?"

"No, sir. Only caught a glimpse of one or two coming through the jungle. Feels like a whole lot more, though."

Joe Youngblood popped off two quick rounds from his M1. "There," he said. "That's two less chasing you now."

Jock asked, "Did you see any besides those two, Youngblood?"

"Yes, sir. A whole lot more...but they dropped out of sight real quick."

"All right, then," Jock said, "let's get moving back to the trail, *on the double*."

"Wait a bloody minute, Jock," Jillian said, blocking his path. "That poor boy...aren't you going to go get him?"

"Ordinarily...hell yeah we would, Jill. But we're in kind of deep shit right now."

"That's the thanks he gets?" she replied. "You're just going to leave him there? Not even try to bury him?"

"Jill, listen to me, dammit. I've got no choice."

"Bullshit," she replied, standing her ground, spitting fire. "It's not bloody fair, Jock. You know what they'll do to him, especially since he's...you know..."

"Knock this shit off, Jill. I can't lose anyone else over a dead man. Now get moving."

He tried to grab her waist and steer her toward the others. She batted his hands away. As she did, the pain from her shoulders made her wince.

She joined the column without saying another word.

You know what they'll do to him...Jillian's words kept ringing in the ears of Jock and his men. They had very clear memories of how the Japanese could desecrate a body. They'd seen it with their own eyes at Buna. The horror of finding those cannibalized bodies— both American and Japanese—was burned into their souls forever.

Let's hope them sumbitches ain't real hungry,
Bogater Boudreau told himself.

Hadley unslung the extra Thompson he was
carrying—Deuce's Thompson—and offered it to Jock,
asking, "What do you want to do with this weapon, sir?"

Jock took the Thompson and passed it to Jillian.
"Jill," he said, "you remember how to use one of these,
right?"

"Of course I bloody remember."

"Good. You carry it, then. Give Anne Marie that
pistol and show her how it works. Don't actually fire it,
though. Don't give our position away…until we have no
choice."

She gave him a dirty look and replied, "You don't
think I'm that bloody stupid, do you, Yank?"

Chapter Twenty-Four

It was almost high noon—1200 hours—when Jock's team reached a ridge overlooking the trail to Mount Dremsel. As they had moved west, the jungle yielded to rainforest. They could make faster progress now—they didn't need to hack through dense curtains of green anymore. One thing hadn't changed, though: just like in the jungle, little sunlight reached the forest floor through the dense canopy of treetops. Their world was still as dreary as a crypt.

The ridge was a good place for a brief rest, affording the protection and advantage of high ground above the trail. From there, they could see the tail end of the Japanese column slogging its way toward the mountain on foot. The few bicycles visible were being pushed rather than ridden. No longer a rapid means of mobility for the troops, they functioned now as improvised cargo carriers. "Well," Jock said, "the good news is we slowed them down quite a bit…"

He didn't need to announce the bad news, though. Everyone knew it: there was no way they could shield Patchett and his boys on the mountain now.

As Jock hunched over the map, Hadley asked, "You think Patchett's still even at the OP? I thought the fleet was supposed to be out of sight around 1000 hours. Maybe they're on their way back to the boats already."

They took a look at Dremsel in the distance, its peak shrouded in storm clouds. "We don't know how long that storm's been up there," Jock said, "but you can bet they can't see a damn thing from the OP right now. You know as well as I do that Patch won't pull up stakes until he's sure the fleet's out of sight."

Or the Japs kick him off, Hadley thought, but decided not to say out loud.

The map study revealed something interesting. "We're only about three miles as the crow flies from the peak," Jock said. "With the height of their antenna up on that mountain, you don't suppose we could raise them on the walkie-talkie, do you?"

Hadley replied, "Sir, the book says the transmitters in these things have a range of one mile *in optimum conditions.* Besides, I'm not even sure it's still working. We didn't get to monitor them last night at 2200, remember? We were busy with our little *jailbreak.*"

"Yeah, Tom...but the book doesn't cover every little thing. It can't hurt to try. If we can't block the Japs, at least we can let Patch know they're coming."

Hadley wasn't convinced. "Well, all right, sir. Just give me a minute to put in fresh batteries. I've got one set left."

"Only one, Tom? What happened to the rest of them?"

"Got torched in McMillen's pack. Probably why his back got burned so bad."

The rest stop finally allowed Anne Marie the chance to improve on the improvised first aid the GIs had applied. She was putting the finishing touches on McMillen's dressing; it looked like she had used a mile of rolled bandage, expertly wrapped like a garment around his torso to cover the burns on his back. "Just as well," McMillen said, smiling as he surveyed her handiwork. "I needed a new shirt, anyway."

Anne Marie replied, "We'll have to change those dressings frequently, Sergeant. You know how quickly infections can fester in the jungle."

"I wouldn't worry about it, Miss Smits," McMillen replied. "By tomorrow night, we're all gonna be outta this sewer. We'll be the US Navy's problem then." He looked at Joe Youngblood and added, "Hey, *chief*...you're the only guy here who doesn't need patching up. You must lead a charmed life, pal."

Youngblood had nothing to say. He took a pained glance at Jillian and thought, *Don't bet on it, Sarge. I believe my time's coming.*

The walkie-talkie had its new batteries. Hadley keyed the transmitter: "*Lost Boy Eight*, this is *Lost Boy Six*, over."

He waited for a reply he felt certain wouldn't come...

And it didn't.

"Call them again," Jock said.

"You sure, sir? We're too far away. We're just going to waste our juice."

"Do it, Tom. Now."

Hadley repeated the call. Again there was no answer. He shrugged, as if telling Jock, *See? I told you.*

"Call them one more time."

"But, sir, it's not—"

Jock cut him off. "Was I not clear enough, First Sergeant?"

Hadley transmitted once again...and nearly dropped the walkie-talkie with surprise when the reply came. A voice—*Stu Botkin's voice*—was banging in loud and clear, saying:

"*Lost Boy Six,* this is *Lost Boy Eight.* You're weak but readable, over.*"

Hadley asked Jock, "What do I tell him, sir?"

"Ask him where the *rubber ducks* are."

Rubber ducks: code for the fleet.

Hadley didn't need to relay the reply. Botkin's voice boomed from the walkie-talkie's earpiece: "Hidden right now, but possible *ducks* could be around for one to two hours more, over."

"Shit," Jock said. "The fucking Navy's behind schedule. Japs could be all over that OP in two hours."

It didn't take him more than a few seconds to come to a decision. "Tell them they've got trouble coming, so *burn down the mission*."

Burn down the mission: code for *destroy the tower*...and get the hell out of there.

"We'd better get our asses moving, too," Jock said, "just in case those *cyclists* happen to have a direction finder with them."

Melvin Patchett smiled as the radio exchange with Jock's team came to an end. "As I live and breathe," he said, "the major didn't go and get hisself killed after all...and he ain't forgot about our sorry asses, neither."

Walking through the wind-driven rain pelting the mountain top, he found Cotton Allred right where he was supposed to be, covering the final, skyward twist of the *spiral staircase*.

"When them Japs come," Allred said, "I sure ain't gonna be able to see much of 'em in this pea soup."

"Don't worry yourself none about it, son," Patchett replied. "Good as you shoot, you don't need to see much. And they won't be seeing much of you, neither, 'cause you probably ain't even gonna be here when they show up."

"What do you mean, Sergeant Major?"

"It means Botkin and Ace are gonna cut down that li'l ol' tower, son, and then all of us are gonna get the fuck outta here."

When Patchett got back to the base of the tower, Botkin and Ace were tying hand grenades to two of its rickety wooden legs. Unimpressed, he roared, "THAT AIN'T WHAT I TOLD YOU TO DO NOW, IS IT?"

"But Sergeant Major," Botkin replied, "this ought to bring it down real easy."

"Sure it will, Sergeant Botkin...but it also wastes four grenades we just might need for their usual purpose before we get off this rock. Now do what I told you to. Pick up them axes them Jap bastards were nice enough to leave behind and hack through that leg on the leeward side. Strong as that wind's blowing, this thing'll crumble like a house of cards in no time flat."

"But it might fall on *us*," Ace Nishimoto said.

"Not if you keep your head out of your ass, son. Now let's see you two make like Paul Bunyan. We ain't got all fucking day."

It didn't take many swings of the axes. As soon as the slow, mournful *groan* of wood rending itself began, Botkin and Ace fled from beneath the mass of lumber swaying above them. The leg they had hacked almost all the way through flexed, twisted, bowed, and finally snapped. The tower tottered for an agonizing moment as if thinking whether it could still stand on its three unscathed legs—and decided it couldn't. With ear-splitting *CRACKS* sounding like gunshots, those legs failed, too. The tower collapsed, transforming itself from a tall, once proud structure to a jagged line of timber scattered among the downwind trees.

Ace seemed stunned by the whole affair. As he picked wood splinters the size of daggers out of his clothing and web gear, he asked Patchett, "Why'd we just do that, Sergeant Major?"

"Why, son? Take a look around you. What do you see?"

"Just trees."

"And that's all them Japs are gonna see when they get up here. Now let's get a move on, boys. It's time to get *The Squad* all together again. Oh, and one more thing…Sergeant Botkin, rip something *critical* outta that Jap radio before we go so it ain't never gonna work again."

Chapter Twenty-Five

Patchett and his three men raced through the pouring rain down the *spiral staircase*, doing their best to keep their footing on the muddy, tractionless trail. To slip could mean a deadly plunge down the mountainside—but being beaten to the mountain's base by the Japanese coming from Lorengau could prove just as deadly.

They were almost to the bottom. Rounding the last curve, Patchett said, "All right...slow it down and get into them trees. If them Nips are already down there, let's not fuck up and run right into their arms."

The base of the trail was in view now. The truck was still there, less than a hundred yards away. So were the bodies of the four men Patchett and Allred had killed early that morning...

And so were three more Japanese soldiers, very much alive and bewildered by the scene of death before them.

"They can't hear us coming in this rain," Patchett said. "Allred, you got a clear shot at all of 'em?"

"Yeah...but I better take out the one on the other side of the truck first, so he don't use it for cover."

"Good plan, son. Do it quick but don't shoot up the fucking truck. I'm thinking we just might need it all of a sudden."

It took two seconds—and two bullets—for Allred to drop the first two Japanese in their tracks. The third man slipped in the mud as he tried to run away. That slip prolonged his life one more second as the third shot splattered harmlessly beside him.

But the fourth bullet was dead on target.

"Let's move it," Patchett said. "Y'all get in that *vee-hickle*."

As they closed the distance to the truck on the dead run, Botkin asked, "How do we know it's even going to start?"

"It ran just fine yesterday, son," Patchett replied. "How the fuck do you think it got here?"

"But it's a *Japanese* truck, Sergeant Major."

"It looks like a li'l ol' Dodge to me," Patchett replied as he climbed into the driver's seat. "Get in...the whole damn Imperial Japanese Army can't be too far off."

Patchett hit the starter button and the engine rumbled to life. With a *growl* of gears, the truck lurched forward—and they were on their way, careening down the narrow trail.

Botkin, in the cab with Patchett, asked, "Aren't we headed straight toward the Japs coming to the OP?"

"Yep," Patchett replied, flooring the accelerator. "Tell the boys in the back to get their asses down in that bed. See if you can raise the major on that walkie-talkie. He can't be far from here."

Botkin stuck the short whip antenna out his side window and called *Lost Boy Six*. Hadley's voice answered immediately.

Patchett asked Botkin, "So what does the major want us to do?"

"He wants to know if we can be at *Rally Point Charlie* within an hour."

Patchett laughed as he navigated a sharp curve at breakneck speed, the truck's wheels spinning and sliding through the mud. "Shit, son...tell the man we'll be there in five minutes, *if the Good Lord's willing and the creek don't rise.*"

They wheeled around another curve—and drove straight into the Japanese column. The truck mowed down—and then jolted over—a dozen screaming men and a handful of bicycles.

Those farther back in the column flung themselves to safety off the trail. They hit the ground and came up firing.

"I guess they figured out we ain't Japanese," Patchett said over the sound of bullets *pinging* off the truck's tailgate.

Then a bullet went over the tailgate, *hissed* through the cab's open rear, snatched the walkie-talkie from Botkin's hands, and shattered the windshield in front of his face on the way out.

With a violent spin of the steering wheel, Patchett skidded the truck through another tight curve. They were clear of the line of fire now.

"You okay, son?"

Trying to wring the stinging sensation from his hands, Botkin replied, "Yeah, I'm good. The radio's had it, though."

"Check the boys in the back."

Allred and Ace were still clawing the bed of the truck as if trying to dig deeper into its metal cocoon.

"They're shitting their pants," Botkin reported, "but they're okay."

"Outstanding," Patchett replied. "Now, this *Rally Point Charlie*...that's right near the village of—"

"WE'RE ON FIRE," Allred shrieked, his panicked face thrust inside the cab. "WE GOTTA GET OFF BEFORE SHE BLOWS."

They all jumped before the truck even slowed down. It sped on, leaving a ribbon of burning gasoline floating on the muddy trail.

"Musta got us in the gas tank," Patchett said.

The truck left the trail at the next curve, coming to a stop as it smashed into a tree.

A second later, it blew up, spewing a column of thick black smoke high into the air—a perfect target marker.

"Can everybody run?" Patchett asked.

His three men nodded.

"Then let's get the hell away from here, *on the double.*"

The Japanese captain was sure he'd be severely punished when he returned to Lorengau. He'd lost forty of his sixty men since leaving there this morning, all to an elusive enemy. Never before during the Japanese juggernaut had his unit suffered so badly. His men had found the body of only one of these attackers. The man's face was so badly disfigured he could never be identified, but his uniform and weapon marked him as a soldier in the American Army.

But not just any American soldier. An English-speaking sergeant had read the dead man's identification tags, stamped with a Japanese surname.

A traitor, no doubt, who deserved to die.

But we still haven't reached the top of Mount Dremsel. At least it's finally stopped raining...and our radio is still working.

Right now, that radio was equal parts *curse* and

blessing. It had shamed him to send that radio message back to Lorengau, informing Headquarters of the *great American force* that had infiltrated Manus Island. In the hope of delaying his disgrace a bit longer, the message had conveniently omitted the catastrophic casualty figures.

But if they send reinforcements quickly, maybe we can still prevail...and somehow reverse my fate.

His lieutenant approached. "Captain, I have assembled a party to pursue the Americans. They can't be far from—"

The captain cut him off with a sharp slap to the face. "We have not completed our mission yet, idiot. We will secure the mountaintop without further delay. Get the men moving immediately."

Tom Hadley laid the walkie-talkie down. Patchett and his men weren't answering anymore. There was no point wasting battery power.

He joined Jock, who was huddled over the map. "You know, sir, the boats are less than three miles south of here right now. We can get there with plenty of sunlight left, too. If we keep walking toward the rally point...well, that's damn near the opposite direction."

"I hear what you're saying, Tom," Jock replied, "but we've got to try to link up with Patchett."

"Don't you think he can find the boats on his own...?" Hadley didn't finish the sentence, because the rest of it would've been, *if they're still alive.* Instead, he added, "This mission's done, sir. All we've got to do now is lay low until tomorrow night and then float our battered asses out of here."

"I'm not leaving Patchett and his guys behind, Tom." It was Jock's turn to leave words unsaid: *We've already had to leave one man behind...and that's one too many.*

"And Tom...I want you to keep transmitting regularly, even if they don't reply. Botkin's got the DF loop—maybe he can home in on us. They can't be too far away."

"But sir, won't that let the Japs home in on us, too?"

"As long as we keep moving, I'll take that risk."

"But the batteries, sir—"

"I don't want to hear any more crap about the batteries running down, either, First Sergeant. Right now, the only thing that juice is good for is finding the rest of our guys."

It was nearly 1400 hours when the Japanese captain and his men reached the OP atop Mount Dremsel. The skies had cleared, but they could see little of the horizon through the trees. Without the tower, this peak was practically useless as an observation post. It was, at the moment, little more than a lofty cemetery, with seven fresh graves and the still-exposed bodies of two Korean privates.

"Lieutenant," the captain said, "climb that tree and search for enemy vessels." The tree to which he pointed—the tallest on the peak—was a spindly specimen whose crown swayed wildly in the sweet, post-storm breeze.

The lieutenant replied, "But sir, I don't think it will

hold my weight."

The Captain slapped his face. "I have given you an order. Climb."

As ordered, the lieutenant shimmied up the narrow trunk to the top, until his head poked above the canopy. The limb to which he clung for dear life swung like a pendulum with his weight. But he could clearly take in a wide expanse of the Bismarck Sea to the south of the island.

The captain called to him, "What can you see?"

"Nothing, sir…just lots of water."

"Use your binoculars, idiot."

That was the last thing the lieutenant wanted to do, because it would mean releasing one hand from its death grip on the limb to snatch the binoculars from their pouch. The range of the pendulum's oscillation was increasing with each swing.

Yet, he managed to get the binoculars to his eyes. He gave the horizon one broad sweep, hesitating for a moment as he looked southwest:

Was it a low cloud, far in the distance? Or was it smoke from a ship…or many ships? I can't tell…this damned swaying!

No…like those storms that just passed, it must be a cloud.

It must be.

The captain called to him again. "What do you see, Lieutenant?"

"I see…I see nothing, sir."

With a loud *snap*, the limb suddenly swung down, flicking the lieutenant out of the tree like some irritating insect.

He crashed through several branches as he fell,

failing to grab any of them for more than an instant…

And then plummeted straight down.

The impact with the ground broke his neck.

The captain stood over his lifeless body, kicked it, and muttered, "Idiot."

Chapter Twenty-Six

The low, slanting rays of the late afternoon sun brightened the usual gloom of the rainforest, casting between the trees vivid channels of orange light that seemed like pathways to heaven. Bathed in this warm and inviting glow, Jock's party caught their first view of *Rally Point Charlie*—a piece of high ground in the rainforest overlooking the Lorengau trail and the collection of grass shacks known as the village of Buyang. It was one of four points Jock had designated as places to reorganize should *The Squad* ever become separated...

Like it was right now.

Hadley, in his usual place at the rear of the column, told himself, *I guess I'll try calling them one last time.* He keyed the walkie-talkie: "*Lost Boy Eight*, this is *Lost Boy Six*, over."

At first, he thought the voice answering was coming from the radio's earpiece. *But it sounds so undistorted...so natural.*

He turned and saw Melvin Patchett standing not ten feet behind him.

"Where the hell did you come from, Sergeant Major?" Hadley asked.

"Same place as you, son...out of this damn forest."

"Did you hear me calling you?"

"Naw, our radio's all shot up. Didn't hear you until we was in earshot. By the way, you gotta talk a little more quieter into that thing. Heard you a long ways off."

Hadley's relief at seeing Patchett multiplied as Ace, Allred, and Botkin emerged from the woods. "We've got one hell of a surprise for you guys," he told them.

Patchett could see Jock's entire party stretched out in column before him. With one glance, Patchett got a pretty good idea what the surprise was. "As I live and breathe," he said, "ain't that Miss Forbes up there?"

"Sure is, Sergeant Major."

"Well, don't that beat all."

Those first moments with everyone on the rally point were a frenzy of greetings and joyous reunions. Patchett was nearly toppled by the crush of Jillian's bear hug. "I'd squeeze you even tighter, you old bastard," she said, "but my shoulders are killing me at the moment."

"I knew them Nips weren't no match for the likes of you, young lady," Patchett told her, his voice coming closer than anyone could remember to choking with emotion.

"Only the good die young, Sergeant Major," she replied, "so you and I have nothing to worry about."

Jock let them have their fun for a few moments more. Then it was back to business. He asked Patchett, "Any Japs following you, Top?"

"Don't think so, sir. I'm guessing they went up the mountain to reclaim the OP."

Jock said, "I don't expect they're going to forget about us for long, though."

"That's for damn sure, sir."

"Do you think they saw anything of the fleet when they got up there, Top?"

"Don't rightly know. When we left, it was still like looking into a pot of pea soup. We did give the Navy a couple extra hours to get out of sight, though..."

"Yeah. Let's hope to hell that was enough..."

"Amen to that, sir."

Patchett looked around, taking in the wound dressings on every one of Jock's men except Joe Youngblood, and said, "Been pretty slow going for y'all, I reckon?"

"Yeah. We're not exactly in tip-top shape at the moment. If it wasn't for Miss Smits nursing us, we'd be hurting a whole lot worse."

"So I'm supposing we ain't gonna try to make the boats before nightfall, sir?"

"You suppose right, Top. If the Japs ain't on our heels by now, I don't think we'll be seeing them before morning. Oscar, our guide, is down in the village now, negotiating for us to spend the night there. It'd be our last chance to sleep dry before we get the hell out of here tomorrow night."

"*Oscar*? You picked yourself up a *native guide* along the way, sir?"

"Real long story, Top. But he's in the worst shape of all of us, I think. Nasty gash on his head. Concussed pretty bad…gets pretty disoriented sometimes. Leg wound, too. I wanted to evacuate him with us when we go—get him some good medical help—but he's refusing. Says his place is here."

"Sounds like y'all had some tough breaks, sir…but you slowed 'em down best you could, I reckon. Nothing y'all could do for that poor feller Deuce, though?"

"Not a damn thing, Top. Hadley tells me he put up one hell of a fight. Saved his ass and McMillen's, too."

Just then, it dawned on Jock their two captives were nowhere to be seen. In all that had happened, he'd forgotten about them. "Wait a minute. What happened to the Koreans?"

"Ace caught 'em going for some weapons.

Cancelled their tickets on the spot. Couldn't have done better myself."

Down in the village, Oscar was waving his arms at them, signaling, *Come on in! Welcome!*

As they settled into the village for the night, Patchett asked Jock, "How much security you want to set out, sir?"

Before Jock could answer, Oscar proposed, "No need for security. Buyang village looks out for Japs every day and night. They warn us if *soldia* come."

"Just the same," Jock replied, "we'll lend them a helping hand. Put two of our guys covering the trail approaches and one on the back door."

Patchett nodded and asked, "Three-hour rotation okay with you, sir?"

"Yeah. That's fine."

Just then, Bogater Boudreau walked up, lugging the captured knee mortar. "I think I found a good place to set this thing up, sir," he said. "Should be able to fire in any direction without bouncing 'em off the trees."

Patchett said, "Where in blue blazes did you pick up that thing?"

"Took it off the Japs at that fight back on the trail," Boudreau replied.

"Yeah," Jock added, "and that's how you and Oscar almost bought the farm, too, Bogater."

Boudreau's face twisted into a sly grin. "You want me to give it back, sir?"

"No, it's come in real handy once already. Let's keep it."

Patchett asked, "How many rounds we got for it?"

Bogater held up three fingers.

"Better than nothing," Patchett said. "Kinda makes me feel bad about spiking that bunch of Arisakas we found up on the OP instead of carrying 'em out."

"Nah, you made the right call, Sergeant Major," Jock replied. "You didn't need some big, heavy rifles slowing you down."

"Maybe so, sir. Maybe so. Sun's nearly down...I'm gonna get the night watches set up."

As everyone scattered to go about their business, Jock stood alone in the middle of the village. Tom Hadley saw him and thought, *This is my chance.*

There was a pained look on Hadley's face as he approached and asked, "A word, sir?"

"Sure, First Sergeant. What's up?"

"I just want...no, I *need* to apologize for the way I was acting before, sir...making it sound like we should cut and run and not try to find Patchett. I feel like the biggest asshole in the world for even thinking it now...especially after...after...you know..."

Jock knew what he was trying to say but couldn't: *Especially after leaving Deuce behind.*

"There's no need to apologize, Tom...because the thing is, you might have been right."

"*The Squad's* all squared away, sir," Patchett reported. "Everyone's chowed down on some of that roast pig and there's plenty of water. The *high mucketymuck* in this village moved some folks around, so Boudreau's team's bedding down in that shack over

yonder. McMillen's team'll be in this one right here."
He pointed to a third grass shack—little more than a
thatched roof on poles—and added, "That one there,
we'll use it for the CP. Hadley and me'll bunk there."

"We're putting people out of their homes, Top?"

"They're glad to do it, sir. They heard about the
thrashing we gave them Japs. The local chatter is all
about them slant-eyed bastards still hauling bodies off
the trail. Us GIs are like gods to them at the moment."

"All right...but what about the women, Top?"

"Miss Smits is staying with the elder's family, sir.
They got wind she was a nurse and put a claim on her
right away. Now, you and Miss Forbes...well, I'll let
Mister Solo explain that one." He snapped his fingers
and Oscar limped out of the night shadows.

"I'll leave you two to talk," Patchett said, and then
vanished into the shadows.

"Major Jock," Oscar began, "you and Miss
Forbes—you are *married*, no?"

"We're not married, Oscar."

"But you *stay together*, yes?"

"Well, sure...when we can, but—"

"Then you are *married* in this place." Oscar pointed
to a shack at the edge of the village. "You two stay there
tonight, okay?"

Jock found Jillian sitting outside *their* hut. "Pretty
clever sleeping arrangements, Yank," she said with a big
smile. "How'd you pull it off?"

He dropped his gear and sat down next to her. "I
had nothing to do with it, Jill."

"I'll bet, you wanker."

"No, really. Consider it a gift from the village, I guess."

Snuggling up against him, she said, "Bloody wonderful gift, if you ask me."

They sat quietly, enjoying the serenity of nightfall, pushing aside for a brief moment the memories of terrors past and the apprehension over those yet to come. Jillian finally broke the silence.

"Thank you for finding me, Jock."

"I wish I could say it was planned, Jill, but it was just dumb luck."

"It doesn't matter," she said, and kissed him. "I'll take dumb luck like that any day."

She stirred in his arms, suddenly unsettled as if seeking some comfort just out of reach.

"Something on your mind, Jill?"

He immediately wished he hadn't said it. It sounded incongruous. Even stupid. *Of course there's something on her mind, you idiot. She's been a POW for a year. Will I ever fully know or understand the hell she's been through? And we're not out of the woods yet, that's for damn sure. She knows as well as I do this could all turn to shit in a heartbeat.*

But when she spoke again, her words startled him. "Jock, that sniper of yours—Joe Youngblood. He doesn't like me very much, does he?"

"It's not that he doesn't *like* you, Jill. It's just…well…he's *afraid* of you."

"Afraid? Why?"

Jock proceeded to tell her the story of *The Woman in White*—and the nightmare on the submarine that brought Joe Youngblood to believe she was the spirit sent to claim his life.

When Jock was finished, she said, "That poor lad—as if being in your Army isn't enough trouble for him right now." She stood, grabbed the skirt of her shift with both hands and flared it like some high fashion model. "But how he could see this filthy Australian girl dressed in rice sacks as some soul-taking spirit? That's just beyond me."

"But that's what he believes, Jill."

She paced back and forth a few moments, deep in thought, before saying, "Let me talk to him."

"Okay, I'll have him brought over here and we can all have a chat."

"No, Jock. Let me talk to him alone. I know where he is."

Joe Youngblood was cleaning his rifle in the glow of the cook fire when he was startled by Jillian looming out of the darkness. He lurched as if wanting to run away, but seemed fastened in place by the need to scoop up the parts of the M1 spread on a towel before him.

"Wait, Joe," she called out, "I need to talk to you."

He said nothing, just stopped his frantic reassembling of the rifle and sat still, resigned to this chat with *death herself*.

"Can I sit with you?" she asked.

"Yes, ma'am," he replied, sounding as if he didn't think he had any choice in the matter.

"You know," she began, "I understand what you're feeling. I've spent my whole life around aboriginals quite like you. I know how powerful their belief in the storylines can be."

"That's funny," Joe said. "I've never heard anyone come right out and say that I, or any other American Indian, was an *aboriginal* before." He mulled it over a few moments more as he slipped the rifle's parts back into place. "But I suppose we do fit the proper definition of the word."

"Yes, you do, Joe. It's something to be proud of...and I meant no offense."

"I know that, Miss Forbes. No offense taken. None at all. But those storylines you talk about...do you believe in them?"

"Some of them...yes."

"Do you believe in *my* story, Miss Forbes?"

"Joe, how can I? I'm not some spirit. I'm just an ordinary, mortal woman."

"No, Miss Forbes, you're not ordinary at all. I've heard the things you've done—how you've made miracles happen for these guys before. That's what spirits do."

The fire's light cast deep shadows across the hollows of his face, making the pleading look in his eyes all the more desperate. "I don't want to believe in this story," he said, "but the dream...I can't get that dream out of my head..."

"Joe, you don't have to believe in anything you don't want to."

A sad but earnest look came over his face. It broke her heart as he replied, with all the certainty in the world, "Yes, Miss Forbes, I do. I have no choice."

Chapter Twenty-Seven

They'd been too exhausted to even think about
making love. It was enough for Jock and Jillian just to
lie in each other's arms, thoughts churning with the
uncertainties the new day would bring, while their
battered bodies cried for the deep, healing slumber that
would never come—not here, not now.

When they heard the heavy, urgent footsteps
coming straight for their hut, they were on their feet
before Patchett's voice pierced the darkness: "We got
trouble coming, sir. You gotta come see this right now."

"Japs?"

"Who else?"

"Jill," Jock said, "get everybody up and ready to
move." Then he turned to Patchett. "Do the villagers
know what's going on?"

"They showed *us*, sir."

"Okay…now show *me*."

Patchett led Jock clear of the huts for a better view.
Deep in the blackness of the rainforest at night, clustered
points of light—a hundred, maybe more—blinked on
and off like fireflies, still some indefinite distance away
but moving *en masse* toward the village.

"What do you make of that, Top?"

"Bicyclists—with lanterns swinging from the
handlebars, sir. Sight in on one with your binoculars and
you'll see what I mean. They're on the trail, for sure."

"Yeah, I got it," Jock said. "Every time one of them
passes behind a tree, you lose its light for a second…and
there must be a million trees between them and us.
That's why they look like they're blinking."

"They're between us and the boats, too, sir. If we let 'em stay there, we're in deep shit."

"Yeah, but we don't want a fight right here in Buyang, either, Top. These villagers don't deserve that."

"I wouldn't worry about them, sir. I reckon they learned the drill back when the Aussies got kicked out—they're already packing up and heading into the woods to get the hell out of the way."

"Good," Jock said. "One less thing to worry about right now." He took an azimuth with his compass, then pulled the map from his helmet. "You're right, Top. They've got to be on the trail—and they've got to be up on the plateau, too, or we wouldn't be able to see them at all." He drew a line on the map. "But at this azimuth, they're still about eight hundred yards away, give or take."

"So what do you got in mind, sir?"

"Let them keep coming until they're in range of that little mortar we've got—about a hundred and fifty yards or so. Then we drop a round or two on them and get the hell out of here."

"I like that, sir. Outnumbered bad as we are, we can't be getting in no gun fights in the dark if we don't have to. A little mortar fire oughta shake 'em up long enough for us to get around and behind them."

"And when the sun comes up, we run south like hell for the boats...and then hide out until we hit the water at sundown."

"Good plan, sir...but who's gonna do the honors with that knee mortar? I don't reckon any of us are good enough to be dead on with that thing in the dark."

"I'll do it, Top. I had some pretty good luck the last time we used it. When the azimuth to those lights gets to one two zero degrees, I'll let her rip. How about you and Bogater spotting the rounds for me?"

"Affirmative, sir. But just one thing...if there's any more of them coming down that trail behind this bunch, we're fucked."

The lights grew closer, blinking less now that fewer trees blocked their glow as the trail straightened toward the village. The mortar, positioned in the small clearing Bogater Boudreau had picked out, was manned by Jock and Sergeant Botkin. Boudreau and Patchett, acting as forward observers, were set up at the edge of the village, closest to the trail and the approaching Japanese. Jillian and Anne Marie strung themselves between those two points to be voice relays for the mortar fire commands.

Nervous about her role, Anne Marie asked Jillian, "Why can't they use radios to talk to each other?"

"Because they've only got one."

"But what if I misunderstand and say something wrong?"

"There's nothing to understand, sweetie," Jillian replied. "Just repeat *exactly* what the Yanks say."

Patchett swung his compass toward the lights, waiting a moment for the floating dial to settle before reading the phosphorescent numerals on its face. "I got one one five degrees, Bogater. Check or hold?"

"Check. Right on the money."

Patchett muttered, "C'mon, you bastards...get a little bit closer now."

At the mortar, Botkin was trying to come to grips with the gunnery. "How the hell are you going to aim this thing, sir?"

"It's pretty crude, I know," Jock replied, "but I've got the tube's direction of fire lined up with that hut over there. That'll lob the round over the village and straight down the trail. Setting the range is a little trickier. The last time I shot this thing, I was aiming for about a hundred fifty yards out, just like now. I tilted the tube at a forty-five degree angle—just like this—set this knob about midway—that varies the range by changing the chamber size—and the round landed right where I wanted it."

"I think I've got it, sir," Botkin replied, ready to drop the round in his hands into the tube. "Just tell me when to load this thing."

Patchett steadied his compass again. "What you got, Bogater?"

"One two zero. Check or hold?"

"Check," Patchett replied. He turned toward Anne Marie and said, "Miss Smits...*Fire.*"

"*Fire,*" she repeated to Jillian, telling herself, *That was easy enough.*

Two seconds later, when Jillian's relay reached the mortar crew, Jock told Botkin, "Drop it in."

With a jerk of the firing lanyard—and a *THUMP* that seemed loud enough to be heard across the entire island—the round was on its way.

His voice on edge, Botkin asked, "You think the Japs heard that shot, sir?"

"Depends on how much noise their bicycles make, I guess."

Eight seconds passed before there was the *CRUMP* of impact far down the trail...

"Where the hell did it hit?" Bogater asked. "I didn't

see it."

The bicycles kept coming. They seemed to be moving faster now and close enough to make out the faint silhouettes of the riders in the glow of their lanterns.

"It had to go long," Patchett said. "It *had* to be." He turned into the darkness concealing Anne Marie and said, "Miss Smits...*Drop Fifty*."

Passing the command to Jillian, Anne Marie felt buoyed, telling herself, *I'm doing this! I can do this!*

As soon as Jillian's relay reached the mortar crew, Jock was cranking the range knob. "For less range, dial in a bigger chamber," he told Botkin. "Okay, drop it in."

The second round went flying toward the advancing Japanese.

"We've only got one round left, sir," Botkin said.

"I know, Stu...I know."

The *CRUMP* of impact was closer this time—and more effective.

When it struck, some of the lights streaked skyward like sparks off a grinding wheel. They faded quickly to nothing in the night sky.

The relentless advance of the lead ranks stopped. There was much shouting in Japanese.

A few small fires flared where shattered lanterns had spilled flaming oil. They illuminated the confused scene better than any parachute flare overhead could.

Soldiers who survived the blast were abandoning their bicycles on the trail and seeking cover behind sturdy tree trunks.

But lights still well down the trail hadn't stopped coming.

"I reckon them Nips farther back ain't figured out

what happened yet," Patchett said. "Let's drop that last round in the same damn place. They'll ride right into it."

"Roger," Bogater replied.

"Miss Smits," Patchett said, "*Repeat!*"

In a few seconds, their final round was on its way.

As that round impacted, Patchett and Bogater once again saw lanterns streak away like sparks into the air.

But this time, the glow of the fires showed them something more: the bodies of cyclists caught in the blast flung away like rag dolls...there one second, gone the next.

The Japanese weren't all dead, though—not by a long shot.

A Nambu machine gun opened up from well down the trail, its yellow tracers arcing blindly through the night sky...

Aimed at nothing but the gunner's fear...

And hitting no one.

Throughout the village, they could hear Jock's shouted command: "RAINBOW, RAINBOW, RAINBOW," the signal to escape the village and regroup at *Rally Point Charlie*.

The Squad moved quickly through the forest, each member seeing nothing in this opaque box of night but the faint outline of the man—or woman—ahead.

Leading the column, Tom Hadley said, "Weapons on *safe*, pass it down."

Private Allred, the man right behind Hadley, couldn't believe what he was hearing. "I ain't putting no damn weapon on safe," he muttered. "We got Japs up our ass."

Hadley replied, "In case you missed my drift, Private, it's so you don't fall down and shoot yourself or the poor bastard in front of you by accident. Do what I tell you and do it right fucking now."

Just a few steps later, Allred tripped over some invisible obstacle and went sprawling. He thanked his lucky stars his M1 was on *safe* because it came out of his hands as he fell and bounced along the ground—an accidental discharge begging to happen.

"Good way to illustrate my point, Private," Hadley said as he helped the man to his feet. "And by the way, you just made my permanent shit list."

They walked uphill—but didn't dare run—until Hadley guessed they'd covered the right distance. The terrain seemed to be leveling out, too, just like it should if they had actually reached the high ground of *Rally Point Charlie*. He brought the column to a halt and waited for Jock to catch up.

"I think we're here, sir," Hadley said. "I just can't tell if we've actually climbed high enough, though. If there's still some terrain looking down on us, and the Japs are on it…"

"Let's get organized first," Jock replied, "then we'll worry about where we are. Get a perimeter set up while we wait for Boudreau and the sergeant major to show up."

Patchett's voice floated out of the shadows: "Already here, sir. We should be the tail end. I'll get a headcount going…see if we're missing anyone. Miss

Forbes and Miss Smits…are they here?"

Jock replied, "Yeah, got them both."

The Japanese down on the trail had tired of firing their machine gun at phantoms. They'd doused the lantern lights. The fires had burned out, too.

I think we got around them, Jock told himself, *but they're still out there…somewhere…and they're not going to stand still, either.*

He took a long look around, trying to get his bearings. All he saw was the sylvan darkness. *Hadley's right. Can't tell exactly what ground we're standing on…not without some light.*

But we can't sit on our asses, waiting for the sun to come up. We've got to keep moving.

Patchett returned and said, "We got one man missing—your boy Oscar. McMillen says he saw him right before we pulled out of the village. Said he was setting booby traps for the Japs."

"Booby traps? Made from what?"

"Beats the hell out of me, sir. We gonna wait for him?"

After hesitating for a troubled moment, Jock said, "No, Top, we can't. If he wanted to be evacuated with us, it'd be a different story, but…"

"No need to explain, sir."

There was a dull, distant *powww* of a small explosion coming from the direction of the village…

And then another.

"Maybe ol' Oscar's got them booby traps of his working real good," Patchett said. "When do you wanna move out, sir?"

"Let's take five more minutes to catch our breath, then we'll go. Me and Hadley up front with McMillen's team, you bring up the rear with Boudreau's team. Women in the middle."

"Very well, sir. You got a good walking azimuth to the boats?"

"I pray the hell I do, Top."

Jock checked his wristwatch. It read 0200.

About five miles to go, he told himself, *and sixteen hours to do it in.*

The Japanese major stood ramrod straight in the middle of Buyang village as if he was impervious to death itself. Two of his soldiers were on the ground, shrieking like wounded animals, each with a leg blown off below the knee. Several more had been wounded by fragments from the same explosions.

A lieutenant scurried up with more bad news: "Major, we've found more booby traps. They're using our grenades...they pulled the pins and hid them below wooden boards. When a man steps on the board—"

"I know how grenades work," the major interrupted. "Search the entire village, Lieutenant. Clear it of booby traps. Bring any of those savages you find to me...*alive.*"

The major eyed a large hut across the village. *That will be perfect for my quarters this evening,* he thought as he walked briskly toward it, *while my men hunt down the Yankee gangsters.*

Passing between two large trees, he felt something momentarily snag his ankle.

All at once, there was a *snap*...a rustle of leaves...a sense of movement...a *swish*...

The blow to the chest that knocked him backward off his feet and carried him through the air...

And then dragged his impaled body forward, back to where it all started, like a pendulum drained of momentum.

He dangled from the thick chunk of log affixed to his chest by two wooden spikes run cleanly through his body.

Like dance partners, they twirled slowly on the rope suspending the log, the major's feet sweeping the ground but no longer supporting his weight.

In his last moment of life, it all came to make sense:

I snagged a trip wire. This spiked log swung down like a wrecking ball...

And killed me.

The Squad's rest period ended all too soon. Weary legs and aching backs shouldered gear once again as they set off into the black void, one behind the other like a human chain, blind beyond an arm's length. Their sense of isolation from everything outside this little universe was complete. The only thing keeping them tethered to the reality of their mission was fear.

They had only been walking a minute or two when a faint orange glow tinged the sky at their backs. Sergeant McMillen asked, "You think those booby traps of Oscar's are doing that?"

"I don't think so, Mike," Jock replied. "It looks more like the Japs decided to burn down the village...those miserable sons of bitches."

Chapter Twenty-Eight

Two hours of cross-country walking was taking its toll on *The Squad*. The ache of wounds to exhausted bodies grew steadily worse. Everyone had tripped and fallen more than once. The same fallen branch or tangled vine, invisible in the darkness, had often claimed multiple victims. Each tumble sapped a few more ounces of energy from men and women already running on empty. They were nearly out of water again. Patchett's quick inventory revealed they had, at best, one K ration meal per person left.

It was still two hours to sunrise. Jock and his people took comfort in one simple fact: *At least we haven't run into any Japs…not yet, anyway.*

He wasn't sure when he'd started limping. The seemingly minor leg wound he'd ignored for so many hours couldn't be ignored anymore. The leg had stiffened and grown tender, making him wince with every step. He could sense he wasn't the only one struggling to keep up with the snail's pace of their march.

The terrain remained fairly level—a small gift to faltering legs—but Jock knew a new physical challenge loomed ahead. "We can't be far from the ridge line," he told Patchett. "The gentlest downhill slope is along the trail, but going anywhere near there will probably mean running right into the Japs."

Patchett took a look at the map in the flashlight's dim glow. "No matter where we go down the ridge, it's gonna be pretty steep. Remember what it was like when we climbed up it? And that was the *best* spot."

When they climbed up it—five days that seemed an eternity ago.

"Yeah, I remember," Jock said. "We're not even going to try it in the dark. We're in no shape for that."

"So you wanna stop here until sunrise?"

"Yep."

"Amen to that, sir. We could sure use the rest."

The sunrise brought a few surprises. First, they found they had camped less than twenty feet from the precipice—a steep cliff dropping over a hundred feet straight down. Mike McMillen, who'd been the point man on their journey to this spot, would have been the first one to step unwittingly over the brink in the darkness.

"You're one lucky son of a bitch," Patchett told him. "If the major hadn't stopped us when he did, we'd be scraping you and Lord knows who else off the valley floor right now."

"Yeah, swell," McMillen replied, "but I still think he cut it too damn close."

"A miss is as good as a mile, son."

The second surprise was more troubling: a compass fix to Mount Dremsel's peak confirmed their journey in the darkness had been well off course.

"Dammit," Jock said, "we're way off to the north, half a mile, maybe more…and too damn close to the Lorengau trail."

"I don't get it, sir," McMillen said. "I stuck to that azimuth you gave me like glue. And you double-checked me a bunch of times. How could we be this far off?"

They all knew the probable answer, but it was Tom Hadley who voiced it: "It's got to be my fault. We really weren't at *Rally Point Charlie* last night. We must've been well north of it."

"Y'all knock off that crying now," Patchett said. "Ain't no one spilled no milk yet."

Just then, the growls of vehicle engines pierced the stillness of the early morning air. They could only be Japanese vehicles.

"Listen to that," Jock said. "We could hit the trail with a damn rock."

Patchett asked, "So what're we gonna do, sir?"

"We're going to walk south along the top of the ridge, until we come to the same place we climbed up on our way in. We'll make the descent there."

Patchett scanned the cloudless sky. "We need water bad, sir. Only place we're gonna get it is down on the valley floor. Ain't gonna be no rain for a spell, that's for damn sure."

"Of course we need water, Sergeant Major…but for all we know, there's a battalion or two of Japs a couple of hundred yards away. Let's bear with being thirsty for a little bit longer, until we put some distance between us and them, okay?"

"Yessir. Didn't mean to—"

"I know you didn't. Let's get moving, right fucking now."

"How about we put Bogater on point, sir," Patchett said.

"Sure. It's his turn, isn't it?"

As the sergeants quickly pulled the column together, Jock saw Jillian's shoulders being ministered to by Anne Marie once again. "Jill," he said, "we're going to have to descend the face of this ridge going hand over hand down a rope. Are your shoulders going to be able to handle that?"

"Anything you can do, I can do, Yank." She sounded as if she was trying to convince herself, too.

He shook his head. "No, never mind. We'll lower you down first. We've only got so much rope left, and it's got to get strung to the valley floor, anyway, so the rest of us can get down."

She was too tired to argue. "Whatever you say, Jock."

"But you'll be down there by yourself for a couple of minutes," he added. "Think you can handle that?"

She patted the Thompson lying beside her. "You know bloody well I can handle it."

"Anne Marie," he said, "how about you? Think you can handle a slide down the rope?"

"I was rope-climbing champion in my gymnasium, Major. It won't be a problem."

It didn't take long to reach the planned point of descent down the ridge. Bogater Boudreau, the point man, spotted the *Hansel and Gretel* markings Hadley had carved on a tree trunk five days ago, when they first passed this way. He peered over the edge of the near-vertical drop, checking for Japanese on the valley floor below. There was nothing to see down there but more trees and the twinkle of morning sunlight reflecting off a stream winding its way toward the Warra River. He could taste its cool, delicious water already.

A large loop was tied in the end of the rope for

Jillian to sit in while being lowered down the cliff's face. As she slid into the loop, Jock told her, "Remember, all you've got to do is hang on to the rope and use your feet to keep yourself facing the cliff. That way, you won't spin and keep slamming into it on the way down."

"Sounds easy enough," she said.

He slung the Thompson across her back, adding, "Keep this thing on safe while you're going down so it won't fire if the trigger snags a branch or something."

Patchett approached with a necklace of six empty canteens strung together with wire. "Might as well take these down with you, too, ma'am. They're light, and you can be filling 'em while you wait for the rest of us. He shook one of the canteens—it made a rattling sound. "This one's got the Halazone tablets you'll need in it."

Poised on the brink, Jillian said, "Lower away, lads."

Playing *tug of war* with gravity, the four men on the rope eased her to the valley floor, a trip that took almost three minutes. "Okay, she's clear," Jock said. "Youngblood, you're next."

First, the top end of the rope had to be secured to the sturdiest tree in reach. That took a few minutes. Meanwhile, Jillian walked the short distance to the stream, set the Thompson down on the bank, waded in up to her ankles, and began filling the canteens.

Once the rope was tied off, Joe Youngblood began an effortless descent, hands and feet churning smoothly and rapidly, keeping his body nearly perpendicular to the slope. He was on the valley floor in little over a minute. He looked up to see the next man, Bogater Boudreau, beginning his downhill run.

Youngblood turned and began to walk toward

Jillian, watching as *The Woman in White* filled the last canteen and then set it in line with the others. She began to drop the Halazone tablets into each canteen in turn.

She prepared the life-giving water as if performing a sacrament, he thought. She seemed happy, content—there was a definite glow about her. Maybe it was just the bright morning sun playing off the white fabric of her dress. But maybe it was something else—something *supernatural*. She had never seemed more like a *spirit—a worker of miracles*—to Joe Youngblood than at that moment. Very soon, he would drink that sweet, refreshing gift she had taken so lovingly from nature for him and the other GIs.

I can almost forgive her, he thought.

When he saw the first Japanese soldier rise from the underbrush, time seemed to freeze around him.

It felt like being in a dream paused by some god-like hand...

A landscape in suspended animation...

Yet he was still running.

Then there were many Japanese—diminutive warriors who seemed larger than life—not thirty yards away...

Now she saw them, too. Still on her knees, she looked to her Thompson, so near yet too far...

And then she looked to Joe Youngblood, splashing past her, toward the Japanese.

He gave her one last glance, his face resolute, without anger or fear...

A look that said, *Now I am a spirit, too.*

Then he turned away...

And met the bullet meant for her.

He lay gasping, floundering in the blood-tinged

water, as Jillian claimed her Thompson and spewed its hatred at the Japanese.

Bogater flung himself from the rope, falling the last ten feet as enemy bullets *pinged* around him.

He hit the ground hard. Oblivious to the pain, he rolled to a firing position and started shooting.

The curses he screamed at the Japanese nearly drowned out the staccato roar of his submachine gun.

The GIs still on the ridge let loose a torrent of plunging fire on an enemy still hidden to them by the trees.

Hadley tried to take the rope next but Jock pushed him out of the way and cut Bogater's time to the valley floor in half.

But by the time he got there, the Japanese were pulling back into the shelter of the woods, dragging their dead and wounded with them.

Jock raced to Jillian as she dragged Youngblood from the stream to safety behind a broad tree trunk. "He doesn't need to bloody drown, too," she said, her words and eyes ablaze with adrenaline.

Hadley had come down now. Anne Marie was right behind him. She rushed to Joe Youngblood as the others, still on the ridge, took the rope in rapid succession.

She worked quickly, silently—but once she had peeled his shirt away, her efforts came to a reluctant stop. The only thing she could do was cradle him in her arms, trying to lend some small comfort in his last moments on this earth.

There was nothing else anyone could do.

Jillian took Joe Youngblood's hand in hers and clasped it tightly.

He acknowledged her with a weak smile, a slight,

reverent nod…

And then he rolled his head toward Jock. In a voice barely a whisper, he said, "I told you so, sir."

Anne Marie gently released his lifeless body. Neither she, nor Jillian, nor Jock could find words to say or a voice with which to say them.

Patchett's voice filled that silence, dragging them back to cold reality: "Where the hell's Bogater?"

"I saw him cross the stream and go into the woods," McMillen said. "He was firing the whole way."

Patchett asked, "When was that, Mike?"

"Just when I came off the rope."

"Ahh, shit," Patchett said. "Why the hell would that crazy Cajun go and do a damn fool thing like that?"

"We've got to go get him, sir," McMillen pleaded.

"Damn right we do," Jillian added, slapping a fresh magazine into her Thompson.

"Let's do this," Hadley said. "I'll take two guys and—"

"No, we can't," Jock interrupted. "Knock it off, all of you. Nobody's chasing after him. We stay together and fight together…let's not make it easy for them to pick us off one by one. Now form up…we're moving south on the double. I need two men to carry Youngblood's body."

Confused and angry, McMillen said, "Why are we dragging him around and not helping out Bogater?"

Patchett's face registered pure displeasure. "Let me handle this one, sir," he said.

"Be my guest, Sergeant Major."

Patchett grabbed McMillen by a shoulder strap and roughly pulled him away from the others. The young sergeant didn't dare resist. Once they were far enough away not to be overheard, Patchett got right in McMillen's face.

"I don't never again want to hear one of my sergeants sound like some sniveling li'l sack o' shit like you just did, McMillen. I didn't say a damn thing when I heard you and Hadley left Deuce behind. I wasn't there, so I don't know what happened…figured y'all had your reasons…and I hope to hell they were real good ones."

"But, Sergeant Major, I—"

"Shut the fuck up. I ain't finished yet. Now I may not have seen what happened with Deuce but I sure as shit saw what happened here. We're gonna take care of that young man like decent human beings oughta."

"So you agree with the Major? We're gonna cut out and forget about Bogater…just so we can bury some Indian?"

Patchett's eyes took on a sadness McMillen had never seen.

"You got it wrong, Mike. Ain't nobody forgetting about Bogater, but the major's right. We can't go chasing after him like a bunch of dumbass rookies. We got ourselves enough dead heroes already."

"That just ain't right, Sergeant Major."

"Mike, the only thing *just ain't right* at the moment is Bogater leaving us down another man when we're already outgunned. Damn fool shoulda known better than to get all *Sergeant York* on us. Now you get yourself back over there and go help Ace carry that man's body."

Chapter Twenty-Nine

Somewhere to the north, not so far away, a war was going on in which they had no part. They could hear it clearly: intermittent doses of Arisaka rifles firing in what seemed a musical *call and response* to the rhythmic chatter of a Nambu machine gun. These outbursts had erupted with languid frequency for the past two hours—the time it took to move south to the headwaters of the Warra River, find the rubber boats unscathed in their well-concealed nest, and bury Joe Youngblood.

"Who the hell's fighting who?" Tom Hadley asked. "I don't hear anything that sounds like a GI weapon or even an Aussie one."

Patchett replied, "Whoever it is, let them kill each other all they want. Better we just lay low here and keep praying we get left alone." He checked his watch—it was just after 1200 hours. "All we gotta do is hold out until dark and then take ourselves a little boat ride."

"That's pie in the sky talk, Sergeant Major," McMillen said. "If you think we're just going to sit here all day and not get hit, you're dreaming."

"I didn't say we wasn't gonna get hit, son. I said we gotta *hold out*."

The forest had been mercifully quiet for nearly an hour, long enough to sow the seeds of false security in every member of *The Squad*.

That's why the two explosions—just seconds apart—made them all practically jump out of their skin.

A few moments later, they could see a column of thick black smoke rising skyward some distance to the north.

"I reckon that smoke's coming from the Lorengau trail," Patchett said. "That'd put it about two miles away."

"Looks right to me," Jock replied. "Funny, though…that sounded like something just got bombed. You'd think there'd be airplanes flying around…"

But when the echoes died, there was nothing but the silence of the forest once again.

Another hour passed before blessed rain began to fall. Jillian had sensed it coming—she and Anne Marie were awaiting it with ground sheets strung to act as water collectors. Beneath those sheets, empty canteens were lined up. The deluge filled them all quickly.

As Jillian passed the canteens out to the men along the perimeter, she got an idea. "Jock," she said, "you don't really *need* me and Anne Marie in the trenches. Your lads have the lookout duty covered…"

"What are you getting at, Jill?"

"Why don't I go and catch us some dinner? There's a river right there…and I do know a little about the fishing business, don't I?"

He had to admit someone who owned and captained a fleet of fishing boats back in Australia probably knew a fair bit about catching fish. "Of course you do," he replied.

"So what do you say, Yank? Shall I fetch us all a proper supper? Considering we're down to our last crackers and all."

"Actually, Jill, that's sounds pretty damn wonderful. Take the Thompson with you, though."

"Of course I'm going to take the bloody Thompson, silly boy. Oh, and I'll need to borrow your bayonet, too."

Jillian swept her latest catch from the river, a huge catfish impaled on the spear she'd whittled from a fallen branch. Anne Marie sat nearby on the bank collecting the steadily growing catch, using Jock's bayonet to sharpen more branches into spears. She was keeping a sharp lookout for crocs and water snakes, too.

Stopping a moment to rub her aching shoulders, Jillian gazed across the river. She was startled as a tree's branch snapped off suddenly, as if cleaved by some invisible scythe.

Before she could blink, she heard the rifle shot...

And realized it was a bullet, faster than the sound of its own, distant firing, that had just pruned that branch.

Before she could take another breath, what sounded like a thousand guns began to sing their terrifying chorus.

"GET DOWN," she screamed to Anne Marie, who was bewildered and still sitting upright despite the bullets zipping past her.

She heeded the warning and threw herself to the ground. Jillian crawled to her, took the .45 pistol from the pocket of Anne Marie's dress and placed it in the nurse's hands.

"Remember what I showed you," Jillian said, "hold it tight with both hands or it'll kick back and hit you in the face. Just stay here behind this log and lay low. Shoot any Jap that comes near you." She began to crawl away toward Jock and his men but stopped to offer one last instruction: "But for pity sake, Anne Marie, don't shoot Ace."

By the time she'd crawled to Jock, the fight had ebbed to random shots, each sounding like it was trying to get in the last word in a lethal argument.

"They're pulling back," Jock told her.

"How many were there?"

"Sounded like a hundred...probably just a handful." She asked, "Anybody hit?"

"I don't think so."

Patchett scampered down the line, shouting, "If you got a grenade left, throw the fucking thing right now as far as you can. Then everybody stay the hell down. It ain't over yet. This is when they lob mortars at you, while they're breaking off contact."

Jock said, "Jill, get in that hole over there and keep your head down."

"Where are you going to be?"

"Right on top of you."

A few seconds later, the first mortar round crashed in, just yards in front of *The Squad's* position.

Patchett mumbled, "I hate being so goddamn right all the time."

Another round landed, this time behind them.

"It's gotta be only one mortar," Patchett said. "Not much volume of fire."

Then the third round came...and a man began to scream to his mother, to God, to anyone he prayed might save him.

A long burst from a Nambu machine gun sent all

their faces back into the dirt…

Until they realized the strangest thing:

Not one of its bullets had flown through their position.

But the GI was still screaming.

It was Mike McMillen. He'd been closest to the impact of the last mortar round.

Its blast had sheared off his right leg just above the knee.

The severed limb lay mangled and bloody a few feet away…

Right where McMillen could see it.

Patchett pulled off his belt and used it to fashion a tourniquet around McMillen's thigh. "We need Miss Smits, right fucking now," he said, shouting over the wounded man's howls as he slid a hefty stick beneath the belt to lever it tight.

"I'll get her," Jillian replied, and hurried away.

McMillen had stopped begging, but his rant continued, taking a new tack. "I hope you're fucking happy now," he said, looking straight at Jock.

"*At ease*, son," Patchett said, and then turned to Jock. "Let me help him, sir, while you go check on the rest of the men, okay?"

Jock nodded. He'd listened to gravely wounded men ramble in their delirium many times before, blurting out things they'd regret later if they even remembered saying them at all. He didn't need that distraction right now.

With Jock gone, Patchett continued, "No call for talk like that, Mike. Besides, you're gonna be just fine."

"JUST FINE? How the fuck can I be *just fine*, Sergeant Major? My fucking leg!"

"It's just the fear talking, Mike. We're gonna take real good care of you. It could be worse, you know."

"HOW THE FUCK COULD IT BE WORSE?"

"They could've got your pecker, son."

"Oh, yeah? Who gives a shit about my goddamn pecker? The only pecker that matters around here is *the major's*. And what does he give a shit? He's got his girlfriend back now. He don't care he got us all fucked up doing it...two guys dead, probably three, and I'm going to be dead any fucking second, too. All this bullshit, just so he can get his *cooch* back."

Patchett pulled the tourniquet tighter and said, "That's about enough out of you, Sergeant. You're wrong as wrong can be about that man. But we're gonna cut you a little slack right now, seeing as how you're hurt and all...but if I was you, I'd choose my words *real careful* for a while."

"It's too tight, Sergeant Major! Loosen it up, please! It's hurting like hell."

"It's gotta be tight, son. And it's gonna hurt a lot worse before it gets better."

Jillian returned with Anne Marie, who took one look at McMillen and said, "He needs morphia."

Patchett asked, "Do you have any?"

She knelt down and opened her medical kit. "Of course I do, Sergeant Major. When I steal, I steal *everything*."

She pulled the syringe from her bag—and more: Jock's bayonet and a box of matches.

"We need to start a small fire," she said.

Patchett nodded. He understood fully. "You're gonna heat up that knife and cauterize, I reckon?"

She smiled as she replied, "Ahh, you've had

training."

"Somebody's coming," Hadley said as he and Jock huddled behind a felled tree on the perimeter. They raised their Thompsons...

Held their breath...

And watched as Bogater Boudreau came into view.

He was toting a Nambu machine gun and a rucksack full of ammunition for it.

"Holy shit," Jock said. "That Nambu doing all that shooting...that was you?"

"Yessir," Bogater replied. "Picked it up off a dead Jap a while back when I ran out of Thompson ammo. Fires a whole lot faster than one of them bolt-action Arisaka pieces of shit. Real handy when you're on your own, believe you me."

Jock couldn't contain his amazement. "So you've been in a running gun battle with the Japs ever since we came off the ridge?"

"Pretty much, sir."

"How many Japs are out there?"

"Now? Not a one, sir. Looked to be about a platoon's worth, though, at the beginning."

"And you killed them all?"

"Not all, sir. You guys got a couple of them here and there, I reckon. Did you hear them trucks go up a while back?"

"Those explosions? That was your doing, too, Bogater?"

"Yessir. Damn fools oughta know better than to leave their vehicles unattended. A grenade in the gas tanks did the trick. They even left me some rope to pull the pins with, so I could be far away when they blew. I just did one little thing wrong, sir..."

"You did? What?"

"The Thompson," Bogater said. "I lost it. Went looking for it but can't find it no more. I know that's a court-martial offense and all."

He was startled when Jock and Hadley burst out in incredulous laughter.

"I wouldn't worry about it, Sergeant Boudreau," Jock said. "If we live long enough to write an After Action Report, it'll be in the *Destroyed In Contact With The Enemy* column. Now come with me. There's a whole bunch of guys who can't wait to see you again."

McMillen was their first stop. When he saw Bogater, he said through his morphine haze, "Son of a bitch. Someone's raising the dead around here."

Jock filled Patchett in on Boudreau's exploits. When he was finished, Patchett turned to the blond Cajun and said, "Damn fine job, Bogater. But don't you fucking never go running off by yourself again, you hear?"

The fire Anne Marie kindled was now put to a different use: cooking the fish Jillian caught. Even though Patchett was stuffing pieces of catfish into his mouth, it didn't stop him from grousing, "Them Japs gonna smell this little fish fry ten miles away."

"They ain't gonna smell shit," Bogater replied, "because there ain't no Japs anywhere near here."

Patchett cut him a nasty look and said, "That ain't

knowledge, son...that's faith. You better keep your damn eyes peeled."

Ace was huddled nearby with the walkie-talkie. He slid the headphones off his ears and said, "If there are any Japs around here—besides me, of course—they sure as hell don't have a working radio. Lorengau's going crazy trying to raise someone...*anyone*."

Jock's wristwatch confirmed what the low sun was already telling them: it was time to get the two rubber boats ready. Once night fell, they'd have three hours to row up the Warra and out into the Bismarck Sea. If all went as planned, the submarine would meet them two miles offshore.

"It's going to be a hard row once we're in the open sea, Jock," Jillian said. "The wind and current will try to push us northwest, back toward Manus. It'd be so much better if we had proper boats, instead of these two oversized life preservers."

"Believe me, Jill, if I had *proper boats*, I'd use them."

"We'd better pray some croc doesn't take a fancy to them while we're on the river. One bite and—"

"Now see here, Miss," he said, mimicking her Aussie accent, "I'm told by the US Navy that crocodiles don't eat rubber."

"It's not the rubber they want, you wanker. It's the flesh inside. Tell that to your bloody Navy. And by the way, sweetheart, you bloody illiterate Yanks shouldn't be mocking the way others talk."

Bogater asked, "How come we gotta row two miles to get picked up when they dropped us off a mile offshore?"

"Full moon tonight," Jock replied. "The silhouette

of a sub only a mile out will probably be seen plain as day from shore."

Even doped up on morphine, McMillen was growing more unsettled. When Anne Marie knelt by his improvised stretcher to check on him, he begged, "It hurts so bad. I need some more morphine."

She didn't need to check the time of the last dose written on his forehead in grease pencil—she'd made that mark herself. "It's not time yet, Sergeant. Not even close."

"You know, it's your fault it hurts so fucking bad," he slurred. "The way you burned me with that knife…"

"I had to do that, or you would have bled to death. I wasn't equipped to do anything else."

"Still," he said, "I hope you're fucking happy."

"Fucking happy? That I saved your fucking life? You can be sure I'm fucking happy about that, Sergeant McMillen. Now if you'll excuse me, I've got to check on the others."

McMillen watched the boats being prepared. He listened as Jock and Patchett worked out the passenger list for each boat.

He never heard his name mentioned.

"Major Miles," he called out, "you're not going to leave me here, are you?"

Before Jock could answer, McMillen began to cry. Words tumbled from his mouth: "I'm sorry, sir…I'm so sorry. I didn't mean all that shit I said about you and Miss Forbes. Don't leave me here. Oh God please don't leave me!"

Patchett gave Jock that look that said, *You want me to handle this, sir?*

Jock waved him off. *No, Top…I've got this one.*

He knelt next to McMillen, put a comforting hand on his shoulder, and said, "Mike, nobody's leaving you behind. You're the *given*—you're going to be in the second boat. It's everyone else we've got to figure out a place for."

"Don't bullshit a bullshitter, sir. You're gonna dump me in the ocean once we get out there."

Jock smiled and shook his head. "That doesn't make any sense, Mike. Why would we go through all that trouble just to get rid of you?"

The stricken look slowly vanished from McMillen's face. Even in his doped-up state, Jock's attempt at humor did have a certain logic about it that couldn't be denied.

Chapter Thirty

They'd been on the river for almost an hour, two rubber boats groping their way toward the sea by the stark light of the full moon. In the lead boat, Botkin played with the direction-finding loop on the walkie-talkie, searching for a signal from the submarine tasked with picking them up. Jock asked him, "You got anything yet?"

"Nothing yet, sir."

"It's still early," Jock said. "They're not expecting us for at least an hour." He'd tried to sound optimistic, but the words still came out as more of a hope than a certainty.

Hadley and Ace were on the oars. Ace had grown strangely quiet since the last fight with the Japs at the riverhead. Hadley asked, "Something on your mind, Ace?"

"It's nothing, First Sergeant."

"Oh, come on. That look on your puss...something's eating at you. It helps to talk about it, you know."

Ace turned his head away, not saying a word.

Hadley asked, "You worried about the major hearing us? Just talk quiet. Keep it between you and me. He's real busy...he won't hear."

There was no reply.

"You upset about losing Deuce? You were good buddies and all."

"No...that's not it. We both knew the risks when we volunteered for this mission."

Hadley waited for him to say more but nothing was

offered.

"Well, if that's not it, Ace, then what is it?"

Hadley thought the Nisei would slip into silence once again, but after a few moments, the words slowly began to come.

"It just seems kind of strange, First Sergeant. That last fight we were in—I emptied four magazines but never had a clue who I was shooting at. Never saw the first Japanese soldier…"

"Yeah," Hadley said, "that's the way it is most of the time."

"But not always," Ace replied. "Those two Koreans I killed…I saw them. I saw them plain as day…and I never asked them what they were doing. I was the only one who could speak to them but I didn't even bother. I just gunned them down. They didn't want to be in this war any more than we do. Maybe they were just trying to help us out—switch sides, fight the Japs and all—but I never even thought about asking."

"Wait a minute," Hadley cut in. "Any prisoner stupid enough to go for a weapon deserves what he gets. You did the right thing, Ace."

"Yeah, that's what the sergeant major said, too. But I'll never know that for sure, will I?"

"I think you need to put those thoughts right out of your head. Like you said, you knew the risks—this isn't some *Boy Scout* hike we've been on. It's a damn war."

There were a few moments of silence before Ace asked, "Don't they court martial GIs who shoot POWs? That's murder, isn't it?"

"I don't know what kind of legal-eagle bullshit they fed you back at HQ, but out here, anybody going for a gun isn't a prisoner. He's a combatant. You did the right thing, dammit. Put a lid on this crap."

In the distance, the shadowy outlines of mangroves overhanging the river's banks were yielding to a wide, dark emptiness that could only be the Bismarck Sea. A few more minutes of rowing and the boats would be clear of the river's mouth. "We're right on schedule," Jock said.

Botkin stood on wobbly, landlubber legs in the stern of the lead boat, holding the walkie-talkie high over his head, trying to stretch for every inch of antenna height while searching for the submarine's signal. Jock didn't have to ask—he could tell his radioman hadn't found that signal yet.

Jillian stood in the bow with Jock's compass. "If we don't have a radio bearing," she said, "which way should we steer?"

"South-southeast," Jock replied. "That should be about right."

"You don't sound very sure of that," she said.

"It's as sure as I can be, Jill. If we don't—"

He was cut off by her upraised hand, an emphatic, wordless command to *shut up!*

She'd heard it first—a different sound on the air...

Different from the *swish* of the oars slicing the water's surface...

Different from the *hiss* of the sea breeze through the mangroves...

The noisy *chug* of a boat's motor.

"Do you hear that?" she asked.

"I do now. That sure as hell isn't any submarine."

He told Hadley and Ace to row into the shelter of the mangroves. Waving his red flashlight, he signaled the second boat to do the same.

"Keep a lookout for the bloody crocs," Jillian said. "They'll be right at home around here."

The boats nestled together among the stilt roots of the mangrove not a moment too soon. The roots hid them from the searchlight's beam sweeping the river mouth.

Jillian crawled onto the raised roots, spying the intruder through binoculars. "Bloody hell," she said, "it's a patrol boat. I count five, maybe six Japs on deck."

Jock crawled alongside her. She handed him the binoculars.

"Holy shit," he said, "it looks like it's got at least two mounted machine guns."

"It's just an old workboat, Jock. No more than a fifty-footer. See that boom on the aft deck? Probably used to be a shellfish boat that the Nips impressed into service."

"Old workboat or not, Jill, it's armed to the teeth. Can that thing come into the river?"

"I doubt it. Takes too much water."

Jillian was right—the patrol boat circled off the river mouth, showing no intention of coming upstream.

But it showed no intention of leaving, either.

Patchett had clambered from the second boat to join them. Once he got a good look at the patrol boat, he said, "What do you wanna do, sir?"

Jock replied, "We're going to give her ten minutes to clear out."

"And if she don't?"

"I'm still working on that one, Top. Got any ideas?"

"Nothing that don't get us all sunk," Patchett said.

The ten minutes passed. The patrol boat was still circling the river mouth.

And there was still no radio signal from the submarine.

"Time's a-wasting, sir," Patchett said.

"No kidding," Jock replied. "Jill...that boat's wooden, right?"

"Yes...most every working boat in this part of the world is."

"Where would the fuel tank be?"

"In the stern, near the engine."

"Can you tell if it's a diesel or not?"

"It doesn't sound like a diesel, Jock. I'm pretty sure it burns petrol."

"So it'll burn easily?"

"Of course. Much easier than diesel will."

"Top, we still have those tracer rounds for the M1s?"

"Yessir, one box. Haven't fired a round out of it yet. What you got in mind?"

"Here's the plan," Jock said. "They haven't turned that damn searchlight on for a while...and I'm guessing they won't unless they get spooked. It ruins their night vision just like it ruins ours. And with this moon tonight, who the hell needs it?"

Every member of *The Squad*—their faces washed in its pale blue glow—nodded in agreement.

"So this is what we'll do," Jock continued. "Bogater and I will take the lead boat with the Nambu and an M1.

We'll get as close as we can…and then set that Jap boat on fire with tracers to the gas tank. The rest of you lay low right here in the second boat."

Patchett said, "You sure that's enough firepower, sir?"

"With the Nambu, yeah…that's enough *accurate* firepower. It'll keep their heads down while the tracers light the candle."

Patchett had another concern: "How close you think you're gonna get to that boat with that moon and all?"

"If we stick close to the mangroves, we can cut the distance in half and still have a pretty good chance of not being seen. Okay…everyone but me and Bogater out of this first boat."

Jillian didn't budge.

"That means you, too, Jill."

"I'm not going bloody anywhere, Jock. You need me. I'm a better shot than any of you Yanks. And you've got another M1 for me, right?"

There was another M1—the one Joe Youngblood used to carry.

"Dammit, Jill, I said *no*. The last time you went on a little *nautical adventure*, you ended up a POW."

"That's true…and I'd do it again if it meant keeping you alive."

"Jill…Jillian…nobody's doubting your courage…or your shooting ability. But—"

She continued her argument, stepping on his words as if he wasn't even speaking.

"Besides," she said, "none of you can handle a boat better than I can."

She left him no room to counter. There was no denying anything she'd said.

And there was no time for debate, either.

"All right," Jock said. "Hand her the other M1."

Bogater picked up one oar while Jillian grabbed the other.

"No," Jock said. "Your shoulders aren't up to rowing, Jill. Give me that oar."

She waved him off. "Never you mind, Yank. Just get on that bloody machine gun."

"All right, fine," Jock said. "Let's go."

As they pulled away from the other boat, Patchett said, "Sir, all the croc wranglers are in your boat. What do we do if one comes and pays us a *little visit*? If we shoot it, that'll give us all away."

Jillian handled the reply. "Just sharpen up some of those long sticks laying around the mangrove. If a croc comes at you, stab the bloody bastard in the eye before it rips that silly boat to shreds."

Bogater told her, "Couldn't've said that better myself, ma'am."

Another minute of paddling and they'd be free of the river mouth, out in open water, away from the shield of the mangrove. The patrol boat presented a perfect profile as it coasted slowly. They could still see the Japanese on deck—all five of them— plus one man, presumably their leader, who looked to be shouting orders from the helm in the tiny wheelhouse.

Jillian had an idea. "Jock," she whispered, "suppose we just shoot those blokes and seize the bloody boat? There's only a handful of them."

"What if there are more below deck, Jill? Even one

guy with a weapon down there would make boarding pretty risky…and I'm not going to risk anyone's life worse than I already am for a boat I don't need."

"Fine, then," she replied. "We'll blow the bloody thing up. Bogater, see where that boom attaches to the deck?"

"Yes, ma'am."

"The petrol tank should be just below and slightly aft. If nothing flares up after the first few rounds, we'll move our shots forward up the hull. We've only got twenty tracers between us, so we've got to make every one count."

"Got it," Boudreau replied. "What do you make the range at, ma'am?"

"Two hundred yards…maybe a little less. What do you think, Jock?"

"Two hundred sounds just about right to me, Jill. When I start sweeping the deck clean with the Nambu, you two do your stuff. Just remember—tracers work both ways. If they can see them coming, they'll know exactly where we are."

"Amen to that, sir," Boudreau said.

"Bogater, you're starting to sound just like Sergeant Major Patchett."

"I reckon I could sound a lot worse, sir."

Jock held the gunner on the bow in his sights, adjusting for the rise and fall of the rubber boat on the modest swells. *This thing better shoot as flat a trajectory as everyone says it does,* he told himself, *because if I miss high or wide, I won't know where those rounds went.*

Jillian lay snug against him on his left, Bogater the same to his right. Both had their M1s trained on the patrol boat's stern.

Here goes nothing, Jock told himself...

And squeezed the Nambu's trigger.

He expected the roar of the machine gun to wake the dead...

But he hadn't expected to be blinded by the vivid muzzle flash.

I can't see if I'm hitting anything or not!

"YOU'RE LOW, JOCK," Jillian yelled. "YOU'RE HITTING THE WATER."

And then the Nambu fell silent.

Shit! Jammed!

Jillian and Bogater had pumped five rounds each into the stern...

But there was no onboard fire yet.

The patrol boat began to turn hard toward them.

Jock ripped the magazine from the Nambu. When he did, the round that had jammed fell into the sloshing water at the bottom of the rubber boat. It danced about like a mischievous child caught red-handed yet protesting its innocence. He gave up trying to grab it and reached for a new magazine.

As he did, he caught sight of the strangest thing: two men on the patrol boat's deck were on fire, dancing in crazy pirouettes as flames consumed their torsos.

Jillian fired again, the tracer a white-hot pinpoint of light streaking to hit a third man on the deck. He, too, began to burn.

"I got no shot at the stern," Bogater said.

"Then don't waste your tracers," Jock replied. "Help me reload this damn Nambu. I can't get it right."

"I had trouble the first time, too, sir," Bogater said as he deftly slipped the magazine into place. "Gotta get that front edge hooked in before the back'll lock down."

The patrol boat was headed straight for them. The machine gun on its bow began to fire simultaneously with Jock's Nambu.

The next seconds were a festival of hideous mayhem as the two automatic weapons fought a watery duel to the death.

Jillian and Bogater buried their heads at the bottom of the boat, clutching the dubious protection of rubber tubes filled with air.

They could sense the bullets flying close above them like angry winged insects, even hearing their quiet *pffit* in those infinitesimal moments of silence between the Nambu's shots.

The rounds from the patrol boat that went short showered them with little geysers of seawater.

Then the Nambu stopped firing again. It wasn't another jam—this time the magazine was empty.

But the machine gun on the patrol boat had stopped firing, too. The only sound was the indifferent putter of the patrol boat's engine as the vessel barreled toward them.

There wasn't a soul visible on the deck. Even the burning men were gone.

Probably threw themselves into the water, Jock thought. *Some choice...bleed to death, burn to death, or both.*

"I believe we got 'em all," Bogater said, more surprise than certainty in his voice.

"Let's board her," Jillian said. "Start paddling— she's going to pass very close."

Bogater jumped on her bandwagon, adding, "Yeah, why not? We got two Thompsons. They're perfect for a close fight if need be."

"Not so fast," Jock said. He pointed to the stern of the rubber boat. It was already awash—what had once been the buoyant aft tube was now ragged and airless, punctured in any number of places.

But the front half of their boat was still afloat, at least for the time being.

Jillian was adamant. "We can still make it, Jock."

She had a point. The patrol boat's track would bring her to within about ten yards of where they lay in the water. It wouldn't take much paddling to drag their foundering craft into a position to intercept.

Seizing the patrol boat was suddenly a very tempting option.

"Okay," Jock said, "let's do it. Jill, grab a Thompson and cover that boat. Bogater, you and me on the oars."

Thirty seconds of furious rowing and the rubber boat had barely moved. "It's like we got an anchor holding us back," Bogater said.

There was a rope dangling over the side of the patrol boat's low afterdeck. Jillian was ready to snag it...provided it was in arm's reach.

"Come on, you wankers," Jillian said, "get me just a little closer."

Jock gritted his teeth. Every stroke of the oar— every twist of his kneeling body—caused jolts of pain from his wounded leg. His strength flagging, the oar began to thrash uselessly at the water's surface.

But on his side, Bogater was pumping his oar with what seemed superhuman strength—so much that their sluggish craft began to pivot, swinging Jillian away from the approaching patrol boat.

"STRAIGHTEN OUT, YOU KNOBS," she yelled, not realizing that was now physically impossible for Jock.

It was a losing game. As the patrol boat grew near—thirty yards, twenty-five yards—that rope hanging from the afterdeck was still out of reach...and it was going to stay that way.

Before disappointment had a chance to wash over her, she saw the flames—just a flicker at first—playing along the afterdeck.

The flicker became a blaze in mere seconds.

"GET UNDER," she screamed to Jock and Bogater—but their swamping boat had seen to that already. Only their heads bobbed above the surface.

"SHE'S GOING TO BLOW," Jillian said, and then dove underwater.

From the safety of the mangrove, Patchett and company watched as the patrol boat dissolved in a fireball, spitting flying matchsticks in all directions. The explosion seemed to consume everything—and everyone—in the water around it.

Chapter Thirty-One

The second rubber boat threaded carefully through a sea full of charred, broken wood—the burned-out remnants of the Jap patrol boat. Torn, jagged planks of her hull would loom suddenly out of the darkness like floating spears, threatening to puncture the soft, fragile craft. As he batted more dangerous flotsam out of their way, Patchett mumbled, "Some fucking rescue we got going on here. We're gonna get our asses sunk just like the major and them if we don't watch our step real careful-like."

He'd called out several times to the lost trio but gotten no answer. McMillen, in his morphine stupor, was convinced he knew why: "They're all fucking dead. Got the shit blown out of them. Ain't that just a fucking perfect ending?"

"Shut the hell up a minute," Hadley said, straining to hear. "Way over there…I think that's Bogater's voice yelling."

A few minutes later, as the rubber boat came alongside, Bogater Boudreau said, "Good thing y'all heard me. I'm running out of steam here."

He'd nearly exhausted himself being guardian angel to Jock and Jillian. Both of them were barely able to hang on to the floating plank that was their makeshift life preserver. Jock's wounded leg had become nothing more than a useless appendage, searing with pain. The chronic ache in Jillian's shoulders had snowballed to debilitating discomfort. For them, swimming—even treading water—was out of the question. Only Bogater's steadfast grip kept them from slipping under.

As Patchett and Ace lifted Jock into the boat, he managed a weak smile and said, "At least we didn't get ourselves cooked."

"Amen to that, sir," Patchett replied, "but we got ourselves another little problem."

"Let me guess...nothing from the sub?"

"Not a damn thing, sir."

Jock looked to Botkin and asked, "Are we sure that radio's even working?"

"Positive, sir. I can still pick up Lorengau."

"Good," Jock replied. "We'll need that bearing to find the rendezvous point."

Patchett asked, "You still wanna look for that sub, sir?"

"Well, we're not going back to Manus, that's for damn sure. Let me see your map, Top. Mine sunk with my helmet."

He studied the map for a few moments, and then, teeth gritted with pain, dragged himself over and around the others to the stern of the boat, where Jillian was sitting. "Jill," he said, "I need some sailor's advice. Are you up to giving me a hand here for a minute?"

She couldn't quite mask the pain in her voice as she replied, "Of course I am. Just don't ask me to lift any bloody barbells right now."

He laid the map before her and said, "Tell me about the wind and current again."

When her explanation was done, he said, "Okay, that's what I needed to know."

Then he addressed everyone on board. "Here's the plan. We're going to continue rowing this boat as near as we can reckon to the rendezvous point with the sub, with or without its radio signal. And if the sub doesn't show by sunrise, we're going to turn west and row with the current to one of the small, uninhabited islands a couple of miles off Manus. They're just a few miles from here. We'll see them clearly in the daylight. Unfortunately, if any more patrol boats show up, they'll see us clearly, too, so we'll have to be quick about it. Once we're there, we'll figure out our next move. Any questions?"

"Just one, sir," Hadley said as he grabbed for an oar. "What compass heading do you want us to row?"

In a few minutes they were making good headway through the open sea, finally clear of the debris field left by the shattered patrol boat. Patchett finished taking stock of their equipment. He told Jock, "Well, sir, we got no food, only about a sip of water per person, morphine's running low, ammo's getting tight, the Nambu's gone, and the rest of our weapons will be jammed up tight as padlocks if we don't get 'em clean and dry real soon."

Jock tried a little gallows humor: "But aside from that, Top…"

Patchett was in no joking mood. "Aside from that, sir, we got a C.O. who I reckon can't walk, a lady who can't lift her arms over her head no more, and a man without a leg who ain't long for this world if we don't get picked up right quick."

"Well, on the bright side, Top, I won't have to worry about walking as long as we're all crammed onto this damn little boat."

"Walking ain't the half of it, sir. I can smell the gangrene coming on you."

They never thought they'd be praying for rain, not after all the drenchings they'd endured in the jungles and rainforests of Manus. When they saw the flashes of lightning illuminating distant storm clouds from within, like Chinese lanterns, it seemed their prayers were about to be answered. Even when the storm grew closer, the lightning now splashing down on the sea's surface, the air thick with the stink of ozone and the danger of electrocution very real, they still wanted it to come. Ready for the deluge, they sat in their little rubber boat with helmets upturned and waiting to be filled. They were *that* thirsty.

But the thunderstorm swept wide of them without delivering a drop—all fury, no salvation...

And it was hours past the scheduled rendezvous with the submarine. Botkin had kept up his unfailing vigil on the radio, but there was still no signal.

"This battery's going to be dead pretty soon, sir," Botkin said. "After that, I've only got one more...if all this water hasn't ruined it already."

"We got a couple hours to sunrise, sir," Patchett added, his voice low, trying to keep the conversation as private as possible in this boat crowded shoulder to shoulder. "Wanna start rowing toward them islands now? You know, get us a head start on this *Robinson Crusoe* shit. We'll get out of that baking sun quicker. I mean, parched as we are..."

"No, Top," Jock replied. "We're going to wait."

"All due respect, sir, may I ask *why*?"

"Because things may look a whole lot different in daylight, Sergeant Major...for us, and any swabbies that just might be looking for us."

There was a long, tense pause before Patchett replied, "As you wish, sir...as you wish. But if that's the way you want it, we might as well just leave one man on watch and let everyone else get some shuteye for now, if they can."

"Good idea. I've got first watch."

"But sir, don't you need a little—"

"I need a lot of things right now, Top, but sleep isn't one of them. And don't worry about my leg. All I've got to do is sit here."

Jock could tell there was something else on Patchett's mind, though. Usually, you never had to tell an old soldier twice to take a nap. But the sergeant major lingered, staring into the night as he searched for the right words to say.

"You know, sir, this wouldn't be the first time the brass decided to just *forget* about a li'l ol' unit like ours...like getting them back wasn't hardly worth the trouble."

"I'm not buying that, Top. Not for a minute. We've been walking around in enemy territory for six days. They're going to want to know what we saw."

"I sure do hope you're right, sir. I surely do."

Not everyone fell asleep. Mike McMillen drifted in and out of the morphine's grip, mumbling what sounded like curses on President Roosevelt, the United States Army, and every *swinging dick* in it.

Jillian wasn't sleeping, either. She snuggled up to Jock and said, "I suppose I'm not a target of Sergeant

McMillen's wrath at the moment, seeing as I don't possess a *swinging dick*." She slipped her hand into his. "I'd put my arms around you if I could, you know. You'll have to settle for this."

They sat quietly, just holding hands for a few minutes, until—her voice very soft—she asked, "Could Patchett be right? Could they really just write off you lot?"

"I hope to hell not, Jill."

She put her head on his shoulder. "Whatever happens, we'll get through this, Jock. One bloody way or the other. I know we will."

Chapter Thirty-Two

The last time they could actually see Manus from offshore, it was through the narrow and water-sloshed point of view of a submarine's periscope. The island seemed such a tiny place then: drab, unimposing, unthreatening. Now, as the rising sun lifted the blindfold of night from their eyes, the view from the rubber boat was unsettling. The island soared from the sea like an evil god ready to suck them back to a primal hell that was all too familiar. And it seemed closer than any of the GIs had envisioned.

"All that rowing," Patchett said, "and damn if it don't look like we ain't gone nowhere."

"It's just our perspective," Jillian said, trying to be reassuring. "We're really about three miles offshore."

"It still feels too damn close," Patchett replied.

Jock looked west, to the cluster of small offshore islands they'd soon be rowing toward. Though they were the same distance from their rubber boat as Manus— some three miles—they seemed tiny and incredibly far away. Nothing about them suggested safe haven. Even rowing with the prevailing wind and current, it seemed unlikely they'd reach them anytime soon.

"Let's get one more three-sixty scan with the binos," Jock said. "If we don't see anything, we start rowing west."

He left the scanning to Patchett and Hadley. He'd lost his binoculars last night in the battle with the Jap patrol boat, along with everything else but his waterlogged Thompson. The two top sergeants were better suited for the task anyway. Lookout duty was best left to tall men who could actually stand, that extra height pushing the horizon out nearly five miles.

It got deathly quiet as Patchett and Hadley, standing back to back, scanned in a slow, synchronous pivot that would have seemed comically choreographed if the stakes weren't so high. The silence was shattered when Private Allred shouted, "HEY, SHE'S GOT WATER. A WHOLE FUCKING BOTTLE OF IT."

He was standing, mouth agape, pointing at Anne Marie. His entire body seemed cast in an accusatory gesture. "AIN'T THIS SOME BULLSHIT," Allred continued, "WHILE THE REST OF US GOT JACKSHIT, SHE'S GOT—"

"That's enough, Private," Jock said.

"Yeah," Patchett added, pushing the silent but still open-mouthed Allred back down in his seat. "Just shut the fuck up, son."

Private Allred was right, though. Anne Marie was cradling Mike McMillen's head in her arm, raising it so he could drink from a glass bottle she had taken from her medical kit.

Jock asked, "What the hell's going on, Anne Marie?"

"This man needs water more than anyone else here," she replied.

"Where'd that water come from?"

"From the rain, Major, just like all the rest. I filled the empty bottles I had when we filled the canteens."

Jock turned to Jillian, giving her an accusing look everyone understood: *You were filling the canteens, too. Did you know what she was doing?*

"Don't blame Jillian," Anne Marie said. "She knew nothing about it."

Jock asked, "Why didn't you tell us you had that water, Anne Marie?"

"I'm a nurse. I'm supposed to be prepared for medical emergencies, and with all the blood he's lost, Sergeant McMillen certainly qualifies as an emergency. A *dire* emergency, Major."

"Ahh, bullshit," Patchett said. "We're all dying of thirst here…and you're hoarding, lady."

"Not hoarding, Sergeant Major. Conserving. And the rest of us are *not* dying of thirst. Not yet. And before you ask, rest assured that I have not drank a drop of it myself."

Patchett shook his head, not wanting to believe her. He asked Jock, "What are you gonna do about this, sir? People get killed for less than what she done."

Jillian slid next to Anne Marie, a solitary show of support amidst a hostile crowd. "She didn't mean any harm, Jock. She's done nothing but help the lot of you this whole time."

"I know that, Jill," Jock replied. He cast a stern glance at his angry men, and then added the innocuous-sounding words they all knew was meant as a warning: "We *all* know that, don't we?"

When there was not even a murmur of obedient response, Jock repeated, louder this time, "*Don't* we?"

It was slow in coming, but Patchett nodded first. The others took their cue from him.

"Listen, Anne Marie," Jock began, "we appreciate your diligence…and we sure do appreciate all the help you've been. But here's the thing—this is a military unit, and when it comes down to deciding what's best for that unit, only one person gets to decide. And that person is me. So I've got to ask you, how much water do you have?"

She pulled two more bottles from her medical kit. "This much, Major...about two liters."

"Two goddamn liters," Patchett mumbled. "Shit...we could all live for a whole fucking day off that."

"Yeah, we could," Jock continued, "so this is what we're going to do. Anne Marie, turn those bottles over to the sergeant major, who will distribute an equal share to every person here, with one exception—Sergeant McMillen will get a double share."

"He'll need much more than that, Major."

"I'm afraid we're *all* going to need much more than that, Anne Marie."

There was a commotion at the front of the boat. Hadley, who'd never stopped searching the horizon, was so excited he almost fell into the water.

"Over there," he said as he pointed to the sky. "Airplanes...two of them...looks like twin-engined jobs..."

"Shit," Patchett replied as he grabbed binoculars, too. "They better not be some Jap bombers."

"Can't tell yet," Hadley said.

What had been just dots to the naked eye a minute ago grew quickly into full-sized aircraft. The markings were still indistinct—but definitely not the red disks of Japan. Their course would take them almost right overhead.

Patchett asked, "How high up you make them?"

"Two thousand feet, maybe," was Hadley's guess.

Botkin struggled to get the radio up and running but it was no use. "That last battery I had...it's no good, sir. The moisture killed it."

"Shit."

"Hot damn! They're Aussie Beaufighters," Hadley said. Like a reflex, he began to wave his arm at the planes.

Jillian couldn't keep the sea captain in her under control. She yelled, "Use those oars like shovels to stir up some foam around us."

Patchett scoffed at her suggestion, telling Jock, "We need to get their attention with them Very flares, sir."

"Don't bother," Jock replied. "They probably won't see those flares from way up there. They'll get lost in the glare of the sun on the water."

Their conversation quickly turned heated. "Dammit, sir...we gotta do something *positive* to get their attention. We're just a little fucking dot in this ocean."

Jock replied, "Just keep waving and churning up the water like she says with everything we've got—oars, gun butts, the works. We've only got two flares left and we just might need them in the dark sometime, so we're going to save them. Do I make myself clear, Sergeant Major?"

Patchett looked ready for a fight. "With all due respect, sir, I just don't think—"

"Put a damn lid on it, Top. You've been on an airplane once in your whole life. I spent the fucking Port Moresby campaign in a goddamn airplane, looking down. I think I know a little better than you how aerial observation works."

The Aussies in the sky seemed eager to prove Jock right. The lead Beaufighter began to turn while dropping down for a closer look. The wingman was close behind.

Patchett cycled the bolt on his Thompson and said, "If them fuckers think they're gonna strafe us..."

"*At ease*, Top," Jock said, "and just keep waving."

Jillian cradled her arms across her chest as tears streamed down her cheeks. Jock asked, "What's wrong?"

"I can't wave," she said. "It hurts so bloody bad."

"That's okay, honey. I think we've got enough arms at work already."

The two planes flashed past them close enough to see the pilots waving back from their cockpits. The leader climbed away while the wingman came back around for a second pass. This time, he dropped a canister on a bright orange parachute before climbing to join his circling leader.

"Just like a jungle drop," Patchett said as the canister splashed down a hundred yards away. "You gotta go find the damn thing. It better not sink."

It didn't. But it was much too big to be pulled into the crowded boat. With all the care their exhausted bodies could muster, they unpacked the canister while it stayed in the water, carefully opening the lid and holding it upright while item after item was brought onto the boat.

There were five boxes of rations, enough to feed them for several days.

One well-stocked medical kit.

A five-gallon can of water marked "POTABLE."

And a handwritten note, which read:

Rescue Cat to arrive within the hour.

We'll keep you company upstairs until fuel runs low.

Use the parachute as a panel marker.
Cheers,
P/O N Saunders, RAAF

The Beaufighters' fuel only lasted another twenty minutes. They were barely out of sight, though, flying south back to New Guinea, when the rumble of the *Cat's* engines began to blow in on the trade wind. The *Cat*—a Royal Australian Air Force Catalina flying boat—lumbered in from the southeast, making a beeline for the rubber boat. Jock's people used the orange parachute as directed, holding it over their heads to aid the Cat's crew in locating them—a spot of contrast in the bright blue sea. The parachute served another, very practical purpose, too: it made a very effective sun screen.

The big flying boat splashed down and, once slowed to taxi speed, doubled back, coasting to a stop with its wingtip just yards away. Crewmen in the open observation blister beckoned them forward with hand signals; there was no point trying to shout over the clatter of the Cat's idling engines. Once they rowed close enough to the blister, ropes were thrown to secure the bobbing boat against the aft fuselage.

Mike McMillen was hoisted aboard first. Then, one by one, the rest climbed through the blister, until only Patchett and Jock were still in the boat. "Up you go, sir," Patchett said, acting as a crutch for his wounded C.O. as the Cat's crewmen took hold of him.

A flight sergeant asked Patchett, "Have you got everything you need from the bloody boat?"

Patchett took a quick glance—there was nothing left onboard but empty ration boxes and the water can they'd already half drained. He almost tossed the can overboard, but then—perhaps replaying the morning's events in his head—handed the can over to the flight sergeant. That done, he opened the boat's scuttle valves and climbed onboard the Cat.

"Good riddance to you," Patchett mumbled as he cut the boat free. He didn't bother to watch it swamp and slip away.

The takeoff run seemed to take miles of bouncing and lurching, but finally they were airborne. Jock took a long look around the cabin. Compared to the Aussie flight crew, freshly washed and in clean uniforms, his tattered, filthy people were crammed into the Cat's tiny cabin like the refugees they were. They gnawed like hungry dogs on the survival rations dropped to them not an hour ago. He wouldn't be surprised if they'd bite anyone foolish enough to try and take their food away.

The flight sergeant who had helped them onboard turned out to be the plane's navigator. "Sir, the flight will last about an hour and a half," he said to Jock. "We're taking you to Cape Sudest, in Papua. Do you know where that is?"

Jock shot him a withering look. "Don't make me laugh, Sergeant. Yeah, we know where the hell it is. But why there and not Milne Bay?"

"Those are our orders, sir...and we've got to get back to a very tight patrol schedule."

Jock yelled across the cabin to Patchett, "HEY, SERGEANT MAJOR, SPREAD THE WORD...THEY'RE TAKING US BACK TO BUNA. AIN'T THAT HOT SHIT?"

Patchett replied with nothing but a tight, pained smile.

Jillian had overhead what Jock said. Her face reflected all of Patchett's pain, but without any trace of a smile.

"Buna," she mumbled. "Bloody hell...not again."

"I'm sorry, sir," the flight sergeant said, and truly meant it. "Did you fight in the Buna Campaign?"

"We fought, we died...the whole bit, Sergeant. Those two ladies were caught up in it, too. But that's ancient history now. Maybe you can tell me something else while we're at it. I don't want to sound ungrateful to you guys, but what happened to the submarine that was supposed to pick us up?"

"I have no idea, sir. But I can tell you this. It looks like your whole Navy's gone west for a big blow-up with the Nip fleet."

"Do you guys know anything about the Hollandia assault?"

"Just rumors, sir."

"Are they good or bad, Sergeant?"

"Good, sir. Definitely good. We hear it's going fairly well."

The navigator returned to his duties on the flight deck. Jock slumped back against the cabin bulkhead and became lost in his thoughts: *What that sergeant just said—"We hear it's going fairly well"—I take that to mean we did our job. The Japs never got a look at the invasion fleet from that mountain on Manus...*

And I found Jillian, too.

If only this damn leg...

He squirmed in the rock-hard seat, his wounded and useless leg stretched out as the pain grew steadily worse:

It feels like I'm getting stabbed with a thousand little knives.

He looked down the cabin at Mike McMillen, lying quietly as Anne Marie tended to him. Jock's viewing perspective was most unfortunate for a man whose own leg wound was steadily worsening: he was looking right at the bottom of McMillen's stump. It was an oozing morass of blood red and crusty black.

Jock had to look away. The longer he looked at that stump, the worse the pain in his leg became.

Chapter Thirty-Three

Cape Sudest—and the entire Buna area stretching inland from its shore—was so different from the swampy battleground it had been a year ago. It was a logistical base now, one of several in Papua serving as supply depots and transportation hubs for MacArthur's push down the north coast of New Guinea. Paved roads and wooden walkways displaced what was once nothing but watery muck. The front line had moved west almost five hundred miles, making the entire area decidedly a *rear echelon*, a bureaucratic jungle manned by paper-shuffling officers and men whose impressions of combat were, save for the few who had actually flown or sailed into harm's way, gleaned entirely from the barroom bravado and the movies they enjoyed when their work day was over. Their war was strictly a sun-up to sun-down affair.

Somewhere in the vast Allied chain of command which ended here at Buna, the ball had definitely been dropped; as Jock and his people struggled to the dock from the launch that met the Cat, there was nobody to collect them. They realized then and there how lucky they were that someone—*somewhere*—had at least remembered to pluck them from the sea off Manus. But that seemed to be as far as the accommodations went for the men of *Operation Blind Spot*.

Troops on stevedore duty gazed uneasily at these bloodied warriors, who might as well have been armed visitors from a strange and savage world. The type of men who'd rip your head off at the first hint of standard military bullshit. The two women didn't look too friendly, either. Patchett easily intimidated a young PFC truck driver, commandeering his deuce-and-a-half to take them to the field hospital. On arrival, a flustered yet pompous second lieutenant—a living manifestation of the high-level communications failure—told Jock, "You people don't belong here. We have no paperwork on you. I can't admit you. For all I know, you're all AWOL." His nose was turned up as if their rank odor offended him.

Speaking from the wheelchair Bogater Boudreau had scrounged, Jock replied. "I'm going to do you a big favor, Lieutenant, and not rip that cute little Quartermaster Corps insignia off your collar and stuff it right down your throat. My people don't need pencil-pushers right now, they need doctors. Now get the fuck out of my way and make yourself useful—get me a landline to Thirty-Second Division HQ, on the double."

The lieutenant was more flustered than ever now. "Where on Earth do I find them, sir?"

"Try Milne Bay, Lieutenant."

"But that's a couple of hundred miles from here."

"No shit," Jock replied. "Now get them on the fucking horn."

This tent-city hospital had no formal triage unit. It hadn't needed one; being so far from actual combat, there was never a flood of casualties. Save for a few malaria and dysentery cases and one unlucky GI who'd fallen off a truck, breaking his arm in the process, the place was deserted at the moment. The wounded in Jock's party were the biggest influx of people seeking emergency medical care since a careless mess sergeant caused a minor epidemic of diarrhea. A nurse in prim whites nearly fainted when she first laid eyes on Mike

McMillen's stump.

The doctor examining McMillen had a stronger stomach. He was a white-haired lieutenant colonel—Jock figured him for an old-school Army doc: *Probably been in since The Great War.* He introduced himself as Doctor Lewis.

"Who did this cauterization?" the doctor asked, gently probing the seared area.

"I did," Anne Marie replied. "There was no other option."

Heavy on the sarcasm, Lewis said, "Is that so? Are you a *doctor*, then?"

"No, sir, I'm a nurse." There wasn't the faintest hint of inferiority or apology in her voice.

"A nurse, eh?" Noting her accent, he added, "You sound German."

"No, sir, I'm Dutch."

"Well, one slip and you could've killed this man outright, little lady...but it looks like you saved his life instead. Excellent job." Turning to his squeamish nurse, the doctor added, "Get this man ready for surgery immediately. Doctor Clancy's been dying to get his hands on an amputation ever since he got here."

The doctor summoned another nurse. "Cut that trouser leg off the major here," he said.

"If it's all the same to you, Colonel," Jock replied, "I have three other wounded people I'd like you to have a look at first."

"If you mean those two bandaged-up sergeants of yours, they walked in all by themselves. I doubt they're critical. You, Major, on the other hand—"

"Don't mean to interrupt, sir, but there's someone else, too. That woman clutching her arms to her chest..."

"Oh, that Aussie rag doll with the *bloody this* and *bloody that* always coming out of her mouth?"

"Yeah, that's her. She was a POW until a few days ago. The Japs tortured her…both her shoulders need medical attention real bad."

"How'd she manage to get herself captured?"

"A real long story, sir…but she was a ship's captain in the Allied Merchant Navy. Got captured during the Buna Campaign last year. Let's just say a whole bunch of us owe the fact we're still alive to her."

The doctor took another long look at Jillian. "A sea captain? No shit?"

"No shit, sir. And I'd owe you one…a *real big one*…if you'd take care of her."

The old doctor was nobody's fool. "She means a hell of a lot to you, doesn't she, son? Maybe a whole hell of a lot?"

"You've got that right, sir."

"Well then, Major Miles, you have my word—my people will fix her up with whatever she needs. But she walked in here under her own steam, too…and you didn't. The rules around here say *the worst first*…and that's you, son. I can smell that leg of yours from ten feet away…and *it don't smell good.*"

"Ahh, there you are, Jock," Colonel Dick Molloy said as he burst into the ward tent. "Sorry this glorified supply dump wasn't ready for you. The idiots running this place could fuck up a wet dream. How long have you been here?"

"A couple of hours, sir," Jock replied, quite

surprised his regimental commander turned up out of nowhere. "But how'd you get here from Milne Bay so fast?"

"I was already on a plane, Jock. The rest of the division's on its way. This is the staging area for our next campaign. In fact, your battalion's on a boat that should be dropping anchor any minute."

"That's real good news, sir. It'll be great to get back with *all* my men again."

The smile faded from Colonel Molloy's face. "Not so fast, Jock. From what I hear, you're out of action for a while…maybe a long while."

"Nah, I'll be okay, sir. Doc Lewis says I'll have to live with a big dent in my thigh, and a bit of a limp, too. But they scooped out most of the dead tissue already. They'll be doing more later."

"Well, you know I've got my fingers crossed. By the way, I got quite a wonderful surprise a few minutes ago…"

"I'm guessing you ran into Jillian, sir?"

"Yes, I did! Our Miss Forbes…back from the dead! And feisty as ever, too. Quite a story you two have to tell."

Jock turned serious and asked, "The Hollandia assault, sir? It is going okay, isn't it?"

"It's going pretty well, Jock. The Japs didn't know we were coming until we were right offshore. You and your boys did one hell of a job on Manus…not to mention liberating POWs while you were at it, too. Now, the general will be here in a minute to begin the debrief, just as soon as he's finished reading the riot act to the deadbeats who dropped the ball and left you hanging like that."

"The *general*, sir? *Which* general?"

"Ted Stanley...a brigadier from MacArthur's G2 shop."

"I've heard the name, sir, but I don't know him. What's he like?"

"He's just like everyone else on the *Supreme Commander's* staff, Jock—a complete asshole."

Jillian's arms were in slings when she returned to Jock's ward tent. The tattered rice-sack shift she'd worn was now discarded. She was scrubbed clean and wearing a fresh set of GI khakis a few sizes too big, cinched up with a belt. On her feet was a brand new pair of GI boots, which fit surprisingly well. "I suppose I have very big feet by Yank standards," she said, proudly showing off her new footwear.

Colonel Molloy excused himself to give them a precious few minutes alone before General Stanley arrived.

"The doctors say I've got torn ligaments in both shoulders," she told Jock. "No big surprise, I suppose."

"How long are you going to be in those slings?"

"A month, maybe. My arms need to be immobile as much as possible. They wanted to wrap me up in plaster but I told them they could go straight to Hell."

Gingerly, she pulled one arm free of its sling and stroked his hair. "I wouldn't be able to do this if I was in plaster, would I?"

There was a shout of *ATTEN-HUT* from the far end of the ward tent. General Stanley strutted in like a peacock with Colonel Molloy and two other officers in his wake.

As she watched the parade approach, Jillian muttered, "Bloody hell, did the wanker lose his brass band?"

Colonel Molloy handled the introductions. When he was done, General Stanley pointed to Jillian and asked, "Is this woman one of the freed POWs?" He made *woman* sound like a dirty word.

"Yes, sir," Molloy replied, "she's—"

Stanley cut him off. "Well, get her the hell out of here, Colonel. No civilians in this debrief."

Surprised but not flustered by the rude, shortsighted remark, Molloy replied, "Sir, I think you'll find Miss Forbes has valuable—"

"Get her out, Colonel. Now."

One of Stanley's lackeys, an eager lieutenant, took the initiative to usher Jillian from the tent, but made the mistake of laying his hands on her. Putting those new boots on her feet to good use, she kicked him squarely in the knee.

The lieutenant toppled over like a table suddenly missing a leg.

"Keep your bloody hands off me, you stupid knob," she said, and then strolled leisurely out of the tent.

"Get up, you imbecile," the General told his lieutenant, still on the floorboards clutching his knee. "A woman couldn't possibly hurt you that much."

Jock and Colonel Molloy tried not to smirk; they knew Jillian Forbes' capabilities far better than any general.

"Let's get down to business," General Stanley said. Turning to the major standing next to him, he added, "Ask the questions, Major Billingsley."

Major Billingsley: Kit Billingsley, the officer who led that first briefing where *Operation Blind Spot* was set in motion. The politically well-connected bonehead Jock had known since West Point was apparently still basking in the good graces of *The Supreme Commander*.

"First off," Billingsley began, "I want to assure both you, Major Miles, and you, Colonel Molloy, that Supreme Allied Headquarters had nothing to do with the foul up over the recovery phase of your mission. That was strictly a local command failure here in the Buna area. It's being dealt with as we speak."

"That comes as a great relief," Jock said, trying not to sound sarcastic. "Nothing like returning from the gates of Hell to be told you're not welcome. But never mind. What do you want to know, Kit?"

"Well, first off, *Major*, we'd like your estimate of the number of Japanese troops on Manus." He'd made the word *major* sound as if the man being addressed was somehow inferior to him, even though they wore the same gold leaf on their collars.

"Can't really tell you, *Kit*. Our mission was to deny the Japanese observation of the convoy en route to Hollandia, not count heads."

"But you were in contact with the Japanese, weren't you?"

"Yes, we were."

"How many of them did you encounter, then?"

"No more than two companies."

General Stanley held up his hand to silence Billingsley. He'd take over the questioning himself. "Only two companies, Major Miles? Our photo recon leads us to believe the Japs have at least a regiment on Manus."

"That may be, General, but like I said, the total number of Japs we tangled with never exceeded two companies."

"So you can't confirm the photo recon estimates?"

"No, sir, I can't…and we were never asked to do so in the first place."

Jock's answer left General Stanley dissatisfied. "Major Miles," he continued, "I understand you deviated from your mission to rescue POWs. Is that true?"

"No, sir. When our mission objective—the OP on Mount Dremsel—was secured well ahead of schedule, I took advantage of the extra time to follow up on intel we got from two impressed Korean soldiers who surrendered to us."

Stanley's face twisted into a scowl. "*Korean* soldiers, Major? How can you be sure they were Koreans?"

"I had two Nisei with me, sir, who debriefed the prisoners in Japanese."

Stanley's scowl grew tighter. "You actually trusted these *Nisei*?"

"With my life, sir."

"And the lives of all your men, too, I might add, Major. Very foolish, if you ask me…a Jap's a Jap. But let's get back to this *intel*. What was it?"

"That the Japanese were preparing to evacuate Manus, sir. Part of those preparations involved executing the POWs they were holding there as well as the Korean troops being used as guards at the prison camp. We were able to at least partially confirm some of that intel, sir— we witnessed the execution of two Australian flyers while observing the camp."

"So, are the Japanese evacuating Manus, Major

Miles?"

"I don't know, sir."

"Why not, Major Miles? Why don't you know? You were on the goddamn island, weren't you? On that goddamn mountaintop."

Colonel Molloy couldn't hold his peace anymore. "Sir," he said, "in all fairness, the mission was to—"

"I wasn't talking to you, Colonel," Stanley said. "I want to hear this major of yours explain himself."

"Very well, sir," Jock replied. "If the Japs were pulling their people out, they'd be embarking at night, with the ships all blacked-out, just like all the other sea movements they've been doing for the past year. We wouldn't have been able to see any of it, even from the mountaintop. We all know their fleet can't afford to be caught standing still in daylight. Our planes will eat them alive."

"Don't presume to lecture me on the operating procedures of the Japanese, Major Miles. But speaking of planes, did you see any Japanese aircraft during your time on Manus?"

"Not a one, sir...in the air or on the ground."

A half-smile crossed Stanley's face. "Finally, some intel we can use."

Dick Molloy took another shot at speaking up. "With all due respect, General, the—"

"I thought I told you to be quiet, Molloy. And I know full well what *with all due respect* really means, so you'd be wise not to say it again."

Returning to Jock, the General continued, "Now, Major Miles, I'm told by Colonel Molloy that you're having a relationship with one of those POW women you rescued. Is that true?"

There was no point in Jock denying it. "Yes, sir. I've had a relationship with Miss Forbes since Australia in '42. But after she went missing a year ago, I grew to accept that she'd been killed. I had no idea—"

"No idea of what, Major? That she was on that island? Of course you didn't. But I'm guessing when you heard there was a POW camp and that it contained women…"

"Sir, we never knew the camp contained women until we got there and saw for ourselves."

"But there was always *that hope*, wasn't there, Major Miles, that maybe—just maybe—you'd find her there. Was there not?"

"I'd be lying if I said there wasn't, sir."

The General's face grew stern, like a reproachful headmaster about to deliver a caning to a misbehaving schoolboy. "This is how it looks to me, Major Miles. When given the opportunity to show some initiative that could've really helped *The Supreme Commander*, you chose to go looking for your girlfriend instead. And that little search cost you two dead and four wounded—two very seriously—out of a ten-man unit. That's a pretty shabby state of affairs in my book. Some might call it a dereliction of duty."

Jock tried to speak but Dick Molloy's gesture was unmistakable: *Shut up…don't say a word you'll regret later.* If there was any *regretting later* to be done, Molloy had made up his mind he'd be the one to risk it. "General," he said, "that's bullshit and you know it. Major Miles accomplished the mission he was given, and more. Your Hollandia operation is off to a great start because of what he and his men did."

The General looked decidedly unimpressed. "Just

doing what you're supposed to do isn't enough. *The Supreme Commander* expects more from his officers...something you should remember, too, Richard."

"All the same, sir," Molloy replied, "none of us have a crystal ball that can read General MacArthur's mind."

General Stanley didn't bother with a reply. He was halfway out of the tent when Jock asked, "Excuse me, General, but I'm a little confused about something. You said *two very seriously wounded*. Sure, Sergeant McMillen's lost a leg...but the rest of us are going to be okay. What makes you think there's another seriously wounded man?"

For once, the general's face seemed to show some small amount of empathy. He shook his head sadly and replied, "Didn't you know? It's *you*, Major Miles. The surgeon tells me you're going to lose that leg."

Chapter Thirty-Four

The men of Jock's 1st Battalion had been ashore at Cape Sudest only a few minutes when Colonel Molloy's jeep roared into their assembly area. "I need a detail, on the double," Molloy told Captain Lee Grossman, the battalion's senior company commander and the first officer he saw. "And I mean *right now*, Captain."

Disembarking a battalion from ship to shore was a difficult enough project, full of plans changing on the fly, missing equipment, frustrated troop leaders, and thoroughly confused troops. The last thing Lee Grossman needed right now was the regimental commander tapping his manpower for some circle-jerk of a work party. When he heard what the detail was all about, though, he wanted to lead it himself.

"It's simple, Captain," Molloy said. "We're going to kidnap Major Miles out of that butcher's shop of a hospital he's stuck in before they hack off what just might be a perfectly good leg. We'll turn him over to our regimental docs, now that they're here, and let them take care of him...the right way."

Sergeant Major Patchett was the one who talked Lee Grossman out of leading the kidnap detail personally. "You'd better not go, Captain," Patchett said. "I shouldn't, neither. Things are fucked up enough as it is at the moment. We gotta stay and keep this circus rolling. We got plenty of others up to the task of rescuing the major."

"Yeah, I guess you're right, Sergeant Major. I think I'll put Theo Papadakis in charge."

"Now you're talking, sir. The *Mad Greek's* just the

guy we need for this job, I reckon. He broke the major out of that hospital back in Australia, too."

"That's exactly why he's getting the job...superior qualifications."

Captain Theo Papadakis thought there were entirely too many MPs hanging around this hospital, especially since it had only a handful of patients. "It's those damn nurses," the *Mad Greek* said to Tom Hadley and Bogater Boudreau, fresh out of that hospital themselves. "Those nightstick-swinging assholes got nothing better to do than hang around the skirts. We gotta divert their attention."

Hadley replied, "So how're we going to do that in broad daylight, sir? We can't afford to wait until dark. They may have whacked off the major's leg by then."

"Damn right," Papadakis said, "so this is how we're gonna play it." He turned to the four privates they had dragged along as *just in case* manpower. "Okay, you guys, listen up. Go over in front of that tent with the flag pole and start fighting each other. Make it look like a real good brawl...lots of pushing and shoving, but don't land any roundhouses, okay? All those idiot MPs will come running. Just do me a big favor and don't kill each other...I'll never get replacements for you. And for Pete's sake, make damn sure none of you hit an MP. Do I make myself clear?"

"Sure, sir, " one of the privates replied, "but what happens when those bastards start cracking our heads with those nightsticks?"

"Not to worry, Private. I'll step in and take charge

of the situation before it ever gets that far. And while I'm pretending to give you all a real good ass-chewing, First Sergeant Hadley and Sergeant Boudreau will snatch the major, sneak him out to the colonel's jeep...and *mission accomplished*."

Another private asked, "So we won't spend the night in the stockade, sir?"

"Nah. You came with me...you'll leave with me."

"Dammit," the private mumbled, "a good night's sleep in a jail cell sounded like the cat's ass right about now."

"Forget about the *cat's* ass," Papadakis said. "It'll be *your* ass if you fuck this up. Now get moving...and start swinging."

The fake brawl erupted exactly as Theo Papadakis planned it. As his four *actors* scuffled and tumbled, the MPs came running from all corners, blood in their eyes. He told Hadley and Boudreau, "I think it's time I go save their bacon."

With Captain Papadakis gone, Hadley said, "Bogater, I believe it's showtime for us, too."

They ducked under the rolled-up side of the ward tent and headed to Jock's cot. He didn't seem to recognize his two sergeants, just gave them a vague smile like you'd give to someone whose name had slipped your mind.

His voice barely above a whisper, Jock said, "Can I help you guys?"

Hadley replied, "No, sir, we're here to help you."

He nudged Bogater toward the other side of the cot

and said, "He's really doped up, like they're going to cut on him any minute. We got here just in time. Lay that IV bag in his lap. We'll do a two-man carry. Lift when I count to—"

A woman's stern voice interrupted their efforts. "Just what do you think you're doing, Sergeant?"

Hadley turned to see an Army nurse—a major in gleaming white—standing a few feet away. She didn't look happy in the least.

"We're just visiting our C.O., ma'am," Hadley replied. "Good thing we're here, too. I think he's got to pee something fierce. We'll just bring him to the latrine and come right back."

"You'll do no such thing, Sergeant. That man needs surgery immediately. What's your name?"

Hadley didn't bother to answer. With Jock cradled between them as if sitting in a chair, they were already headed out of the tent.

The nurse tried to block their path but with a deft side-step, they blew past her.

"I'm putting you on report, Sergeant. Tell me your name...that's an order!"

Outside the tent now, Hadley replied, "The name's Roosevelt, Franklin D., ma'am."

"In a pig's eye it is," she said. "You're in big trouble, both of you. I'm calling the MPs."

Jock was already sprawled in the jeep's back seat. For all he knew, he was on the moon.

"Good luck with that, ma'am," Hadley replied. "You take care, now."

Bogater dropped the jeep into gear and they were gone, speeding back to Regimental HQ.

The sergeant in charge of the hospital's MP detachment was pretty sure his leg was being pulled. It was a *captain* doing the pulling, though…and he looked and talked like one tough little son of a bitch, with the battle scars to prove it.

He asked Theo Papadakis, "You really want to take full responsibility for these four zipperheads, sir?"

"That's what I said, Sergeant. You got something stuck in your ears?"

"No, sir…it's just…I mean, we'll be glad to lock them up for you. I've got a list of charges on them as long as my arm already."

"Oh, that would be just peachy keen, Sergeant. Lock up four jabonies in the cooler who should have shipped out on a combat assault instead. You don't suppose they'd *prefer* to be in the stockade, do you? And just maybe that's what this little *performance* was all about? Find a place with a lot of MPs, act up, get your ass arrested and stashed away in a nice, safe place…with no jungle…and no Japs."

The sergeant hesitated for a moment. If it was bullshit the captain was peddling, it was *first-class* bullshit…and he couldn't help but see the logic in it. Buying into it made him feel shrewder, like he was gaining some of this combat veteran's wisdom without having to actually put his ass on the line. Directing traffic and locking up unruly GIs was so much easier— and a hell of a lot safer—than rooting the Japs out of the rainforests and jungles of New Guinea. He could understand why a GI might do anything he could get away with to stay here, too, rather than ship out to where the shit was flying.

"Okay, Captain," the sergeant said, "I guess they're all yours, then."

As Theo Papadakis marched his men away, he could tell they were still pumped up from the staged melee. One of the privates asked, "So what do we get for putting on that little show, Captain Pop?"

"I'll tell you what you get...you get to stay off my shit list for the rest of the day."

"I won't try to snow you, Jock," the chief regimental surgeon said. "It's bad...but I don't think it's bad enough to amputate. We've cut out any trace of gangrene. If the viable tissue stays healthy for forty-eight hours, I think we'll be out of the woods."

Anne Marie Smits, seated in a corner of the tent with Colonel Molloy, allowed herself a satisfied smile.

"Go ahead and smile, young lady," the surgeon added. "You've earned it. I hear this *rescue mission* was all your idea?"

"A few of the doctors in that other hospital are knife-happy," Anne Marie replied. "You should've seen the look of glee on that Doctor Clancy's face as he was cleaning up Sergeant McMillen's stump. He couldn't wait to carve someone else up, too."

"It really pisses me off," Jock said, "because Doc Lewis had no intention of amputating. But once he went off duty, things got strange real fast."

"Well," the surgeon said, "under combat conditions, it's sometimes safer just to take the limb. But we're not in combat conditions here, so let's not get carried away. Not yet, anyway. But I've got to tell you, even if you keep it—and I think you will—there will be consequences..."

"Are any of them be as bad as losing the leg, Doc?"

"No, of course not, Jock." Turning his attention to Colonel Molloy and Anne Marie, he added, "Let him rest now. He's going to need it. I'll be back to check on him later."

The surgeon gone, Dick Molloy said, "We've got to talk, Jock."

"Yeah, I figured as much, sir...but first, can I ask where Jillian is?"

"Some Aussie war correspondent heard about her story. He's latched on to her...and he's already dubbed her *Lady Lazarus*, like she's returned from the dead."

That news took Jock by surprise. "And she's actually interested in talking to one of those hucksters, sir?"

"Not at first...she told him to *bugger off* a few times...but she's warmed to the idea now. I think she's trying to play it up so the both of you will get a *heroes' tour* back in Australia. Actually, that might not be such a bad idea, Jock. You could sure use the time off."

"*Time off*...I'm guessing that's what you want to talk about, sir?"

"Yeah. Miss Smits, would you excuse us for a few minutes?"

"Certainly, Colonel."

Molloy pulled up a chair. He didn't want to say the words, no more than Jock wanted to hear them. But they had to be said and it was nobody's job but his.

"Jock, the division's shipping out in a week, and

there's no way you're going to be in shape to take your battalion back into combat."

They both knew there was no need to spell it out.

I'm getting relieved. Thrown on the trash heap. Unserviceable. War-weary.

"So who's replacing me, sir? Please tell me you're promoting one of my guys into the job. Grossman...Papadakis..."

The pained silence made it clear that wasn't to be, either.

Finally, Dick Molloy said, "I didn't have a choice here, Jock."

Oh, shit...who are my men getting stuck with?

"I'm putting Kit Billingsley in your slot," Molloy said. "MacArthur's got big plans for the boy, but he needs his ticket punched in a combat command if he's going to get stars pinned on him. It'll be least dangerous for everyone involved to put him with an experienced, savvy unit like yours."

Molloy expected shock, hurt, maybe even an outburst of rage. But when he summoned the courage to look Jock in the eye, he was laughing softly, with a big smile on his face.

"Did I say something funny, Jock?"

"No, sir. I was just thinking, though...they'll eat that numbnuts Billingsley alive. I'd pay good money to watch that."

Chapter Thirty-Five

Jillian relaxed in a deck chair on the veranda of Buna Government House, watching the sun set while she awaited the arrival of the correspondent from the Australian network. A cold Aussie beer sat on the table beside her, a long straw jutting from its neck so she could sip it even with her arms in slings. The beer wasn't the only comfort Government House provided. Not only had she been given a cozy room for her stay at Buna—its length still undetermined—but there was a small stock of women's clothes which, by some miracle, had survived the bitter fighting that raged around the building last year. Some of those clothes fit Jillian perfectly. She'd shed the baggy GI khakis and donned a comfortable skirt and blouse.

A jeep pulled up and expelled a short, plump civilian in tropical whites. He swayed on his feet like a round-bottomed doll trying to settle at its point of equilibrium. Jillian found herself chuckling at his appearance, just like she had when they first met. With his portly, middle-aged body, a fringe of hair circling an otherwise bald head, and calabash pipe that hung like the letter *S* from his mouth, she thought him the living representation of a garden gnome. All he needed to complete the picture was a silly conical hat.

She told herself, *Ladies and gentlemen, Hugh Finchley, war correspondent and lawn ornament, has arrived.*

"Good evening, Miss Forbes," Finchley trumpeted as he waddled up the path to the veranda. It was almost inconceivable that his voice—*that lovely voice*—came out of such a comical body. A sonorous baritone, you would swear its owner must be an attractive, virile man…unless you were actually looking at him. "I have a face for the wireless," he'd said, trying some self-deprecation to break the ice when they'd first met.

"How are those lovely arms doing tonight, my dear?"

"Still attached, Mister Finchley."

He pulled a piece of paper from his battered leather briefcase. "I've heard back from Sydney," he said, waving the dispatch like a flag. "They're captivated by the story of you and your Yank. It's got everything—adventure, romance, a courageous *Lady Lazarus* fighting her way back from the dead, and of course, a happy ending."

"I'm glad they're so sure it's a *happy* ending, Mister Finchley. I don't believe that's been determined yet. And I was never actually dead, you know."

Her downbeat attitude surprised him but he pressed on. "There's already quite a bit of interest in a book, too. Do you fancy writing up your story, Miss Forbes?"

She frowned and allowed her arms a gentle shrug within their slings. "I don't imagine I'll be doing much typing with these for a while."

"I'd be glad to provide whatever assistance you might need, Miss Forbes."

"I assume you're volunteering to be my co-author and not my typist, Mister Finchley. Bloody nice pay envelope in it for you, I suppose."

His voice took on the tones of an actor doing Shakespeare: "Oh, Miss Forbes! You cut me to the quick! It's not about the filthy lucre, I assure you."

She took a long pull on her beer, and then replied,

"In a pig's arse, it's not."

He decided this was not the time to discuss business; there were journalistic matters to settle first. "Sydney is being a stickler on corroboration, though, Miss Forbes. This whole Buna adventure a year ago…your role in the *fire ship* attack that turned the debacle around…it's all a bit fantastical, you must admit. Terrific drama, of course…but we must be able to document the testimony of actual witnesses. I've tried to talk with your Major Miles but the Yank hospital personnel won't let me near him."

"Good on them. He's got an open wound. He doesn't need you and every other journalist in Papua traipsing around trying to infect him now, does he?"

"But I must talk with people who were there, Miss Forbes. Can you give me some idea where I might find them?"

"Mister Finchley, I believe this is your lucky day…"

It was not the start of a beautiful friendship. The ink was barely dry on the orders putting Kit Billingsley in charge of 1st Battalion, but he and Melvin Patchett were already at odds.

"Begging your pardon, sir," Patchett said, "but the custom in these parts is to refer to me as *sergeant major*."

"Negative, *Sergeant*," Billingsley replied. "There is no such rank in the United States Army. You wear six stripes—you are a *master sergeant*. You will be addressed as such. And by the way, remove that diamond from your insignia of rank. You are no longer a first sergeant, either. According to your records, you haven't been one for some time."

"Don't mean to contradict, sir, but Major Miles always felt the *top sergeant* of the battalion deserved—"

"I don't give a hot damn what Major Miles *felt*, Sergeant Patchett. Creating imaginary ranks out of thin air only serves to bastardize the NCO hierarchy...and I won't have it, not in my outfit. I don't see why you care, anyway...the pay's the same."

"It ain't about the pay, sir. It's more important than that."

"Well, Sergeant, I've got some news for you. *I'll* decide what's important around here. Do I make myself clear?"

"Yes, sir. Crystal clear."

"Outstanding. Now what's the next order of business?"

How about we arrange a little "training accident" for you, sir?

But Patchett kept such thoughts to himself. Swallowing his anger, he saved it for another day— another day that would come very soon, he was sure.

"Very well, sir," *Master Sergeant* Patchett said. "Next up, I've got two requests for immediate transfer into the battalion—"

"Did you say *into* the battalion, Sergeant?"

Ain't I speaking English, you dumb shit?

"Yes, sir...*into* the battalion. Two lads from Division HQ who was with us on the Manus mission want to join the flock full time. This Sergeant Botkin here is the best damn signalman I ever known in *this man's army*. We sure could use him around here. And this Corporal Nishimoto is a—"

"Just a minute, Sergeant. This man's name is *Nishimoto?*"

"Yes, sir. We call him *Ace*. He's one of them Nisei troopers. Hell of a good fighter, if I may—"

"You *may not*, Sergeant. There will be no Japanese in my unit. Botkin is approved, the Jap is denied. Next order of business."

It was just past midnight when the medic shook the surgeon awake. "It's Major Miles," he said. "That last debridement we did…the site's hemorrhaging."

"How bad, Corporal?"

"Real bad, Doc."

"Dammit. How much plasma do we have ready to go?"

"About five units."

"Probably not enough. Prepare five more."

A minute later, standing in a growing pool of Jock's blood, his gloved fingers deep into the leg wound feeding that pool, the surgeon asked, "How're you holding up, Jock?"

"I'm a little woozy, to be honest."

"Ahh, here it is," the surgeon said. "Corporal, hemostat."

The medic slapped the instrument into the doctor's open hand.

"Shit…I can't see the bleeder now with all this blood pooling again…and I can't sew up what I can't see. Get more sponges in here, Corporal."

The surgeon struggled to set the clamp for a few

more moments without success. "You still with me, Jock?"

There was no answer.

"We're losing him, Doc," the medic said.

Chapter Thirty-Six

Hugh Finchley asked, "Is it too early in the morning to offer you a beer, Sergeant Major Patchett?"

"Nah, it ain't too early...provided it ain't none of that Japanese piss-water."

"No, sir...only the finest Australian brew is served at Government House."

From his seat on the veranda, Patchett took in the building and meticulous gardens surrounding it. "Funny thing," he said, "last time I saw this place, we was blowing it full of holes."

"Yes, a marvelous job of reconstruction, wouldn't you say? I believe we have you Yanks to thank for that."

Patchett seized the cold bottle eagerly and raised it in a toast to the sunrise. "By the way, Mister Finchley, you don't have to call me *sir.* In fact, you better just call me *sergeant.* This new C.O. we just got don't believe in no such thing as *sergeant majors.*" He took a long pull on his beer, and then added, "Can't remember the last time I had beer for breakfast. Sure tastes fine..."

And I don't give a shit if that jackwad commander of mine smells it on my breath, neither. What's he gonna do? Fire me?

Finchley got down to business. "As you can tell from my note, Sergeant Patchett, I'm looking for people who witnessed the battle that raged here last year. Miss Forbes mentioned you as a prime source of information."

"The lady knows what she's talking about, Mister Finchley, believe you me. We got about fifty men in a couple-mile radius who was in the fight here, me included."

Finchley's pen was poised over his notebook page. "Why don't you tell me what happened then, Sergeant, in your own words."

Patchett regaled Finchley with the whole story—the stalemated campaign against the desperate but well-organized Japanese; the high command's suicidal plan for an amphibious assault to try and break that stalemate; Jillian Forbes' clever *fire ship* diversion that saved the day, making that amphibious assault unnecessary and tipping the scales to an Allied victory at Buna.

By the time Patchett finished talking, Finchley was out of breath with excitement. This was the story that could make him the Edward R. Murrow of the Pacific Theater...and if he could convince Jillian to let him co-author a book with her—or better yet, write it himself— he'd be raking in the gold, too.

He calmed himself enough to ask, "Any one of these men you mentioned can confirm Miss Forbes' role in the battle?"

Patchett nodded. His empty beer bottle clinked as he set it on the table.

Finchley, still clinging to the slender shred of journalistic integrity that hadn't yet been severed by the euphoria of impending wealth, asked, "And each and every one of these men will tell *exactly* the same story you just told me?"

"Affirmative," Patchett replied, "and they're all gonna tell you the same thing I'm fixing to tell you now, too."

"What's that, Sergeant?"

"That every last one of us—every last swinging dick—would be buried in this fucking place, with the

Japs pissing on our mass grave every damn day, if it hadn't been for Jillian Forbes."

"How's our boy doing?" Colonel Molloy asked the surgeon.

"He gave us quite a scare last night. Damn near died on me twice. I hate to say this but taking that leg would have been a whole lot easier…and a whole lot safer for all concerned."

"But he's stabilized now, Doc?"

"Yeah…believe it or not. The only good thing I can say about hemorrhaging is that dead tissue doesn't bleed, so I'm still confident all the necrosis has been removed."

"So you think he's going to make it, Doc?"

The exhausted doctor settled heavily into a chair. He pondered Molloy's question, grappling for an honest answer to something best not asked. There were just too many *ifs*...

He could feel Molloy's eyes boring into him, waiting, expecting—*no, demanding*—a reply.

The best the surgeon could come up with was, "Ask me that question again tomorrow, Dick."

Tom Hadley had the solution for Patchett smelling of beer. He picked up some coconuts that had been lying around on the ground, punched two holes in each one, and poured their milk down Patchett's fatigue shirt. "There," Hadley said, "now you smell like rotten coconuts. Let's see *Major Kitty Kat* smell beer over that."

"I smelled worse, you touch-hole. But I'm soaking fucking wet now, too."

"Hey, we're all sweating like pigs anyway, Top. Who the hell's going to notice?"

Then they waited. Kit Billingsley, their new C.O., was late for the very first morning formation of his new command. Finally, a jeep approached and screeched to a halt. Billingsley tumbled out, looking bleary-eyed, like a man who'd overslept—or never slept at all. "Sergeant Patchett," he said, "my battalion looks like it's standing around with its thumb up its ass...and all I see here are sergeants. Where the hell are my officers?"

"In your CP tent, sir, waiting on you to give them the briefing you scheduled for 0800." Patchett made a grand theatrical gesture of checking his wristwatch. "That would be ten minutes ago by my watch, sir...which is gonna make us late for this morning's training exercise. I'm sure Colonel Molloy's gonna be unhappy about that right off the bat, sir."

Billingsley *harrumphed* and stomped off to the CP.

"The man's a walking, talking disaster, Tom," Patchett said, as they followed at a respectful distance.

"How the hell do we get rid of him, Top?"

"Just bide your time, son...just bide your time. You heard what Colonel Molloy said...he's only gonna be here long enough to get hisself a combat star. Then he'll be back upstairs faster than shit through a goose."

For Hadley, that seemed too long. "And in the meantime?"

Patchett put a comforting hand on Hadley's shoulder. "Tom my boy, our shirts spent more time in the laundry than he's got in a combat zone. While he's busy screwing the pooch, we're gonna be watching out for our men. Like we always done."

"Just like Major Miles taught us, right, Top?"

"No, you dumb shit…just like *I* taught y'all." Patchett broke into a sly grin and added, "With a little help from the major, of course."

It had been the same story at every tactical problem during the day's training. Major Billingsley would brief his company commanders on the problem's objective and his plan to seize it; as soon as he was done, they would collectively shake their heads in dismissal of the plan. One of them—*usually that smartass kike Grossman*, Billingsley fumed—would then speak for the sullen group, saying something like *that's not the way it's done, Major.*

Kit Billingsley knew no matter how their objection was phrased, it contained three implied messages.

The first: *we're combat veterans and you're not.*

The second: *We've already done this shit for real a hundred times…and you haven't done it once yet.*

Last but certainly not least: *That's not the way Major Miles taught us.*

It was nearly 1500 now—time for the last problem of the day before supper back at the bivouac area—and Billingsley was barely into describing his plan of attack before Lee Grossman was voicing the collective objection.

"We're in the wrong position, Major," Grossman said. "That's not the Girua River over there. It's something we named Rabbit Hole Creek, since it never had a name on those crappy maps we had."

"Why'd you call it that, Captain?"

"Because all we did around here was kill Jap snipers hiding out in rabbit holes, sir."

Billingsley plastered that insufferable smirk on his face, the one his officers had grown to hate in the remarkably short time he'd been their C.O. "That's an interesting anecdote, Captain Grossman...but I think your recollection of the geography is a bit faulty. I know this place like the back of my hand, and that's the Girua River."

Trying not to laugh in Billingsley's face, Grossman said, "Would you mind sharing with us how you came to know this place *like the back of your hand*, Major?"

"From map study, of course, Captain."

Lee Grossman didn't hold back his laugh this time. "From maps, sir? These useless maps? Well, we learned this terrain a little differently, I'm afraid...by bleeding and dying on it. So here's the deal, Major—we can launch your screwy *pretend attack* from here and watch the whole battalion bog down in the chest-high swamp. With a little luck, maybe nobody will drown or get taken by a snake or a croc. Then, we can all watch Colonel Molloy chew your ass for *the worst attack he's ever seen.* Or, we can bypass the *sewer diving* and take that nice, dry trail over there to the correct start point and show them once and for all how a combat unit gets it done."

As Grossman finished his sermon, Kit Billingsley didn't respond. He found himself distracted by the actions of the other company commanders. Their attention had shifted to the jeep where Sergeants Botkin and Patchett were huddled anxiously over its radio set.

Billingsley was the only one who didn't know why.

Sergeant Stu Botkin had gone over the *Signals* section of the division's operations order from one end to the other. He'd identified all the frequencies that weren't in use today. Then he designated one frequency—unofficially—as 1st Battalion's *personnel* communications link back to bivouac. Over this frequency, updates on Major Miles' condition would be sent on the hour. It was just seconds shy of 1500.

Botkin pressed the headset against his ears, his head bowed as if in prayer. When he finally popped his head up, he announced, "He's still hanging in there!"

Billingsley could sense the wave of relief sweeping over the men—*his* men.

But they're my men in name only right now, he told himself, *and as long as that fucking Jock Miles draws breath...*

They were all completely ignoring Kit Billingsley now. Bogater Boudreau ambled over to the jeep and asked, loud enough for everyone to hear, "Hey, *Sergeant Major,* if the man keeps his leg, that means we get him back, right?"

Patchett surprised everyone—especially Major Billingsley—with his reply: "Better tone it down a notch or two, son. It don't mean no such thing."

Then he looked Billingsley dead in the eyes and said, "I believe Captain Grossman just laid out one hell of a fine option here. So what're we gonna do, sir?"

Colonel Molloy buttonholed the surgeon in the mess tent as he was scarfing down a hot supper of Spam and lima beans. "At least we finally got some vegetables on the menu, Dick," the surgeon said between mouthfuls. "The men could sure use them." The colonel wasn't here to talk about the chow, though.

"It's been twenty-four hours, Doc," he said. "What's the word on Jock Miles now?"

"Well, a little bit of an infection has popped up. Kind of expected that here in the tropics...but I don't think it's anything we can't knock out with sulfanilamide."

"Give it to me straight, Doc...is he going to keep the leg?"

"Yeah, Dick, he'll keep it. How much use it'll be to him...that's another story."

Melvin Patchett felt ridiculous in the hospital gown, surgical gloves, and mask. "They wouldn't let me in to see you unless I wore this stuff, sir," he told Jock. *"Threat of infection,* they said. Not sure if they meant a threat to you or me. So how the hell you feeling?"

"Been worse, Top. Been better, too."

"I hear tell from Colonel Molloy that all that amputation talk got deep-sixed. That's real good news, sir....real good news. It'll give the men something to feel good about, too, because they sure need something right about now."

"Things not working out too well with the new boss, Top?"

Patchett started to laugh. "The man's only been around a couple days and already I could write a damn book. He got hisself more lost than a ball in high weeds today, nearly marched us straight through the goddamn swamp…until Captain Grossman straightened his ass out. But it was the damnedest thing…even after the Captain read him the riot act, I thought that pig-headed sumbitch would still try and make us do it his own fucked-up way."

"But he didn't," Jock said, "so maybe he's learning?"

"That'll be the day, sir. The way I see it, that man's a perfect sun-riser"

"Sun-riser? What's that, Top?"

"Someone who thinks the sun rises out of his asshole, sir."

"Hey, go easy on me, Top. It hurts when I laugh….it really does. But come to think of it, I thought the gospel according to Melvin Patchett stated that *every* officer thinks the sun rises out of his asshole."

"Not *all* y'all, sir. Just most."

Their laughter turned bittersweet. Neither of them wanted to face the fact their working relationship—one that had helped them survive this war from its earliest days—was now coming to an end.

"Any of the big brass come to see you, sir? Aside from that brigadier who showed up just to bust your balls?"

"No, Top. Not a one."

"Figures. They're gonna ship you home this time, ain't they, sir?"

"Not if I can help it."

"But how in blue blazes you gonna work it so you can stick around?"

"I honestly don't know, Top."

Chapter Thirty-Seven

Anxiety had gotten the better of his appetite. Try as he may, Hugh Finchley couldn't bear to touch a morsel of his supper. Across the table at Government House, though, Jillian Forbes didn't seem to be having any problem polishing off hers. She'd popped her left arm from its sling—*that shoulder aches less today*—and deftly switching from knife to fork, was one-handedly cleaning the tuna steak from her plate with alarming efficiency.

"This is bloody good fish," she said.

"I suppose you know a great deal about fish," Finchley said, "owning that fishing fleet back in Weipa."

Her face took on the *no shit* look she'd seen on so many soldiers—GIs and diggers alike—when someone was belaboring the obvious. To ensure he didn't miss its meaning, she added, "Can't bloody fool you, can we, Mister Finchley?"

She pointed her fork at his still-full plate and added, "What's the matter? You don't fancy the meal?"

"No, I'm sure it's quite wonderful, Miss Forbes. It's just that I'm a bit nervous about the broadcast tonight."

"Why's that?"

"The transcript hasn't gotten the *stamp of approval* from MacArthur's headquarters yet, I'm afraid…"

Jillian finished the sentence for him. "And without that approval, there'll be no broadcast."

Those words stung Hugh Finchley like a slap in the face. "And no book, either."

"I don't care about the bloody book," she replied.

Hugh Finchley did, though. Very much. As long as

this war raged on, *The Supreme Commander* would hold the editorial power over anything written about his campaigns. Jillian Forbes might have her family fortune to fall back on but he did not. A best seller right now could make his life very comfortable. Give him negotiating power with the network and the publishing world he never had before. And most importantly, get him out of this hellhole called Papua once and for all.

Now Jillian seemed to have lost her appetite, too. She wasn't lying when she said she didn't care about the book. There was something she did care about, though, something putting their story over the airwaves could provide:

Without that broadcast, there'll be no possibility of Canberra using our story to bolster morale back in Oz. That means no heroes' tour for me and Jock...

And he gets shipped home.

Without me.

Five minutes to air time: *1955 hours*...and still no word from MacArthur's headquarters giving Hugh Finchley's broadcast a *thumbs up* or *thumbs down*.

The broadcast engineer at the radio relay station, a US Army sergeant, watched the Aussie newsman with great amusement: *He's sweating worse than a whore in church.*

Then the sergeant went back to thumbing through a well-worn copy of *Life* magazine.

Two minutes to go...

The red light on the microphone's desk that, when lit, meant *On The Air*, was still dark.

One minute to go…

The phone on the engineer's desk rang. The conversation was brief. As he hung up, the sergeant looked at Hugh Finchley and shook his head.

The red light never came on.

The sergeant went back to his magazine.

Hugh Finchley retreated to his room and the bottle of whiskey stashed there.

At Government House, Jillian tuned the shortwave to Radio Australia and waited. For the next hour, she listened as the *News Hour* featured segment after segment describing the great Allied victories being won as MacArthur's forces swept down the northern New Guinea coast.

Five minutes were reserved at the end of the program for brief pieces about the war in Europe and the American naval campaign in the Central Pacific.

And then the *News Hour* signed off for the evening.

She never heard Hugh Finchley's voice…

And the world's going to wait until Hell freezes over to hear our story.

By midnight, the whiskey had jacked up Hugh Finchley's courage enough for him to hitch a ride to the Dobodura airfield complex on an American deuce-and-a-half. Once there, he leapt from the truck like a paratrooper while it was still moving—twisting an ankle in the process—and then, limping but undeterred, tried to storm the American Headquarters building. A trio of amused MPs stopped him well short of his goal.

"Maybe you just oughta get lost and sleep it off, pal," the MP sergeant said.

"I will do no such thing," Finchley replied. "I demand to see the general!"

"Look, pal…either get lost or we have to lock you up. Your choice, *amigo*."

"I'm not going anywhere, Yank." He tried to emphasize his point with a whiffed punch, which did no more than stir the humid night air.

"Oh, the hell you're not," the sergeant replied, spinning the unsteady Aussie around and snapping on handcuffs. That's when Hugh Finchley *really* began to make a scene, shouting every swear word and anti-American epithet his sodden mind could conjure.

After a particularly strong chorus of *you bloody miserable Yank son of a bitch fuckers,* the MPs stopped wrestling with him and sprang to attention. Finchley, without the benefit of his handcuffed arms for balance or the brawny MPs holding him up, fell flat on his ass. Bewildered, he looked around, not quite sure what had caused this sudden turn of events.

A commanding voice called from the building's entryway, "What the fuck's going on out there, Sergeant?" The voice belonged to Brigadier General Ted Stanley. He was standing in a silk dressing gown, with a phalanx of lackeys behind him.

"Nothing to concern yourself with, General," the sergeant replied. "This Aussie gentleman's just had a little too much to drink."

"GENERAL?" Finchley said, his voice an alcohol-fired roar. "ARE YOU GENERAL MACARTHUR?"

"No, I'm General Stanley. And who might you be?"

It took three tries—each one spraying the MPs with saliva—before he got past the *F* in Finchley. Once said, though, Stanley realized exactly who this drunk was.

"Finchley, eh? You're the gent who wrote that piece about that Aussie hero woman and her American boyfriend...the pair that seems to be winning this war single-handedly, right?"

"Bloody well right, that's me. How dare you refuse my story, you...you..."

"*General* will suffice for a title, Mister Finchley. You want to know why your story's been shitcanned? Well, I'll tell you why: *nobody* but Douglas MacArthur is going to be given the credit for any of his brilliant tactical campaigns. And I mean *nobody*. Your little piece of fiction about some Aussie *split-tail warrior* will never see the light of day, my friend. So I suggest you crawl back to your typewriter like a good little *mate* and write what you're told."

The whiskey was still pumping chemical courage through Finchley's veins. He replied, "Or what?"

"Or those war correspondent credentials we were charitable enough to grant you just might vanish, Mister Finchley...and you'll be lucky to find yourself in some Outback shithole, reporting on the price of kangaroo meat."

Chapter Thirty-Eight

The old vessel may have been rusty and tired-looking, but Jillian thought the coastal freighter *Esme*—*her* ship: the one still bearing her name on the ownership papers—looked wonderful in the noonday sun. She and Jock sat at quayside of Port Moresby's Fairfax Harbor and watched as deck cranes lowered her war cargo to the wharf.

"The old girl's still beautiful, isn't she, Jock?"

Jock hesitated, searching for a delicate way to express the anxiety reborn with this ship's reappearance. The best he could do was, "You're not actually thinking of becoming her captain again, are you?"

"No, not yet. Not until I'm strong enough for the job." She raised her arms—finally free of the slings they'd worn for the past month—and made slow circles above her head. "Nice to be able to do this again, though."

And it would be really nice not to have you at sea in a war zone again, too, he thought, but didn't dare say out loud. Trying to stay upbeat and hopeful on their last day—and last night—together was proving difficult enough. The prospect of her sailing into harm's way again was more than he could bear, and he told her so.

Upbeat, eager, and without a hint of sarcasm, she replied, "What else am I going to do with myself while we're apart?"

He couldn't see it that way. He cursed the sea, the fact she was so at home on it, and the fact he had nowhere to go now but back to the States.

"Maybe we should just head back to Commander

Shaw's place," he said. "Don't want to be late for *The Last Supper*."

The enthusiasm drained from her face. He wished he hadn't used those words, not meaning for them to sound so cold, so final. Even if they were.

"I suppose you're right," she replied. "We don't want to seem rude now, do we?"

He rose to his feet without using the cane for support. "The leg, Jock...I can tell it's getting stronger every day. You'll be running track and field again before you know it."

"I'd be the first guy with a limp to ever do that."

"Give it time, Yank. Give it some bloody time."

She slipped her hand into his and they walked toward the jeep. He felt the cool, unyielding touch of the thin gold band she wore on her ring finger as their hands laced together. He wore one, too, on the hand clutching the cane. They had wed as soon as they arrived in Port Moresby, he still in his hospital bed, she in the one dress she took from that unclaimed wardrobe at Buna's Government House. An Australian magistrate had performed the brief ceremony, with Trevor Shaw and Ginny Beech as witnesses. So Jock wouldn't feel like the lone Yank in a mob of Aussies, two US Army nurses volunteered to be bridesmaids. He'd half expected the magistrate to say, *Jillian Forbes, do you take this bloody Yank...*

So far, though, their marriage had done nothing but make public a bond so obvious it needed no publicity. They knew the risks of a hasty wartime marriage at the outset, and those risks had raised an administrative snag right off the bat: the US Army was refusing to recognize the marriage.

"You've filed the appeal?" she asked.

"Yeah...but bear in mind it's not going to be the most pressing issue on the G1's desk, Jill. This process is going to take a while...a long while."

Even if the Army did eventually come around while the war still raged, it would be a year, maybe two, before she would be allowed to emigrate to the US as an officer's spouse.

"Of course," she said, "once this bloody war ends, the travel restrictions will be lifted and I'll buy my own bloody ticket to America. The hell with your Army."

And when that time finally comes, Jill, I pray you'll still want to buy that ticket.

They both knew this war was nowhere near over, though...and the assumption the Allies would win it was still anything but a certainty.

"Let me drive, Jill," he said. "I think my leg is up to working the pedals. It'll be just our luck we'll get pulled over by some MP without a sense of humor about a civilian woman driving government property."

With one last, lingering look toward the harbor, she surrendered the driver's seat to him.

When they pulled into the drive of Trevor Shaw's villa, they were surprised to find another jeep parked there. Jillian asked, "You don't suppose MacArthur's moving back in, do you?"

"No...I don't see any of his *palace guard*. He wouldn't be here without them."

As they drove closer, Jock could read the unit identifiers on the jeep's bumper. "That's a Fifth Air

Force jeep," he said. "What the hell are they doing here?"

Trevor Shaw stepped from the house onto the veranda, followed by Ginny Beech and an Air Force colonel Jock recognized instantly, the silver pilot's wings on his chest glistening in the late afternoon sun. "I know that guy," he said. "That's Buck Ziminski. He was in the hospital here in Port Moresby with me for a spell. Appendicitis, of all things. We dogfaces get bullet and shrapnel wounds...flyers get appendicitis and athlete's foot."

Jillian failed to see the humor, adding, "Or they crash...and if they're not killed outright, they get their heads cut off in a POW camp."

Trevor Shaw introduced Jillian to Colonel Ziminski. "Man oh man," the colonel said, his eyes gleaming. "Now I get to see for myself the woman Jock Miles just couldn't stop talking about. It's truly a pleasure to meet you, ma'am."

As Ginny served up cold beers, the conversation quickly got down to business. "Jock, old boy," Ziminski said, "I hear you're looking for work."

Those words were like throwing gasoline on a dying fire. Jock and Jillian couldn't help themselves; the flicker of hope in their souls was suddenly a blazing inferno.

"Yeah," Jock replied, wondering if he was dreaming. "I sure am, sir...but a job here? In *this* theater?"

"Damn right it is," Ziminski replied. "Right here in Port Moresby...for the time being, that is, until we move to Tokyo. General Kenney is getting damn sick and tired of listening to you ground-pounders and cannon-cockers complaining about the maps and aerial photos we provide you guys...*not enough detail,* you say. *Too many surprises, relief not worth a shit*...pardon my French, ladies."

Ginny and Jillian exchanged amused looks. Jock expected one of them to say *No fucking problem, sport,* but the women folded their hands in their laps, held their tongues, and tried like hell not to smile like Christmas had come very, very early this year.

"So I was thinking," Ziminski continued, "I met this Infantry-type who knows his terrain inside out, from up in the air and down on the ground...and he doesn't get airsick, I'm told." He pointed to the cane leaning against Jock's chair, adding, "And this Infantry-type could sure use a *relaxing* job where he didn't need to be slogging through that damn jungle."

Jock thought his heart would melt when he saw the glow of relief on Jillian's face. He knew what she was thinking: *You're not leaving...and you'll be safe, too.*

Colonel Ziminski wasn't finished with his pitch. "Now, Jock, maybe you had your heart set on going home, but—"

"Begging your pardon for interrupting, sir," Jock said, "but I only need to know one thing...where do I sign?"

***

More Novels by William Peter Grasso

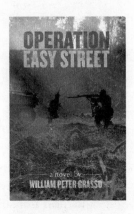

Port Moresby was bad. Buna was worse.

The WW2 alternative history adventure of Jock Miles continues as MacArthur orders American and Australian forces to seize Buna in Papua New Guinea. Once again, the Allied high command underestimates the Japanese defenders, plunging Jock and his men into a battle they're not equipped to win. Worse, jungle diseases, treacherous terrain, and the tactical fantasies of deluded generals become adversaries every bit as deadly as the Japanese. Sick, exhausted, and outgunned, Jock's battalion is ordered to spearhead an amphibious assault against the well-entrenched enemy. It's a suicide mission—but with ingenious help from an unexpected source, there might be a way to avoid the certain slaughter and take Buna. For Jock, though, victory comes at a dreadful price.

Alternative history takes center stage as *Operation Long Jump,* the second book in the Jock Miles World War 2 adventure series, plunges us into the horrors of combat in the rainforests of Papua New Guinea. As a prelude to the Allied invasion, Jock Miles and his men seize the Japanese observation post on the mountain overlooking Port Moresby. The main invasion that follows quickly degenerates to a bloody stalemate, as the inexperienced, demoralized, and poorly led GIs struggle against the stubborn enemy. Seeking a way to crack the impenetrable Japanese defenses, infantry officer Jock finds himself in a new role—aerial observer. He's teamed with rookie pilot John Worth, in a prequel to his role as hero of Grasso's *East Wind Returns.* Together, they struggle to expose the Japanese defenses—while highly exposed themselves—in their slow and vulnerable spotter plane. The enemy is not the only thing troubling Jock: his Australian lover, Jillian Forbes, has found a new and dangerous way to contribute to the war effort.

— WILLIAM PETER GRASSO —

In this alternate history adventure set in WW2's early
days, a crippled US military struggles to defend
vulnerable Australia against the unstoppable Japanese
forces. When a Japanese regiment lands on Australia's
desolate and undefended Cape York Peninsula, Jock
Miles, a US Army captain disgraced despite heroic
actions at Pearl Harbor, is ordered to locate the enemy's
elusive command post.

Conceived in politics rather than sound tactics, the futile
mission is a "show of faith" by the American war
leaders meant to do little more than bolster their flagging
Australian ally. For Jock Miles and the men of his
patrol, it's a death sentence: their enemy is superior in
men, material, firepower, and combat experience. Even
if the Japanese don't kill them, the vast distances they
must cover on foot in the treacherous natural realm of
Cape York just might. When Jock joins forces with
Jillian Forbes, an indomitable woman with her own
checkered past who refused to evacuate in the face of the

Japanese threat, the dim prospects of the Allied war effort begin to brighten in surprising ways.

Congressman. Presidential candidate. Murderer. Leonard Pilcher is all of these things.

As an American pilot interned in Sweden during WWII, he kills one of his own crewmen and gets away with it. Two people have witnessed the murder—American airman Joe Gelardi and his secret Swedish lover, Pola Nilsson-MacLeish—but they cannot speak out without paying a devastating price. Tormented by their guilt and separated by a vast ocean after the war, Joe and Pola maintain the silence that haunts them both...until 1960, when Congressman Pilcher's campaign for his party's nomination for president gains momentum. As he dons the guise of war hero, one female reporter, anxious to break into the "boy's club" of TV news, fights to uncover the truth against the far-reaching power of the Pilcher family's wealth, power that can do any wrong it chooses—even kill—and remain unpunished. Just as the nomination seems within Pilcher's grasp, Pola reappears to enlist Joe's help in finally exposing Pilcher for the criminal he really is. As the passion of their wartime romance rekindles, they must struggle to bring Pilcher down before becoming his next victims.

A young but veteran photo recon pilot in WWII finds the fate of the greatest invasion in history--and the life of the nurse he loves--resting perilously on his shoulders.

"East Wind Returns" is a story of World War II set in July-November 1945 which explores a very different road to that conflict's historic conclusion. The American war leaders grapple with a crippling setback: Their secret atomic bomb does not work. The invasion of Japan seems the only option to bring the war to a close. When those leaders suppress intelligence of a Japanese atomic weapon poised against the invasion forces, it falls to photo reconnaissance pilot John Worth to find the Japanese device. Political intrigue is mixed with passionate romance and exciting aerial action--the terror of enemy fighters, anti-aircraft fire, mechanical malfunctions, deadly weather, and the Kamikaze. When shot down by friendly fire over southern Japan during the American invasion, Worth leads the desperate mission that seeks to deactivate the device.

Made in the USA
Middletown, DE
21 February 2020

85123942R00187